全民英檢
全新!GEPT
單字大全
Vocabulary
中高級

全MP3一次下載

https://globalv.com.tw/mp3-download-9789864544356/

掃描QR碼進入網頁（須先註冊並保持登入）後，按「全書音檔下載請按此」，可一次性下載音檔壓縮檔，或點選檔名線上播放。

全MP3一次下載為zip壓縮檔，部分智慧型手機須先安裝解壓縮app方可開啟，iOS系統請升級至iOS 13以上。

此為大型檔案，建議使用WIFI連線下載，以免占用流量，並請確認連線狀況，以利下載順暢。

使用說明
INTRODUCTION

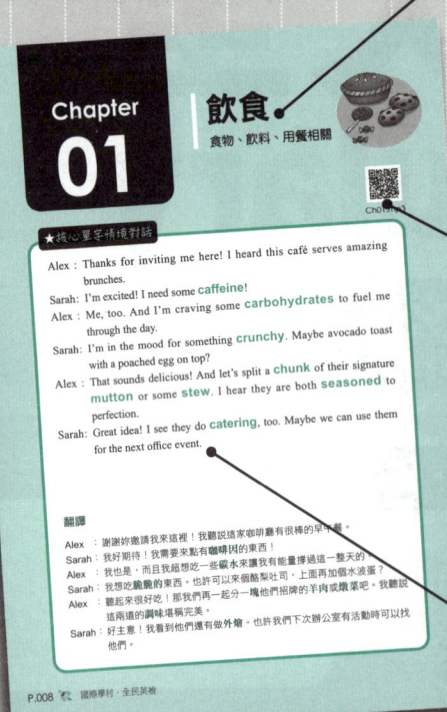

01 常考主題分類
分析實際測驗題目，以必考的 12 大主題精準分類單字，相關主題核心單字一次學會。

02 核心單字美式發音＋中文字義＋英文例句 MP3
搭配音檔邊聽邊唸，加深印象、幫助記憶。

03 核心單字情境對話
針對分類主題，在日常情境對話中實際運用核心單字，在開始深入學習前，先感受核心單字的運用語感！

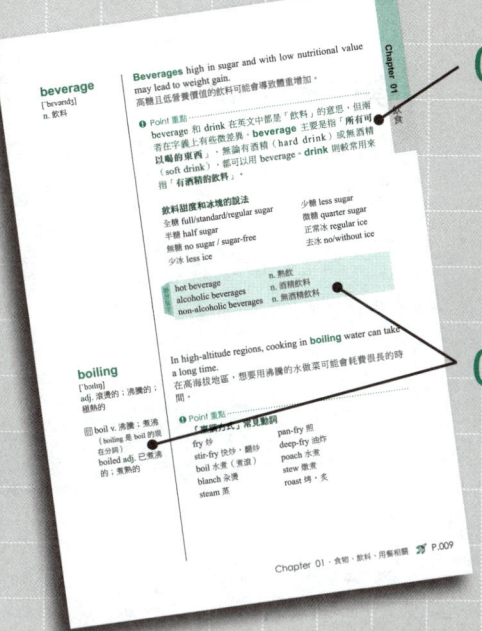

04 | 出題重點詳細解說

詳細解說與各核心單字相關的常考文法、片語、慣用語、相似字義辨析及使用訣竅，考點剖析深入又好懂！

05 | 相關字詞表達一次囊括

一併補充衍生字、同義字、反義字、片語、聯想單字及慣用表達方式，一口氣學會所有相關重點字詞及表達方式！

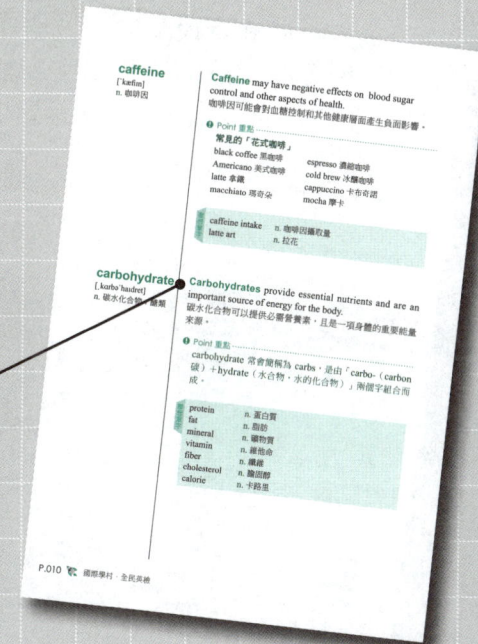

06 | 貼近實際測驗內容的例句

每一個核心單字都搭配符合出題趨勢並模擬實際測驗內容的例句，讀例句就像在練習單字題！

Introduction・使用說明　P.003

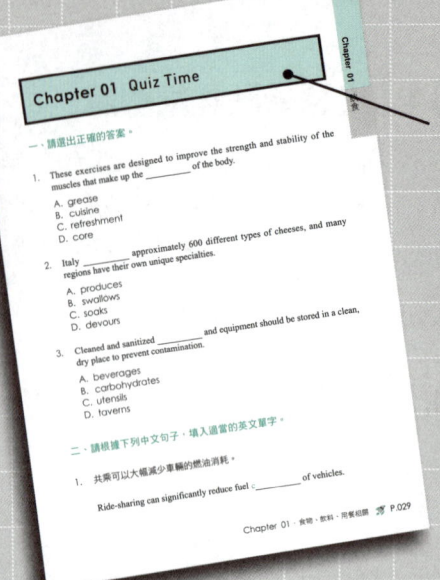

07 | 模擬實際測驗的練習題

特別設計接近實際測驗的字彙題及克漏字，讓考生能運用模擬題複習單字，提升作答手感。

08 | 一併收錄主題分類單字

一併收錄全民英檢官方字庫內與主題相關的分類單字，讓考生學習無遺漏、認字更輕鬆！

09 | 方便好查的單字索引

複習時搭配索引查找，便能快速找出想看的內容，學習效率提升、複習成效更佳！

10 | 學習音檔使用說明

考生可以按照個人學習需求，選擇最適合自己的學習方式，提升學習效率。

★ 本書收錄下列版本學習 MP3

1. **核心單字英中對照**
   先唸一次核心單字的美式英文發音，再唸一次中文字義。
2. **英文例句**
   每個核心單字搭配的英文例句都唸一次。
3. **核心單字英中對照＋英文例句**
   先唸一次核心單字的美式英文發音及中文字義，再接英文例句。
4. **主題分類單字英中對照**
   先唸一次分類單字的美式英文發音，再唸一次中文字義。
5. **核心單字情境對話**
   以美式英文進行一次核心單字情境對話。

本書各章第一頁均附有「核心單字英中對照＋英文例句」的獨立線上音檔 QR 碼，不須切換搜尋便可立即聆聽，亦可掃描本書第一頁上的全書音檔下載 QR 碼，一次下載全書共五個版本的完整 MP3 音檔。

★ 本書標示說明

v. 動詞 ｜ n. 名詞 ｜ adj. 形容詞 ｜ adv. 副詞 ｜

prep. 介系詞 ｜ phr. 片語 ｜ 衍 衍生詞 ｜ 同 同義詞 ｜ 反 反義詞 ｜

[英] 英式英文 ｜ [美] 美式英文 ｜ [口] 口語說法

目錄
CONTENTS

1 飲食 008
食物、飲料、用餐相關

主題分類單字..................027
Quiz Time......................029

2 衣物 031
衣物、配件、顏色、形容詞

主題分類單字..................043
Quiz Time......................044

3 居家 046
房屋、家具、日常用品、家庭

主題分類單字..................065
Quiz Time......................068

4 交通 070
交通工具、運輸方式

主題分類單字..................084
Quiz Time......................085

5 外表 087
身體部位、外貌形容

主題分類單字..................101
Quiz Time......................103

6 性格／特質 105
個性、情緒

主題分類單字..................124
Quiz Time......................127

7 工作 129
職業、工作地點、職場相關

主題分類單字..................145
Quiz Time........................148

8 休閒娛樂 150
興趣、嗜好、運動、購物相關

主題分類單字..................165
Quiz Time........................167

9 教育 169
學校、學科、知識學習相關

主題分類單字..................186
Quiz Time........................189

10 自然 191
動物、昆蟲、環境、景色、天氣、自然現象

主題分類單字..................206
Quiz Time........................209

11 健康 211
疾病、醫院、傷病處理、感受

主題分類單字..................229
Quiz Time........................230

12 量測 232
單位、方位、距離、尺寸、計量、金錢、時間

主題分類單字..................253
Quiz Time........................256

★ 索引..................258

Chapter 01

飲食
食物、飲料、用餐相關

Ch01.mp3

★核心單字情境對話

Alex : Thanks for inviting me here! I heard this café serves amazing brunches.
Sarah: I'm excited! I need some **caffeine**!
Alex : Me, too. And I'm craving some **carbohydrates** to fuel me through the day.
Sarah: I'm in the mood for something **crunchy**. Maybe avocado toast with a poached egg on top?
Alex : That sounds delicious! And let's split a **chunk** of their signature **mutton** or some **stew**. I hear they are both **seasoned** to perfection.
Sarah: Great idea! I see they do **catering**, too. Maybe we can use them for the next office event.

翻譯

Alex ：謝謝妳邀請我來這裡！我聽說這家咖啡廳有很棒的早午餐。
Sarah：我好期待！我需要來點有**咖啡因**的東西！
Alex ：我也是，而且我超想吃一些**碳水**來讓我有能量撐過這一整天的。
Sarah：我想吃**脆脆的**東西。也許可以來個酪梨吐司，上面再加個水波蛋？
Alex ：聽起來很好吃！那我們再一起分一**塊**他們招牌的**羊肉**或一些**燉菜**吧。我聽說這兩道的**調味**堪稱完美。
Sarah：好主意！我看到他們還有做**外燴**。也許我們下次辦公室有活動時可以找他們。

beverage
[ˋbɛvərɪdʒ]
n. 飲料

Beverages high in sugar and with low nutritional value may lead to weight gain.
高糖且低營養價值的飲料可能會導致體重增加。

● Point 重點
beverage 和 drink 在英文中都是「飲料」的意思，但兩者在字義上有些微差異。**beverage** 主要是指「**所有可以喝的東西**」，無論有酒精（hard drink）或無酒精（soft drink），都可以用 beverage。**drink** 則較常用來指「**有酒精的飲料**」。

飲料甜度和冰塊的說法
全糖 full/standard/regular sugar　　少糖 less sugar
半糖 half sugar　　　　　　　　　　微糖 quarter sugar
無糖 no sugar / sugar-free　　　　　正常冰 regular ice
少冰 less ice　　　　　　　　　　　去冰 no/without ice

聯想單字
hot beverage	n. 熱飲
alcoholic beverages	n. 酒精飲料
non-alcoholic beverages	n. 無酒精飲料

boiling
[ˋbɔɪlɪŋ]
adj. 滾燙的；沸騰的；極熱的

衍 boil v. 沸騰；煮沸
（boiling 是 boil 的現在分詞）
boiled adj. 已煮沸的；煮熟的

In high-altitude regions, cooking in **boiling** water can take a long time.
在高海拔地區，想要用沸騰的水做菜可能會耗費很長的時間。

● Point 重點
「烹調方式」常見動詞
fry 炒　　　　　　　　pan-fry 煎
stir-fry 快炒，翻炒　　deep-fry 油炸
boil 水煮（煮滾）　　　poach 水煮
blanch 汆燙　　　　　 stew 燉煮
steam 蒸　　　　　　　roast 烤，炙

Chapter 01・食物、飲料、用餐相關　　P.009

caffeine
[`kæfɪn]
n. 咖啡因

Caffeine may have negative effects on blood sugar control and other aspects of health.
咖啡因可能會對血糖控制和其他健康層面產生負面影響。

 Point 重點

常見的「花式咖啡」
black coffee 黑咖啡　　espresso 濃縮咖啡
Americano 美式咖啡　　cold brew 冰釀咖啡
latte 拿鐵　　　　　　cappuccino 卡布奇諾
macchiato 瑪奇朵　　　mocha 摩卡

聯想單字
caffeine intake　n. 咖啡因攝取量
latte art　　　　n. 拉花

carbohydrate
[ˌkɑrbə`haɪdret]
n. 碳水化合物；醣類

Carbohydrates provide essential nutrients and are an important source of energy for the body.
碳水化合物可以提供必需營養素，且是一項身體的重要能量來源。

 Point 重點

carbohydrate 常會簡稱為 carbs，是由「carbo-（carbon 碳）＋hydrate（水合物，水的化合物）」兩個字組合而成。

聯想單字
protein　　　n. 蛋白質
fat　　　　　n. 脂肪
mineral　　　n. 礦物質
vitamin　　　n. 維他命
fiber　　　　n. 纖維
cholesterol　n. 膽固醇
calorie　　　n. 卡路里

catering
[ˋketərɪŋ]
n. 外燴；餐飲服務

衍 cater v. 提供飲食；
承辦（宴席等）
caterer n. 提供餐飲服務的人（或公司）
self-catering adj. 可以自己做飯的

The hotel offers **catering** for conferences and business meetings.
這家飯店針對會議和商務會面提供餐飲服務。

❶ Point 重點
cater to sb/sth 滿足或迎合某人／某願望或需求
⇨ No longer bound by geographical constraints, online shopping **caters to** the busy lifestyle of modern people.
不再受地理限制，網路購物滿足了現代人忙碌的生活方式。

chunk
[tʃʌŋk]
n. 大塊；厚塊

A large **chunk** of his income is used to pay the rent and bills.
他收入的一大部分都用來付租金和帳單了。

❶ Point 重點
chunk vs. dice vs. cube
chunk 指的是**形狀不規則、具有厚度，且可以切開**的東西，一般會翻譯成「大塊」或「厚塊」。
⇨ He cut the bread into thick **chunks**.
他把麵包切成厚厚的大塊。

dice 有「骰子」的意思，通常會用來形容被**均勻切成小正方塊**、形狀如骰子般的**食物**上。
⇨ The chef sprinkled the soup with **diced** ham.
主廚在湯裡撒了切成小方塊的火腿。

cube 指的通常是**正方體或立方體**，體積會比 dice 更大，且可用來形容**非食物的東西**。
⇨ Add a few ice **cubes** to your drink.
在你的飲料裡加幾塊冰。

聯想單字		
a chunk of	phr. 一大塊
a piece of	phr. 一塊，一片
a slice of	phr. 一片
a scoop of	phr.（用挖勺挖的）一球
a bunch of	phr. 一串，一束

Chapter 01 飲食

consumption
[kənˋsʌmpʃən]
n. 消耗；消費；食用

衍 consume v. 消耗；花費；吃光
consumer n. 消費者；消耗者

Consumption of junk food can lead to a lot of health problems, such as digestive issues and heart disease.
食用垃圾食物可能會導致許多健康問題，例如消化問題和心臟疾病。

❶ Point 重點
consume vs. **eat** vs. **have**
consume 強調「**攝取或消耗的動作**」，通常用於正式的語境。**eat** 是最直接和生理上的「吃」，使用範圍廣泛，而 **have** 則是更加口語化的表達方式，且可表達出「**品嚐**」的意味，但也可泛指飲食的動作，經常會在對話中取代 eat 或 drink。

core
[kor]
n. 核心，關鍵；果核

The **core** of the problem is the contamination of the drinking water system in the factory.
問題的核心是工廠中飲用水系統的污染。

❶ Point 重點
to the core 完完全全的；非常
⇒ The country's political system is rotten **to the core**.
這個國家的政治體制爛到骨子裡了。
I was shocked **to the core** and burst out crying.
我完全嚇壞了，然後大哭了起來。

聯想單字
core value	n. 核心價值
core vocabulary	n. 核心單字
core area	n. 核心領域
core concept	n. 核心概念

crunchy
[ˋkrʌntʃɪ]
adj. 脆的，酥脆的

衍 crunch v. 嘎吱嘎吱地嚼

These pickled **crunchy** vegetables are suitable for all meals.
這些脆脆的醃製蔬菜和所有餐點都很搭。

> **Point 重點**
>
> **表達「口感」的常見單字**
> tender 嫩的（也可以用 soft 表示肉質很軟嫩）
> tough 硬的（可以用來形容肉太硬、太老）
> chewy 有嚼勁的
> stringy（液體）牽絲的；多筋的
> juicy 多汁的

cuisine
[kwɪ`zin]
n. 烹飪方式；（以特定手法做成的）料理

French **cuisine** is famous for its extensive use of cream and cheese.
法國料理以大量使用奶油和起司而聞名。

聯想單字
chef	n. 主廚
delicacy	n.（較珍貴的）精緻美食，珍饈
culinary delights	n. 美食，佳餚
tasty	adj. 美味的
mouth-watering	adj. 令人垂涎的
appetizing	adj. 令人食慾大開的
finger-licking	adj. 令人吮指回味的

devour
[dɪ`vaʊr]
v. 狼吞虎嚥地吃；吞噬

The hungry dog **devoured** the meal set before it in seconds.
那隻飢餓的狗狼吞虎嚥地在幾秒鐘內就把放在眼前的食物吃完了。

> **Point 重點**
>
> **表達「吃相」的常見單字**
> nibble 小口咬
> chew 咀嚼
> munch 大聲咀嚼
> bolt 匆匆吞下
> gulp/gorge/pig out/wolf down/gobble up 狼吞虎嚥

Chapter 01・食物、飲料、用餐相關

disposable

[dɪˋspozəb!]
adj. 拋棄式的，
一次性的
n. 拋棄式的產品

衍 dispose v. 處理，
處置
disposal n. 處理，
處置

Tourists visiting scenic spots often leave behind **disposable** plates and cups, which leads to ecological problems.
造訪風景區的遊客經常將免洗盤杯留在那裡，而這造成了生態問題。

Please use washable and reusable cutlery rather than **disposables**.
請使用可以清洗和重複使用的餐具，不要用免洗的。

❶ Point 重點 ⋯⋯⋯⋯⋯⋯⋯⋯⋯⋯⋯⋯⋯⋯⋯⋯⋯⋯⋯⋯
dispose of (+N.) 處理；擊敗
⇨ The government spent billions researching ways to best **dispose of** nuclear waste.
政府花費數十億元研究處置核廢料的最佳方法。
He spent several years training before he was able to **dispose of** the former world No.1.
在能夠擊敗前世界第一之前，他花費了數年的時間訓練。

at sb's disposal 任憑某人支配或使用
⇨ After selling the house she inherited from her parents, she had a large sum of money **at** her **disposal**.
在賣掉她從父母那邊繼承的房子之後，她手上有一大筆錢可以自由使用。

聯想單字	
disposable tableware/utensils	n. 免洗餐具
disposable chopsticks	n. 免洗筷
disposable gloves	n. 拋棄式手套
daily disposable contacts	n. 日拋隱形眼鏡

grease

[gris]
n. 油脂 v. 用油脂塗

衍 greasy adj. 油膩的

Baking soda is effective in cleaning and can break down **grease**.
小蘇打可以有效清潔並分解油脂。

Another traditional method is to **grease** the baking pan with butter.
另一種傳統的方法是用奶油來為烤盤塗油。

❶ Point 重點
grease sb's palm 向（某人）行賄；收買（某人）
⇨ The police officer arrested the businessman who tried to **grease** his **palm**.
警察逮捕了試圖向他行賄的商人。

elbow grease 體力勞動；下苦功
⇨ It will take a lot of **elbow grease** to clean the kitchen.
清潔廚房需要花費大量的精力。

grease vs. **fat** vs. **oil**
grease 通常指的是**食物經加熱後融出**的油脂，例如煎培根時出現的油。**fat** 指的通常是在**常溫下呈固態**的脂肪，如豬油、牛油、椰子油等。**oil** 則是在**常溫下呈液態**的油，如橄欖油、葵花油或魚油等。

grill
[grɪl]
n. 烤架
v.（用烤架）烤；盤問

You can season the corn before or after cooking it on the **grill**.
你要在把玉米放到烤架上烤的之前或之後來調味都可以。

Grilling filet mignon to perfection requires a little skill.
烤出完美的菲力牛排需要一點技巧。

❶ Point 重點
各式各樣的「烤」
grill 火烤（用烤架烤，熱源來自下方）
roast 烘烤（熱源來自四面八方）
broil 烤（熱源來自上方）
barbecue 戶外燒烤
bake 烘焙（麵包、餅乾等等）

Chapter 01・食物、飲料、用餐相關　P.015

mutton
[ˋmʌtən]
n. 羊肉

Mutton is the meat of choice in Muslim countries where the consumption of pork is forbidden by religion.
在因宗教而禁食豬肉的穆斯林國家裡，羊肉是肉類的首選。

❶ Point 重點
lamb 和 mutton 都是羊肉，但 **lamb** 指的是一歲以前的羊肉，也就是「**羔羊肉**」，**mutton** 則是一歲以後的一般羊肉。

mutton hot pot	n. 羊肉爐
beef	n. 牛肉
pork	n. 豬肉
chicken	n. 雞肉
duck	n. 鴨肉
goose	n. 鵝肉

聯想單字

pastry
[ˋpestrɪ]
n. 油酥類糕點

The café offers homemade sandwiches, toasts, soups, and a selection of cakes and **pastries**.
這間咖啡廳提供自製三明治、烤麵包、湯以及各種可供選擇的蛋糕和糕點。

❶ Point 重點
各種常見的「點心」
tart 塔
cinnamon roll 肉桂捲
croissant 可頌
macaron 馬卡龍
scone 司康
pretzel 椒鹽捲餅，蝴蝶脆餅

cracker	n. 口感薄脆的餅乾
crumb	n.（麵包或餅乾的）屑
crumble	n. 水果酥派
crust	n.（派餅的）硬皮；外殼；麵包皮

聯想單字

produce
[prə`djus]
v. 生產；製作；引起；出示
n.（大量生產的）農產品（發音 [`prɑdjus]）

衍 producer n. 製作人；生產者；生產公司
product n. 產品
productive adj. 多產的；富有成效的
productively adv. 高效地；富有成效地

A company that **produces** men's cologne has been advertising their products in magazines for years.
一家生產男性古龍水的公司多年來都一直在雜誌上廣告他們的產品。

Hokkaido is a popular tourist spot, known for its lakes, mountains, farms, and dairy **produce**.
北海道是一個受歡迎的觀光勝地，以其湖泊、群山、農場和乳製品聞名。

❶ Point 重點
produce 當動詞和名詞時，重音的位置不同，當**動詞**時，重音在第二音節，讀作 [prə`djus]；當**名詞**時，重音在第一音節，讀作 [`prɑdjus]，在聽力和口說時請特別留意。

refreshment
[rɪ`frɛʃmənt]
n. 茶點；有提神作用的東西

衍 refresh v. 使清涼；使重振精神；刷新（網頁等）
refreshing adj. 使人涼爽的；提神的；令人耳目一新的

The workshop will last approximately 2 hours, and coffee, soft drinks and other **refreshments** will be available.
這場工作坊會進行約 2 個小時，且會供應咖啡、無酒精飲料和其他茶點。

聯想單字		
pick-up	n.	（咖啡等）提神的東西
energy drink	n.	（含咖啡因的）能量飲料
soda	n.	[美] 汽水
fizzy drink	n.	[英] 汽水

relish
[`rɛlɪʃ]
v.（津津有味地）享受；喜歡；憧憬
n. 調味料；樂趣

Very few people **relish** cleaning their old home from top to bottom before moving.
很少會有人喜歡在搬家之前把舊家徹底打掃乾淨的這件事。

Most audiences have no **relish** for dirty jokes, so it's best to avoid those topics.
大部分觀眾不喜歡黃色笑話，所以最好避免這些主題。

● Point 重點
relish 和 enjoy 的意思差不多，用法都是在後面搭配名詞或 V-ing。
⇨ We both **relish/enjoy going** for walks, enjoying good food and going on trips.
我們兩個都喜歡散步、享受美食和旅行。

salmon
[ˋsæmən]
n. 鮭魚

The main reason **salmon** swim upstream is to ensure the survival of their offspring.
鮭魚逆流而上的主要原因是為了確保其後代的生存。

聯想單字

cod	n. 鱈魚
flounder	n. 比目魚
tuna	n. 鮪魚
milkfish	n. 虱目魚
tilapia	n. 吳郭魚
marlin	n. 旗魚
trout	n. 鱒魚
perch	n. 鱸魚
grouper	n. 石斑魚

seasoned
[ˋsizənd]
adj. 經驗豐富的；調過味的

衍 season n. 季節
v. 幫～調味
seasonal adj. 季節性的
seasonable adj. 當令的；合於時宜的
seasoning n. 調味品；佐料

We are looking for a **seasoned** expert in the field of product design who has the desire to lead teams.
我們正在尋找一位在產品設計領域經驗豐富且對帶領團隊具強烈意願的專家。

● Point 重點
表達「經驗豐富的」其他常用單字

experienced adj. 經驗豐富的
⇨ 來自名詞 experience（經驗），指因為長期做某事，所以累積了非常豐富的經驗。常以 **experienced in doing sth** 來表達。

skilled adj. 熟練的；技術好的
⇨ 來自名詞 skill（技術），強調擁有某項專業的技術能力。常用的表達為 **skilled at/in (doing) sth**。

sophisticated adj. 老練的；見多識廣的
⇨ 常用來形容人因為累積了豐富的經驗，而「處事老練的」或因此「很有品味的」，也可以用來形容事物是「精密且複雜的」。

veteran adj. 經驗豐富的 n. 老手
⇨ 這個字做為名詞時原指「老兵，退役軍人」，後來衍生為「在某領域經驗豐富的人」，做為形容詞時的字義則是「資深的；經驗豐富的」。

simmer
[ˋsɪmɚ]
v. 燉，煨；醞釀

Next, you should reduce the heat and let the stew **simmer** for approximately 45 minutes.
接下來，你應該把火轉小，然後讓燉菜燉個 45 分鐘左右。

The bad blood between them has been **simmering** for weeks and put their mutual best friend in an uncomfortable position.
兩人之間的嫌隙已經持續了幾週，讓他們的共同好友感到左右為難。

❶ Point 重點
simmer down 平息（怒火或激動的情緒），冷靜下來
⇨ Do you believe the crisis between these two countries will **simmer down**?
你認為這兩國之間的危機會平息嗎？

soak
[sok]
v. 浸濕；浸泡
n. 浸泡；酒鬼；泡澡

衍 soaked adj. 濕透的；浸透的

反 dry adj. 乾的
v. 把～弄乾；變乾

If you want a strong alcohol flavor, you must **soak** the fruit in brandy for at least 12 hours.
如果想要酒味濃郁，那你務必要將水果浸泡在白蘭地裡至少 12 個小時。

Unsmoked hams tend to be salty and need a **soak** before cooking to remove the excess salt.
未煙燻的火腿通常很鹹，所以在料理前得先浸泡來去除多餘的鹽分。

● Point 重點

soak up sth 吸收，吸除；盡情享受；耗盡
⇨ The renovations have turned into a bigger project than we ever imagined and **soaked up** all our time.
這次的整修計畫已經變得比我們所設想的還要龐大，且耗盡了我們所有的時間。

soak vs. **dip** vs. **marinate**
soak 是把物品完全泡到液體之中，讓液體**徹底浸溼**該物品。**dip** 是快速、淺淺地沾一下，讓液體在該物品的**表面沾染**。**marinate** 指的則是醃製食材的**醃泡**。

sober
[ˋsobɚ]
adj. 清醒未醉的；嚴肅冷靜的；色彩樸素的
v.（使）變得嚴肅冷靜；使清醒

衍 sobriety n. 清醒；冷靜

反 drunken adj. 喝醉的

During the party, Peter decided to remain **sober** and not drink any alcohol.
Peter 決定在派對上要保持清醒，滴酒不沾。

Before leaving the bar, he drank a glass of ginger ale to **sober** himself up.
他在離開酒吧前喝了一杯薑汁汽水來讓自己清醒一下。

● Point 重點

sober (sb) up（使某人從酒醉中）清醒
⇨ It is said that black coffee and a cold shower can **sober** you **up** quickly.
據說黑咖啡和沖冷水澡可以讓你醒酒醒很快。

sober vs. **awake**
sober 和 awake 都可以做為動詞或形容詞使用，形容詞的 **sober** 是「沒有喝醉」的意思，當動詞時則常會與 **up** 搭配使用，表達「（使某人從酒醉中）清醒」。
形容詞的 **awake** 指的是「醒著的；沒有睡著的；有意識的」，動詞則是有「從睡夢中或無意識的狀態裡清醒」的語意。

聯想單字
alcohol　　n. 酒；酒精
alcoholic　adj. 含酒精的 n. 酒鬼，酗酒者

stale
[stel]
adj. 不新鮮的；老套的；厭倦的

反 fresh adj. 新鮮的；新的；剛發生的

Do you know how quickly bread goes **stale** when it is left out of the bag?
你知道麵包被從袋子裡拿出來後會多快變不新鮮嗎？

❶ Point 重點
各種「食物壞掉」的說法
go bad/off phr. 變質
turn sour phr. 酸掉
spoil v. 變壞，變質
rotten adj. 腐爛的
moldy adj. 發霉的
expired adj. 過期的

聯想單字		
	refrigerate	v.（在冰箱中）冷藏
	plastic wrap	n. 保鮮膜

stew
[stju]
n. 燉菜 v. 燉煮；生氣

衍 stewpot n. 燉鍋

I often like to prepare a **stew** with the leftover meat and lots of onions.
我常常會喜歡用剩下的肉和大量洋蔥來做燉菜。

My girlfriend is still **stewing** about an incident a few days ago.
我的女朋友還在為幾天前發生的一件事生氣。

❶ Point 重點
stew vs. simmer
stew（燉煮）是一種**料理的方式或菜名**（通常是燉肉或燉菜）；**simmer**（燉，煨）則是**料理製作 stew 的一部分過程**，表示「用小火慢慢煮一段時間」。

swallow
[`swalo]
v. 吞嚥；吞沒
n. 吞嚥；燕子

If you can't **swallow** the pills, open the capsules and mix them into any food or liquid.
如果您無法吞嚥藥丸，請把膠囊打開並將其混入任何食物或液體之中。

The bird took a quick **swallow** of water before flying away.
這隻鳥在飛走之前快速地喝了一口水。

❶ Point 重點

swallow one's words 被迫承認自己說的話不對
（把自己說的話吞回去）
⇨ I knew I had to **swallow** my **words** when she beat me at the game.
當她遊戲打贏我時，我就知道我不得不把自己的話吞回去了。

swallow one's pride 放下自尊去做正確的事
（把自己的自尊吞下去）
⇨ Lisa **swallowed** her **pride** and shook hands with the winner after losing the race.
Lisa 在輸掉比賽後，還是放下了自尊與獲勝者握手。

swallow the bait 上鉤，中圈套
（吞下誘餌）
⇨ The company **swallowed the bait** and signed a contract worth a million pounds with him.
那間公司上鉤了，與他簽訂了一份價值一百萬英鎊的合約。

takeaway
[ˋtekə͵we]
n. 外賣食物；外賣餐館；重點資訊

同 takeout n. 外賣食物；外賣餐館

My wife and I ordered a **takeaway** from a fancy restaurant on Valentine's Day.
我太太和我在情人節那天訂了高級餐廳的外賣。

❶ Point 重點
takeaway 除了指食物以外，也常常會用來在會議中表達「從各式各樣的資訊中所獲得的重點或精華內容」，也就是讓聽眾可以「帶回家、聽完帶走」的資訊。
⇨ The speaker wrapped up the seminar with a few valuable **takeaways**.
這位講者用幾項很寶貴的重點資訊來結束這場研討會。

For here or to go? 內用還是外帶？

內用	外帶
⇨ for here	⇨ to go
dine in	take out
	take away

聯想單字
giveaway	n. 贈品
on the house	phr.（店家請客）免費
complimentary	adj. 免費贈送的
delivery	n. 外送；運送
order	v. 訂購 n. 訂單；訂購的商品

tasteless
[ˋtestlɪs]
adj. 沒味道的；不得體的；沒有品味的

衍 taste n. 味道；味覺 v. 嚐；體驗
tasteful adj. 雅致的；有品味的

Tomato seeds are indigestible and **tasteless** and will pass through the digestive system unharmed.
番茄種子難以消化又沒有味道，且會完好無損地通過消化系統。

tavern
[ˋtævɚn]
n. 小酒館;餐酒館

The **tavern** provides a relaxed and comfortable atmosphere and is a popular destination for a quick bite.
這間小酒館的氣氛放鬆舒適,且是在想簡單吃點東西時很受歡迎的去處。

❶ Point 重點
常見的各種「用餐或聚會場所」
bar 酒吧
pub 傳統酒吧
club 會館,夜總會,俱樂部
bistro 法式餐酒館
café 輕食店,咖啡廳
cafeteria 自助食堂;學生或員工餐廳
diner 美式餐廳
restaurant 餐廳的總稱(在國外多指價格較高的用餐場所)
food court 美食街

utensil
[juˋtɛnsl]
n.(尤指廚房或家用的)器具,用具

The online store specializes in selling electronics, but it also offers a selection of kitchen **utensils**.
這間線上商店專門販售電子產品,但也提供了一系列可供選擇的廚房用具。

❶ Point 重點
tableware 是「**餐具的統稱**」,utensil 泛指器具,所以 **eating/dining utensils** 就是「**用餐的工具(餐具)**」。**cutlery** 是指在吃西餐時會用到的「**刀、叉、湯匙**」等餐具,**silverware** 泛指所有**金屬餐具**。

vintage
[ˋvɪntɪdʒ]
n. 特定年份的上等葡萄酒;釀造年份;同時代生產的東西
adj. 上等的;經典的

The year of the **vintage** is always displayed on the champagne bottle's front label.
葡萄酒的釀造年份一定會顯示在香檳酒瓶的正面標籤上。

When a **vintage** car is purchased in a non-EU country, customs registration is essential.
當古董車是在非歐盟國家購入時,必須辦理海關登記。

> **! Point 重點**
>
> **vintage** vs. **antique** vs. **classic**
> **vintage** 指的是「在過去的某個時期裡製造的高品質事物」，特別是那些「**同類產品中最好的事物**」。穿衣風格分類中的「古著」就是用 vintage 這個字。
>
> **antique** 指的是具有年歲和一定品質，且有著很高價值的事物，也就是「**古董**」的意思。
>
> **classic** 指的是經過足夠長的時間考驗後，被普遍認為是同類產品中品質最高且最出色的事物，表示「**具代表性的經典作品**」或「**傑作**」。

聯想單字		
vintage car	n. 古董車	
retro	adj. 懷舊的；復古的	
antique	n. 古董 adj. 古董的	

walnut
[ˋwɔlnət]
n. 胡桃；胡桃木

The TV stand made of **walnut** wood can be perfectly combined with any modern living style.
以胡桃木製成的電視櫃可以與現今任何居住風格完美結合。

聯想單字	
a walnut tree	n. 核桃樹
a walnut shell/nut	n. 核桃殼／仁
peanut	n. 花生
hazelnut	n. 榛果
pistachio	n. 開心果
almond	n. 杏仁
cashew (nut)	n. 腰果
pumpkin seed	n. 南瓜子
sunflower seed	n. 葵瓜子
chestnut	n. 栗子
pine nut	n. 松子

whiskey

['hwɪskɪ]

n. 威士忌（也可寫成 whisky）

If you opt for **whiskey** on the rocks, the bartender will give you a glass with two ounces of whiskey.
如果您選擇威士忌加冰塊，調酒師會給你一杯兩盎司的威士忌。

❶ Point 重點
「酒吧」相關的慣用表達
on the rocks 加冰塊
neat 不加冰塊
straight (up) 純酒
build/pour 直接倒入杯中
Single or double?（純酒的份數）要一份還是兩份？
bottle or draft（啤酒）瓶裝或杯裝

聯想單字

bartender	n. 調酒師
spirit	n. 烈酒
cocktail	n. 雞尾酒
champagne	n. 香檳
vodka	n. 伏特加
tequila	n. 龍舌蘭
gin	n. 琴酒
rum	n. 蘭姆酒
brandy	n. 白蘭地
rice wine	n. 米酒
sherry	n. 雪莉酒
happy hour	n. 酒吧提供優惠的時段

主題分類單字 食物、飲料、用餐相關

broth	[brɔθ]	n. 高湯
celery	[ˋsɛlərɪ]	n. 芹菜
chili	[ˋtʃɪlɪ]	n. 辣椒
clam	[klæm]	n. 蛤蜊；蚌
clover	[ˋklovɚ]	n. 苜蓿；三葉草
cocoa	[ˋkoko]	n. 可可粉；可可樹；可可色
cork	[kɔrk]	v. 用軟木塞塞住 n. 軟木；軟木塞
curry	[ˋkɝɪ]	n. 咖哩
dilute	[daɪˋlut]	adj. 經稀釋的 v. 稀釋
dough	[do]	n. 麵糰；現金
grocer	[ˋgrosɚ]	n. 食品雜貨商
lime	[laɪm]	n. 石灰；萊姆
lollipop	[ˋlalɪˏpap]	n. 棒棒糖
lunchtime	[ˋlʌntʃˏtaɪm]	n. 午餐時間
mayonnaise	[ˏmeəˋnez]	n. 蛋黃醬，美乃滋
mint	[mɪnt]	n. 薄荷；薄荷糖 v. 鑄造（硬幣）
mustard	[ˋmʌstɚd]	n. 黃芥末；深黃色
oatmeal	[ˋotˏmil]	n. 燕麥片；燕麥粥

單字	音標	詞性與中文
olive	[`alɪv]	adj. 橄欖的；橄欖色的 n. 橄欖；橄欖色
orchard	[`ɔrtʃɚd]	n. 果樹園；果樹林
oyster	[`ɔɪstɚ]	n. 牡蠣
parsley	[`pɑrslɪ]	n. 香芹
pickle	[`pɪkl̩]	n. 醃黃瓜；醬菜 v. 醃製
plantation	[plæn`teʃən]	n. 農園；造林地
poach	[potʃ]	v. 燉，水煮；偷獵；侵占
radish	[`rædɪʃ]	n. 白蘿蔔
starch	[stɑrtʃ]	n. 澱粉
starter	[`stɑrtɚ]	n. 開胃菜；開端
steamer	[`stimɚ]	n. 蒸籠，蒸鍋；汽船
tablespoon	[`tebl̩ˌspun]	n. 大湯匙；一大湯匙的量
taco	[`tako]	n. 墨西哥玉米餅
teaspoon	[`tiˌspun]	n. 茶匙；一茶匙的量
vanilla	[və`nɪlə]	n. 香草；香草精 adj. 香草味的；普通的
vineyard	[`vɪnjɚd]	n. 葡萄園
whisk	[hwɪsk]	v. 攪打；快速帶走 n. 攪拌器

Chapter 01　Quiz Time

一、請選出正確的答案。

1. These exercises are designed to improve the strength and stability of the muscles that make up the _____ of the body.

    A. grease
    B. cuisine
    C. refreshment
    D. core

2. Italy _____ approximately 600 different types of cheeses, and many regions have their own unique specialties.

    A. produces
    B. swallows
    C. soaks
    D. devours

3. Cleaned and sanitized _____ and equipment should be stored in a clean, dry place to prevent contamination.

    A. beverages
    B. carbohydrates
    C. utensils
    D. taverns

二、請根據下列中文句子，填入適當的英文單字。

1. 共乘可以大幅減少車輛的燃油消耗。

    Ride-sharing can significantly reduce fuel c_____ of vehicles.

2. 改用可重複使用而非拋棄式的購物袋會更環保。

   Using reusable grocery bags instead of d_____ ones is more environmentally friendly.

3. 除非你喜歡在炎熱的天氣裡騎腳踏車，不然你最好還是避開夏天的高溫。

   It's best to avoid the high summer temperatures unless you r_____ cycling in hot weather.

4. 在經歷了一整晚的狂歡之後，他隔天酒醒後覺得懊悔。

   After a night of partying, he woke up the next day feeling s_____ and regretful.

5. 古董車可能無法開長途，速度可能也追不上正常車速。

   A v_____ car may not be able to travel long distances, nor keep up to normal traffic speed.

Answer
(一)：1. D 2. A 3. C
(二)：1. consumption 2. disposable 3. relish 4. sober 5. vintage

翻譯：
(一)
1. 這些運動鞋是為了改善身體接觸地面的耗損率為設計的。
2. 乘火車利用西部約 600 種北回歸線路的起訖，且對許多想要離鄉自己的遊門得各。
3. 清潔和消毒車的儀器及設備，廣布在眾所皆避、乾燥的地方以避免污染。

Chapter 02

衣物

衣服、配件、顏色、形容詞

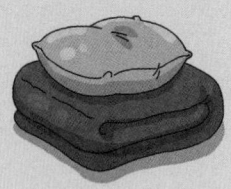

Ch02.mp3

★核心單字情境對話

Ben : Hey, Emily! You're looking very **dressed** up today. I love your **outfit**!

Emily : Thanks, Ben! I just got this **tailor-made garment** from a local boutique. The **fabric** is **exquisite**.

Ben : It's beautiful! I love the **ruby stripes** on the sleeves.

Emily : Yeah, they add a touch of glamour. Oh, have you seen my **backpack**? I can't find it.

Ben : Check the **wardrobe**. You left it there last weekend.

Emily : Oh, right! I need it to pack my **belongings** for this weekend's camping trip.

翻譯

Ben : 嘿,Emily!妳今天看起來**打扮**得非常用心耶。我喜歡妳的**造型**!

Emily : 謝了,Ben!我剛從這邊的一家精品店買了這件**訂製款的衣服**。這件的**布料**很**精緻**。

Ben : 真美!我好愛袖子上的**深紅色條紋**。

Emily : 沒錯,它們有錦上添花的效果。噢,你有看到我的**背包**嗎?我找不到。

Ben : 去看看**衣櫃**吧。妳上週末把它放在那裡了。

Emily : 噢,對!我需要用這個背包來裝我這週末要去露營的**東西**。

armor

[ˋɑrmɚ]
[英] **armour**
n. 盔甲；裝甲部隊

衍 armored adj. 裝甲的，配有裝甲的
army n. 軍隊

The warriors wore **armor** made of metal, which was often polished and gleaming.
戰士們穿著金屬製成的盔甲，這些盔甲通常都被打磨得閃閃發亮。

❶ Point 重點
chink in one's armor（性格或論點中的）弱點
（chink：裂縫；縫隙）
⇨ Jeffrey is brilliant, but his temper is the **chink in his armor**.
Jeffrey 很聰明，但脾氣是他的弱點。

a knight in shining armor 救星；白馬王子
（身穿閃亮盔甲的騎士）
⇨ Ben stopped that man from stealing my bag - he's my **knight in shining armor**!
Ben 阻止了那個男人偷我的包包——他是我的救星！

artifact

[ˋɑrtɪˌfækt]
[英] **artefact**
n. 工藝品

衍 artificial adj. 人工的；假的；不真誠的

The museum's collection includes **artifacts**, documents, photographs and stories of cultural significance to the region.
這間博物館的藏品涵蓋對該地區具有文化重要性的工藝品、文書、照片及新聞報導。

聯想單字	
artificial intelligence	n. 人工智慧
craft	n. 工藝，手藝
craftsman	n. 工匠

backpack

[ˋbækˌpæk]
n.（尤指登山用的）背包
v. 背包旅行

衍 backpacker n. 背包客
backpacking n. 以背包客方式旅行

Wearing a **backpack** incorrectly can lead to more pressure on your neck, shoulders, and back.
揹背包的方式錯誤可能會導致你的脖子、肩膀和背部承受更大的壓力。

We **backpacked** through parts of Australia, South East Asia and Europe.
我們當背包客去了澳洲、東南亞和歐洲的好幾個地方旅行。

❶ Point 重點
常見的各種「包包」
purse 女用手提包
bucket bag 水桶包
shoulder bag 肩揹包
tote bag 托特包
bum bag 腰包
duffle bag 圓筒狀旅行包
drawstring bag 束口包

belongings
[bə`lɔŋɪŋz]
n. 所有物，財產；隨身物品

衍 belong v. 屬於；適合

All the rooms are fully furnished, but you will need to bring personal **belongings** including bedding, towels, tableware and cooking utensils.
所有房間都附有全套家具，但您必須自帶個人物品，包括寢具、毛巾、餐具及廚房用具。

❶ Point 重點
belonging vs. **belongings**
belonging 是 belong（屬於；適合）的**現在分詞及動名詞**，常見於如 **a sense of belonging**（**歸屬感**）等的表達之中。**belongings** 指的則是屬於某人的「物品」，請特別注意**字尾的 s**，belongings 與 possessions 的字義相近。

belong to 屬於
⇨ Do you know who this bike **belongs to**?
你知道這台腳踏車是誰的嗎？

personal belongings	n. 個人所有物；個人隨身物品
possession	n. 擁有；所有物（常複數）
property	n. 財產；所有物；房地產

decorative
[ˋdɛkərətɪv]
adj. 裝飾用的

衍 decorate v. 裝飾
decoration n. 裝飾;裝潢;裝飾品
decoratively adv. 裝飾性地

These **decorative** bookcases can make your room look a bit warmer.
這些裝飾性的書櫃可以讓你的房間看起來溫馨一點。

❶ Point 重點
decoration vs. ornament
decoration 和 ornament 都可以用來指裝飾品，但是 **ornament** 著重於「無實際功能、僅有美化作用」的裝飾，**decoration** 則是「為特殊場合準備」的裝飾。

dressed
[drɛst]
adj. 穿好衣服的；打扮好的

衍 dress v. 幫～穿衣；打扮 n. 洋裝；連身裙
dressed-up adj. 精心打扮的
dresser n. 五斗櫃；餐具櫃
dressing n. 穿衣的動作；打扮的風格；醬料

The kids must make their beds and get **dressed** before breakfast.
孩子們必須在早餐前鋪好床並穿好衣服。

❶ Point 重點
get dressed vs. dress up
get dressed 只是「把衣服穿好」，沒有打扮的意思，而 **dress up** 則是「盛裝打扮」，也就是用心挑選及搭配各種衣物配件，兩者語意完全不一樣，使用時請小心不要搞混囉！

dress up 盛裝打扮
⇒ There will be a competition for who has the best costume, so be sure to **dress up**!
到時會比賽看誰穿得最厲害，所以一定要好好打扮！

be dressed (up) to the nines 盛裝打扮；打扮時髦
⇒ Everyone was **dressed to the nines** for the ceremony with the men in tuxedos and the women in dresses.
大家都為了典禮盛裝打扮，男士們穿上了燕尾服，女士們則穿了禮服。

be dressed to kill 精心打扮而成為全場焦點
⇒ She was **dressed to kill** for the party, wearing a stunning evening gown and accessories.
她為這場派對精心打扮，穿著令人驚豔的晚禮服、配戴著首飾，成為了全場焦點。

聯想單字	dress code	n. 服裝規定；穿著風格
	make-up	n. 化妝品
	attire	n.（特定或正式的）服裝

exquisite
[ˋɛkskwɪzɪt]
adj. 精美的；精緻的；卓越的

衍 exquisitely adv. 精緻地；精美地
exquisiteness n. 精美；精緻

This rug is like an **exquisite** piece of modern art that adds a high-end feel to your home.
這塊小地毯就像一件精美的現代藝術品，可以讓您的家更添高級感。

❶ Point 重點

exquisite vs. **elegant** vs. **elaborate** vs. **delicate**
exquisite 強調美**或技術的極致**，描述人時指的是「品味卓越」，形容事物時則是「作工精美、精緻」的意思；
elegant 則強調**外在顯現的感覺**，如人的外表、衣著或儀態「優雅端莊」或事物看起來感覺「高雅別緻」；
elaborate 表達的則是在**考慮眾多細節**後「精心設計的」；**delicate** 則把重點放在「**脆弱而須小心對待**」的特性，表示某個人事物是「精緻的」或「纖細的」。

fabric
[ˋfæbrɪk]
n. 布料；結構

衍 fabricate v. 捏造；偽造

Clothing for kids should be made of **fabrics** that are soft, comfortable, and kind to sensitive skin.
小孩子的衣物應該要用柔軟、舒適且不會傷害到敏感肌膚的布料來製作。

❶ Point 重點

常見的「布料材質」
cotton 棉   leather 皮革
linen 亞麻   Tencel 天絲
wool 羊毛   denim 牛仔布
silk 蠶絲   cashmere 喀什米爾
nylon 尼龍   polyester 聚脂纖維

聯想單字	textile	n. 紡織品
	cloth	n.（棉、毛、合成纖維等製成的）布料；布
	material	n. 原料；布料

Chapter 02・衣服、配件、顏色、形容詞

fiber
[ˋfaɪbɚ]
[英] fibre
n. 纖維

Natural **fibers** such as cotton, wool, and silk are eco-friendly, biodegradable, and renewable.
棉花、羊毛和蠶絲等天然纖維是環保、可生物分解且可再生的。

garment
[ˋgɑrmənt]
n. 衣著

The company manufactures and sells **garments** and textiles in Taiwan.
這間公司在台灣製造及販售成衣與紡織品。

❶ Point 重點

garment vs. **attire**
garment 指的是 **a piece of clothing**（一件衣物），不論是上衣還是褲子，只要是可以穿的衣物，都可以用 garment 這個字，另外，複數 garments 單一個字就可以用來指整個成衣業（garment industry），不過這是比較正式的用法。

attire 專指在特定場合或為符合特定用途所穿著的「整體服裝」或「服裝類型」，例如 **business attire**（商務服裝）、**casual attire**（休閒服）、**sports attire**（運動服）等等。

glitter
[ˋglɪtɚ]
v. 閃閃發光；閃爍
n. 閃爍；吸引力

The stars **glittered** brilliantly under the cloudless sky of indigo.
星星在一點雲都沒有的靛藍色天空下燦爛地閃閃發光。

The best time to come to this hill is New Year's Eve as you can clearly see the **glitter** of the fireworks from the top of the hill.
跨年夜是來這座山的最佳時機，因為你可以清楚從山頂上看到煙火閃閃發光。

❶ Point 重點

All that glitters is not gold.
閃閃發光的未必都是黃金。
這句話出自莎士比亞的作品《威尼斯商人》，主要表達「不能只看外表來判斷價值」的意思，因為「金玉其外，敗絮其中」的情形其實所在多有。

表達「光彩奪目」的其他常用說法
dazzling 耀眼的；光彩奪目的
splendid 燦爛的；壯麗的
sparkling 閃閃發光的
glistening 閃耀的；閃閃發光的

聯想單字
glimmer	v. 隱約閃爍；發出微光
glow	v. 發出白熱光；容光煥發
shimmer	v. 微弱地閃爍

handicraft
[ˋhændɪˌkræft]
n. 手工藝；手工藝品

衍 handcraft n. 手工藝；手工藝品
v. 手工製作
handcrafted adj. 手工製作的

There are **handicrafts** made by local people from different ethnic groups around the world.
這裡有來自世界各地不同民族的當地人製作的手工藝品。

聯想單字
handmade	adj. 手工的
homemade	adj. 自製的；在家裡做的
handpicked	adj. 精心挑選出來的
craft	n. 工藝 v.（技藝純熟地）製作
craftsman	n. 工匠；工藝師

hood
[hʊd]
n. 衣服上的帽子；遮罩；引擎蓋

Depending on the weather and your styling, you can also detach the **hood** of the coat.
隨著天氣和造型而定，你也可以把這件大衣的帽子拆掉。

● Point 重點
經常看到的名詞字尾 **-hood**，意思是「**做為某種事物的狀態**」。
baby**hood** 嬰兒時期
child**hood** 童年時期
man**hood**/adult**hood** 成年時期
neighbor**hood** 街坊；左鄰右舍

其他常見的「休閒服飾」
sweatshirt 大學 T　　jumper [英] 毛衣
hoodie 連帽 T 恤　　pullover 套頭毛衣
turtleneck 高圓領　　cardigan 開襟衫
tank top 無袖背心　　leather jacket 皮衣
sweater [美] 毛衣　　trench coat 風衣

metallic
[məˋtælɪk]
adj. 有金屬特性的；含金屬的

衍 metal n. 金屬
　　　 adj. 金屬製的

A sharp **metallic** sound coming from the outside frightened me.
我被外面傳來的一聲尖銳的金屬聲嚇了一跳。

❶ Point 重點
常見的「原料及材質」
metallic 金屬的　　leather 皮製的
wooden 木製的　　cotton 棉花的
steel 鋼鐵的　　　silk 絲質的
plastic 塑膠的　　ceramic 陶瓷的

outfit
[ˋaʊt͵fɪt]
n. 全套服裝；全套裝備
v. 裝備；配備

You can wear scarves in different styles to create stunning winter **outfits**.
你可以用不同的風格圍圍巾，打造出令人驚豔的冬季穿搭。

The new truck is **outfitted** with the latest navigation system.
新的卡車裝備了最新的導航系統。

❶ Point 重點
常見的其他「成套服裝」
suit 套裝，西裝
business suit 商務套裝
morning suit 早禮服（男）
evening suit 晚禮服（男）
tuxedo 半正式晚禮服（男）
tailcoat 燕尾服
evening gown/evening dress 晚禮服（女）

ragged
[ˋrægɪd]
adj.（衣服）破舊的；衣衫襤褸的

衍 rag n. 舊布；破布
　　v. 戲弄；對～惡作劇

A **ragged** homeless man begged on the street with a bowl.
一個衣衫襤褸的流浪漢在街頭拿著碗乞討。

ruby
[ˋrubɪ]
n. 紅寶石；深紅色

Some couples may opt for a **ruby** ring as rubies are less common than traditional diamond engagement rings.
有些情侶可能會選擇紅寶石戒指，因為紅寶石不像傳統的鑽石訂婚戒指那麼普通。

❶ Point 重點
常見的其他「寶石」
diamond 鑽石　　　opal 蛋白石
sapphire 藍寶石　　amber 琥珀
emerald 祖母綠　　pearl 珍珠

聯想單字
ruby wedding　　n. 結婚 40 週年

strap
[stræp]
n. 帶子；皮帶
v. 用帶子綑綁；束縛

衍 strapped adj.
　手頭緊的，缺錢的
　cash-strapped adj.
　缺錢的，財務困難的
　strapping adj.
　魁梧的
　strapless adj.
　無肩帶的

To keep your helmet in place, please fasten the **strap** under your chin.
為了避免安全帽移位，請把帶子繫在你的下巴下面。

They **strapped** the surfboard to the roof before heading to the beach.
在去海灘之前，他們把衝浪板綁在了車頂上面。

❶ Point 重點
strap sb in 為（某人）繫好安全帶
⇨ To keep your dog safe, it's important to **strap** them **in** with a doggy seat belt.
為了確保你家狗的安全，幫牠們繫好狗用安全帶是很重要的事。

strap up sth 用繃帶或懸帶綁好（某物）
⇨ After an X-ray, he was given a sling to **strap up** his arm and stabilize it.
在照過 X 光後，他拿到了一條懸帶，用來綁好並固定他的手臂。

> 聯想單字
> shoulder strap　n. 肩帶；揹帶
> spaghetti strap　n. 細肩帶

stripe
[straɪp]
n. 條紋，斑紋；線條

The shop sells fabric with **stripes** in various shades of blue.
這家店有賣各式各樣不同深淺的藍色條紋布料。

● Point 重點
其他常見的「服裝花樣」
plaid/checked 格子花紋　　houndstooth 千鳥紋
leopard print 豹紋　　　　zebra print 斑馬紋
polka dot pattern 圓點花紋　floral pattern 花卉圖案

tailor-made
[ˋtelɚ͵med]
adj. 特製的；客製化的

衍 tailor n. 裁縫師
v. 裁製；修改（以符合特定需求）
tailored adj.（經修改而）合身的；量身打造的

This innovative online educational platform provides **tailor-made** courses to individuals as well as to private companies.
這個創新的線上教育平台為個人和私人公司提供客製化課程。

● Point 重點
be tailor-made for sth 非常適合（某事）
⇨ If your target audience is aged 19-29 years, then this social media app **is tailor-made for** you.
如果你的目標受眾是 19 到 29 歲的年紀，那麼這款社群媒體應用程式就非常適合你。

> 聯想單字
> custom-made　adj.（衣服等）訂做的，客製化的
> customized　　adj. 客製化的，訂做的

tan
[tæn]
n. 淺褐色的膚色
adj. 淺褐色的
v. 把皮膚曬成淺褐色

If you want to get a dark **tan**, you should exfoliate your skin the night before with a bath sponge.
如果你想把皮膚曬成古銅色，那麼你應該在前一天晚上用沐浴海綿把皮膚去角質。

The women's **tan** shoes from this brand are all handcrafted in Italy and are competitively priced with other brands.
這個牌子的淺褐色女鞋全都是義大利手工製作的，而且價格相對於其他品牌更具有競爭力。

You should avoid using bar soaps, high pH shower products or oil-based products at least 24 hours before **tanning**.
在去把皮膚曬成淺褐色之前的至少 24 個小時，你應該要避免使用肥皂、高 pH 值的沐浴產品或油性產品。

❶ Point 重點
當要形容人的**膚色**時，不可以直接用「white/black」，因為 skin color（white/black/yellow）的說法帶有「人種」的意涵，而應用 **skin tone**（fair/light/dark）來表達。
⇨ Your skin is **fair**.
你的皮膚好白。
Everyone in my family is **fair-skinned**.
我們全家人的皮膚都很白。
He has **dark** skin.
他的皮膚很黑。

「曬黑」的其他常見說法
catch the sun 曬到紅紅的
⇨ I **caught the sun** on my nose and cheeks this weekend.
這個週末我的鼻子和臉頰都曬到紅紅的了。

get tanned 曬黑
⇨ I hate getting too tanned and I will slather myself with sunscreen to prevent it.
我討厭曬得太黑，所以我會幫自己塗上厚厚的防曬乳來防曬。

聯想單字		
suntan	n. （皮膚）曬黑
tan line	n. 曬痕
sunburn	n. 曬傷
tanning salon	n. 助曬沙龍
tanning lotion	n. 助曬乳
a golden/dark tan	n. 古銅色的膚色

textile
[ˋtɛkstaɪl]
n. 紡織品

The government has provided financial incentives to **textile** companies.
政府對紡織公司提供了財務獎勵措施。

聯想單字		
textile industry	n. 紡織業

texture
[ˋtɛkstʃɚ]
n. 質地；紋理；（文章等的）筆觸

This artificial fabric has a **texture** similar to the softness of natural leather.
這種人造布料的質地與天然皮革差不多柔軟。

❶ Point 重點
其他常見的「質地」形容詞
furry 毛茸茸的　　velvety 天鵝絨般的
smooth 光滑的　　rough 粗糙的
silky 絲綢般的　　woolly 羊毛製的

undo
[ʌnˋdu]
v. 解開；鬆開；拆開；消除

The tightness of the clothes bothered him, so he **undid** his belt.
衣服緊得讓他不舒服，所以他把皮帶鬆開了。

wardrobe
[ˋwɔrd͵rob]
n. 衣櫥，衣櫃；（個人的）全部服裝

Spring has arrived and this means that we can leave duvets and coats in the **wardrobe** and opt for lighter garments.
春天的到來意味著我們可以把羽絨被和大衣留在衣櫃裡，然後改穿更輕便的衣服了。

主題分類單字
衣服、配件、顏色、形容詞相關

Ch02.mp3

Chapter 02 衣物

brassiere	[brəˋzɪr]	n. 胸罩
brooch	[brotʃ]	n.（女用）胸針
cardinal	[ˋkɑrdənəl]	adj. 主要的；深紅的 n. 深紅色
charcoal	[ˋtʃɑr͵kol]	n. 木炭；炭筆；深灰色
coral	[ˋkɔrəl]	adj. 珊瑚的；珊瑚色的 n. 珊瑚
jade	[dʒed]	n. 玉；玉製品；翡翠色 adj. 玉的，玉製的；翠玉色的
jasmine	[ˋdʒæsmɪn]	n. 茉莉；淡黃色
necktie	[ˋnɛk͵taɪ]	n. 領帶
sandal	[ˋsændḷ]	n. 涼鞋
sandy	[ˋsændɪ]	adj. 含沙的；多沙的；沙色的
sulfur	[ˋsʌlfɚ]	n. 硫磺；硫磺色
tint	[tɪnt]	n.（淡淡的）色調
velvet	[ˋvɛlvɪt]	n. 天鵝絨；絲絨
wig	[wɪg]	n. 假髮

Chapter 02・衣服、配件、顏色、形容詞　P.043

Chapter 02 Quiz Time

一、請選出正確的答案。

1. These _____ handmade creations showcase the talent and dedication of the craftsman.
    A. ragged
    B. dressed
    C. hood
    D. exquisite

2. No personal _____ are allowed in the testing area, but lockers will be provided for the storage of any items.
    A. garments
    B. belongings
    C. straps
    D. stripes

3. The course is _____ for individuals who wish to pursue careers in the IT sector.
    A. decorative
    B. fabric
    C. metallic
    D. tailor-made

二、請根據下列中文句子，填入適當的英文單字。

1. 你可以在這裡用非常低的價格買到一些手工藝品和紀念品。

    You can buy some h_____ and souvenirs at really low prices here.

2. 我在派對上穿的那套衣服完全就是一場災難，而且我甚至連我的項鍊都弄丟了。

   My o_____ for the party was a complete disaster and I even lost my necklace.

3. 質地是包裝材料的關鍵，因為它必須符合消費者的期待。

   T_____ is a key factor in packaging as it needs to meet consumer expectations.

4. 那名教練當時正在沙灘上向女士們炫耀自己曬成淺褐的膚色。

   The coach was showing off his t_____ to the ladies at the beach.

5. 沙發上方增添了裝飾性的畫作，以提升座位區對顧客的吸引力。

   D_____ paintings were added above the sofa to make the seating area more attractive to customers.

Answer
（一）：1. D 2. B 3. D
（二）：1. handicrafts 2. outfit 3. texture 4. tan 5. Decorative

翻譯：
（一）
1. 這家精美的手藝品店販售了工匠的手藝和設入。
2. 個人勿品不僅僅是收藏寶藏，也承載此實物櫃來存放任何物品。
3. 苗準課程若為您提供未來在其領域接事顧工作的人所需門販技的。

Chapter 02．衣服、配件、顏色、形容詞　P.045

Chapter 03

居家
房屋、家具、
日常用品、家庭

Ch03.mp3

★ 核心單字情境對話

Tom : Lily, what do you think of moving up north to the city **outskirts**?
Lily : The **residential** areas there do seem so **spacious** and **cozy** compared to our cramped apartment.
Tom : And the **vicinity** is much quieter and more **hospitable** - a **haven** away from the hustle and bustle.
Lily : It would be nice to **lounge** in peace after a long day.
Tom : And the **architectural** designs of the houses up there are stunning.
Lily : Maybe we could **lease** first and find the perfect place to **inhabit** for the rest of our lives.

翻譯

Tom ： Lily，妳覺得我們往北搬到**市郊**怎麼樣？
Lily ： 和我們擁擠的公寓相比，那裡的**住宅區**的確看起來**空間**超大又**舒適**。
Tom ： 而且那**附近**安靜多了，也更**適合住人**——就是一個遠離塵囂的**避風港**。
Lily ： 如果在忙了一天之後能**待在**一個地方好好休息，那一定很棒。
Tom ： 而且北邊那裡的房屋**建築**設計很讓人驚艷。
Lily ： 也許我們可以先用**租**的，然後再找個適合我們下半輩子**居住**的好地方。

aisle
[aɪl]
n. 走廊；通道

You'll find soaps and shampoos in the second **aisle** from the exit.
您可以在從出口數過來的第二條走道找到肥皂和洗髮精。

❗ Point 重點
get/have/leave sb rolling in the aisles（或 **be rolling in the aisles**）笑得人仰馬翻
⇨ The comedian's joke **had the audience rolling in the aisles**.
這位喜劇演員的笑話讓觀眾笑到不行。

aisle vs. **hallway** vs. **corridor**
aisle 通常是**座位之間的通道**，例如火車、禮堂或小教室中的走道。

corridor 一般是**大型建築裡的走道**，用來**連接兩個不同區域**，且兩側或一側常設有通向其他房間的門，例如醫院或飯店的走廊。

hallway 則是**小型建築裡通往其他房間的走道**，也有可能是指「**玄關**」，例如一般住家中從門口通往客廳或從房間通往浴室的走廊。

聯想單字
aisle seat　　n. 靠走道的座位
window seat　n. 靠窗的座位

architectural
[ˌɑrkəˈtɛktʃərəl]
adj. 建築的；建築學的

衍 architect n. 建築師
　 architecture n. 建築學；建築風格

Architectural style refers to the unique design elements that define a specific period, region, or culture.
建築風格是指定義某特定時期、地區或文化的獨特設計元素。

❗ Point 重點
常見的各種「建築物」
building 大樓　　　　　　　stadium 體育場；運動場
apartment complex 公寓社區　arena 競技場；活動場地
skyscraper 摩天大樓　　　　dome 穹頂建築；巨蛋

Chapter 03・居家

Chapter 03・房屋、家具、日常用品、家庭

聯想單字
structure	n. 結構；建築物
renovate	v. 翻新；整修
construction	n. 建造；建設；建築物
pillar	n. 梁柱
cathedral	n. 大教堂

auditorium
[ˌɔdə`torɪəm]
n. 禮堂；演藝廳

衍 auditory adj. 聽覺的
audition n. 聽力；
（演員等的）試鏡

The beautiful and historic **auditorium** seats 900 people.
這座美麗且歷史悠久的禮堂可容納 900 人。

聯想單字
hall	n. 會堂；大廳
theater	n. 劇場，戲院
opera house	n. 歌劇院

clinch
[klɪntʃ]
v. 獲得；最終贏得
n.（打架時的）扭抱；擁抱

The team **clinched** the first game of the best-of-seven series against the other team.
這隊在七戰四勝系列賽的第一場比賽中擊敗了另一支隊伍。

The two boxers were in a **clinch** when the bell rang to announce the end of the second round.
當宣布第二回合結束的鈴聲響起時，這兩名拳擊手正扭抱在一起。

❶ Point 重點
clinch it 使最終決定；使下定決心
⇒ Many voters claimed that televised debates between candidates could be what **clinches it** for them.
很多選民聲稱，候選人電視辯論會可能會左右他們的最終決定。

commodity
[kə`mɑdətɪ]
n. 大宗商品；貨物

Palm oil is one of the most important **commodities** for the Malaysian economy.
對於馬來西亞的經濟來說，棕櫚油是最重要的商品之一。

> **Point 重點**
>
> **commodity** vs. **goods** vs. **product** vs. **merchandise**
> **commodity** 是由供應商進行買賣的「**大宗商品**」，這些商品通常都是沒有經過太多加工、同質性高的原物料，如大豆、小麥、石油等等。
>
> **goods** 泛指一般人在日常生活中銷售或購入的「**實體商品財貨**」，因為是泛稱，所以無特定指稱商品或產業。
>
> **product** 指的是針對消費者或市場，經過設計、製造、加工等流程所生產出來的「**產品**」。
>
> **merchandise** 是「拿出來賣的商品」，重點放在「銷售」上，通常指**零售或批發的商品**。

聯想單字
agricultural commodities	n. 大宗農產品
necessity	n. 必需品

cosmetic
[kɑz`mɛtɪk]
n. 化妝品（恆複數）
adj. 化妝用的；表面的

衍 cosmetically adv.
　　表面地；美容地

Their products cover a wide range of **cosmetics** and skincare essentials designed to meet the needs of the public.
他們的產品涵蓋各式各樣設計來滿足大眾需求的化妝品和保養必需品。

South Korea is the market leader in **cosmetic** surgery, with a 25% share of the global market.
韓國是整形手術市場中的領頭羊，擁有 25% 的全球市占率。

> **Point 重點**
>
> **cosmetics** vs. **make-up**
> **cosmetics** 指的不只是化妝品，只要是具有美容效果、可以改善外觀的產品，就算是保養品也可以用 cosmetics 這個字。
>
> **make-up** 這個字來自動詞片語 make up（上妝），因此專指粉底、口紅等彩妝用品。

常見的「化妝品」相關單字

foundation 粉底　　　　lip stick 唇膏
concealer 遮瑕　　　　eyebrow pencil 眉筆
blusher 腮紅　　　　　eyeliner 眼線
highlighter 打亮　　　 eye shadow 眼影
setting powder 蜜粉　　mascara 睫毛膏

聯想單字

apply/put on makeup　phr. 上妝
wear makeup　　　　 phr. 帶妝

---

cozy
[ˋkozɪ]
[英] cosy
adj. 溫暖舒適的；
愜意的

Floor heaters can help keep indoor areas warm and **cozy** in the winter.
地暖能讓室內區域在冬天保持溫暖舒適。

dwell
[dwɛl]
v. 居住

衍 dwelling n. 住處，
　　住宅
　dweller n. 居民；
　　居住者

They **dwell** in a cozy cottage by the lake and enjoy their retirement.
他們住在湖畔一間舒適的小屋裡，享受退休生活。

❶ Point 重點 ⋯⋯⋯⋯⋯⋯⋯⋯⋯⋯⋯⋯⋯⋯⋯⋯⋯⋯⋯⋯⋯⋯

dwell in 居住於～
⇒ I used to **dwell in** that small town when I was a child.
　我小時候曾住在那個小鎮上。

dwell on 耽溺於（尤指負面的事）
⇒ She is still **dwelling on** her friend's betrayal and can't fully forgive her.
　她對於朋友的背叛仍然耿耿於懷，無法完全原諒她。

live vs. dwell vs. inhabit vs. reside
最常用來描述一個人「**生活**」或「**居住**」在哪裡的字是 **live**，**dwell** 則是較正式的用字，表示「**在某地長時間居住**」或「**以某種特殊的方式生活**」。有著「**動物在某處棲**

P.050　國際學村・全民英檢

息」意味的 **inhabit**，多半在談論自然生態時才會使用。如果有**合法的永久居住地**，則會使用 **reside** 這個字。

emigrate
[ˋɛməˌgret]
v. 移居外國；移民

衍 emigration n. 移民（出境）
emigrant n.（移居國外的）移民

反 immigrate v. 從外地遷入

Her mother **emigrated** from Taiwan to settle in the U.S. decades ago.
她的母親數十年前從台灣移民到美國定居了。

❶ Point 重點
emigrate vs. **immigrate** vs. **migrate**
emigrate 是**從本國移出**（字首 **e = ex = out**，向外），
immigrate 是**從他國移入**（字首 **im = in**，向內）。
emigrate 和 immigrate 都只能用在人身上，而 **migrate**（開頭是 **m**，可以用 **move** 這個字來聯想）通常指**動物的遷徙或人的移居**。

enclosure
[ɪnˋkloʒɚ]
n. 圍起來的區域；圈地；（信的）附件

衍 enclose v. 把～圍起來；圍住；隨信附上
enclosed adj. 附上的；圍住的

That large **enclosure** is dedicated to growing high-value crops such as cocoa.
那邊圍起來的一大塊地是專門用來種植像可可之類的高價作物。

evacuate
[ɪˋvækjʊˌet]
v.（把人從危險的地方）撤離，撤出，疏散

衍 evacuation n. 撤離，撤出，疏散

The police **evacuated** crowds following an anonymous bomb threat.
在接到匿名炸彈威脅後，警方疏散了群眾。

> ❶ Point 重點
> **evacuated from** 從～（某地）撤離
> （只能使用被動語態）
> ⇨ More than a thousand people were **evacuated from** local towns and villages because of flooding.
> 因為淹水，超過一千人從當地城鎮和村莊中撤離。

聯想單字
relocate	v. 遷移～（到某處）重新安置
flee	v. 逃跑；逃出國外
rescue	v. 救援；解救

fireproof
[ˋfaɪrˋpruf]
adj. 防火的

The material is **fireproof** and can stand high temperatures of up to 1000°C.
這種材料防火，可承受高達 1000°C 的高溫。

聯想單字
waterproof	adj. 防水的
soundproof	adj. 隔音的
bulletproof	adj. 防彈的

haven
[ˋhevən]
n. 避風港；避難之處

The organization requests that the government enact laws to provide safe **havens** for abandoned babies.
該組織要求政府頒布法律，為棄嬰提供安全的避風港。

> ❶ Point 重點
> haven 的後面經常搭配**介系詞片語 from sth**，以表示該避風港是為「**遠離某事物**」而存在。
> ⇨ The place has always been considered a **haven from** stress and anxiety.
> 這個地方一直被認為是遠離壓力和焦慮的避風港。

聯想單字
tax haven	n. 避稅天堂
shelter	n. 收容所 v. 收容
asylum	n.（政治性）庇護
refuge	n. 庇護；收容所；避難所

hospitable

[ˈhɑspɪtəbl]
adj. 好客的；（氣候、環境等）宜人的

衍 hospitality n. 好客；殷勤款待

反 inhospitable adj. 不好客的；（地區）難以居住，條件惡劣的

According to research, the most **hospitable** regions in the world are the Middle East and Latin America.
根據研究，世界上最好客的區域是中東和拉丁美洲。

❶ Point 重點
hospitable（好客的）和 hospital（醫院）的字根都是 **host-**（主人；接待），拼法很類似，小心不要混淆了哦！

hospitable to/towards 對～好客；殷勤接待
⇨ The restaurant owner is always very **hospitable to** his guests.
這位餐廳老闆總是非常殷勤地接待他的客人。

聯想單字		
friendly	adj. 友善的
hospitality industry	n. 餐旅業

inhabit

[ɪnˈhæbɪt]
v. 居住於；棲息於

衍 inhabitant n. 居民；棲息的動物
inhabitable adj. 適合居住的，可居住的

Deserts are **inhabited** by several animal species, and each has its own methods of adapting to water shortage.
在沙漠裡棲息的動物有好幾種，而牠們各有各的方法來應對缺水的環境。

❶ Point 重點
inhabit 和 live 在語意上相似，但用法不同。
live 的後面要接**介系詞 in**，但是 inhabit 不用。
⇨ Wild animals **live in** the woods.
Wild animals **inhabit** the woods.
野生動物居住在森林裡。

聯想單字		
cohabit	v. 同居
habitat	n.（動植物的）生長地，棲息地
habitation	n. 居住
habitant	n.（某個地方的）居民，居住者

Chapter 03・房屋、家具、日常用品、家庭

lease
[lis]
v. 租賃 n. 租約

衍 leasehold n. 租賃權
leaseholder n. 承租人，租賃人

These floors are currently **leased** to a restaurant, with a monthly rent of approximately US$4,000.
這些樓層目前出租給一家餐廳，每月租金約 4,000 美元。

Landlords should offer tenants a lease renewal notice 60 days before the **lease** expires.
房東應在租約到期前的 60 天向承租人發出續約通知。

❶ Point 重點

lease vs. **rent** vs. **borrow** vs. **lend**
lease 是指按照租約出租或租用**不動產**，如土地或房屋。
rent 出租或租用的則**不只不動產，也包含動產**，如跑車、金飾等。這兩字均**涉及租約**，因此在法律層面上會用到的通常是這兩個單字。
borrow（借入）和 **lend**（借出）一般都是**短時間**的行為，且不一定有租賃合約。另一方面，無論是借入還是借出，都可以用 lease 和 rent，關鍵在於後面接的介系詞是 **from**（從～借入）還是 **to**（借出給～）。

聯想單字
tenant	n. 房客；承租人
sublet	v. 轉租；分租
landlord	n. 房東

legacy
[ˋlɛɡəsɪ]
n. 遺產；遺留給後人的東西

Alice received a **legacy** from her uncle and purchased a property.
Alice 從她叔叔那裡得到了一筆遺產，然後購買了房地產。

❶ Point 重點

leave sb a legacy 留給某人一筆遺產
⇒ Although his father **left** him **a** small **legacy**, Thomas squandered much of it on gambling.
儘管 Thomas 的父親有留一小筆遺產給他，但他把其中的大部分都揮霍在賭博上了。

inheritance vs. **legacy** vs. **heritage**
如果指的是法律上的「遺產（現金、不動產等有形資產）」，必須使用可數的 inheritance，不過這個字也有

「遺傳（基因等生物特質）」的意思。同是可數名詞的 legacy，雖然也常指有形資產，但更常用來表達會造成深遠影響的「無形資產（如價值觀、作風等）」。heritage 則是不可數名詞，表示「具有群體共同意義的資產」，多指如 cultural heritage（文化遺產）等的無形資產。

聯想單字
endowment	n. 捐贈基金
pass down	phr. 傳承
inherit	v. 繼承
succession	n. 繼承

lifelong
[ˋlaɪf͵lɔŋ]
adj. 終身的，一輩子的

My **lifelong** ambition is to become a veterinarian and contribute to wildlife conservation.
我的畢生志向是成為一名獸醫，並為野生動植物保育做出貢獻。

❶ Point 重點
表示「時間長久」的其他常用字彙

permanent 永久的；長久的
➩ 強調狀態的持久及穩定，例如 permanent resident（永久居民）即是長久不變的情況和地位。

lasting 持續的；持久的
➩ 表示狀態的持續，語氣比 permanent 更加強烈，如 lasting relationships（持續的關係）。

everlasting 永久的；永恆的
➩ 指不受時間影響，永遠存在且不會發生變化，語氣比 lasting 更強烈，如 everlasting love（永恆的愛）。

eternal 永恆的；不朽的
➩ 這個字較正式，表示在過去、現在、未來都會一直存在、永恆不變的事物，如 eternal truth（永恆的真理）。

聯想單字
lifelong learning	n. 終身學習
lifelong habit	n. 終身的習慣
lifelong member	n. 終身會員

lodge

[lɑdʒ]

v. 投宿；提出（索賠或抗議等）

n.（鄉間或山上的）小屋；（團體的）會所

衍 lodging n. 暫時住處

During my freshman year, I temporarily **lodged** at my cousin's house due to renovations in the dormitory.
我在大一的時候，因為宿舍整修而暫時住在了我表弟家。

A ski **lodge** refers to a mountain hotel that provides accommodation for skiers.
滑雪小屋是指為滑雪者提供住宿的山區旅館。

❶ Point 重點
其他常見的「暫時住處」
cabin 小木屋
hostel（較便宜的）旅社
inn 小型旅館
cottage（鄉村中的）小屋

聯想單字

put sb up　　phr. 為（某人）暫時提供住宿

lounge

[laʊndʒ]

n.（飯店、機場等的）休息室，貴賓室；客廳

Before your flight, you can relax in the airport **lounge** and enjoy complimentary food and drinks in a calming and comfortable environment.
在上機之前，你可以在機場休息室裡休息，並在平靜舒適的環境中享用免費的食物和飲料。

❶ Point 重點
lounge around (sth)（在～）悠閒地待著
⇒ We **lounged around** this beautiful hotel and checked out the pool and gym.
　我們在這間漂亮的飯店裡悠閒地待著，還去用了游泳池和健身房。

聯想單字

lounge bar　　n. 酒廊
lounge suit　　n. 商務套裝
lounge chair　　n. 躺椅

migrate
[ˈmaɪˌgret]
v. (動物)遷徙;移居;轉移

衍 migration n. (動物)遷徙;移居;遷移
migrant n. 移民;遷徙動物 adj. 遷移的;遷徙的
migratory adj. (動物、候鳥或人)移居的,遷居的

Billions of birds **migrate** every year, crossing oceans, deserts, mountains, and even hemispheres in search of better weather and food.
每年有數十億隻鳥為了尋找更好的氣候和食物而遷徙,牠們會飛越海洋、沙漠、山脈,甚至跨越半球。

❶ Point 重點

migrate vs. **immigrate** vs. **emigrate**
migrate 指的是「**暫時性**」的移動,描述人或動物都可以,以動物來說就是遷徙,在人身上則是如因工作等因素而進行的暫時性移居。
⇨ About 20% of all bird species **migrate** every year **to** warmer areas.
在所有鳥類之中,約有 20% 會每年遷徙到溫暖的地區。
A large number of temporary workers **migrated into** big cities.
大量的臨時工移居到了大都市。

immigrate 只能用來描述**人**,字首 im- 有 into(進入到~)的意思,表示「進入或移入某地並**長期**」生活,也就是「**移民遷入**」。
⇨ He **immigrated** with his parents and younger brother **to** Canada **from** Taiwan.
他與父母和弟弟一起從台灣移民到加拿大。

emigrate 只能用在**人**的身上,字首 e- 有 exit(出去)的意思,表示「離開家鄉去到另一個地方**長期**生活」,也就是「**移民遷出**」。
⇨ A Hong Kong couple who **emigrated to** Taiwan four years ago opened a café in Tainan.
四年前移居台灣的一對香港夫婦在台南開了一家咖啡館。

outskirts
[ˋaʊtˏskɝts]
n. 市郊，郊區

反 urban adj. 都市的

Children living in the **outskirts** of the town are too far away to attend classes.
住在郊區的孩子們因為距離太遠而無法上課。

❶ Point 重點
outskirts vs. **suburbs**
outskirts 多指城市或城鎮的外圍及邊界地區，一般都不是單純的住宅區，而是會混雜商舖設施，出入人口較複雜，且通常開發程度不高，常以 **on the outskirts** 的表達方式來使用。

suburbs 專指離市中心不遠的「近郊住宅區」，通常社區規劃完善、房價高昂，經常搭配介系詞 **in**，構成 **in the suburbs** 的表達方式來使用。

聯想單字		
downtown	adj. / adv. 在市中心（的）
country	n. 鄉村，鄉下
rural	adj. 農村的；似鄉村的

populate
[ˋpɑpjəˏlet]
v. 居住於；構成～的人口（或總數）

衍 populated adj. 有人居住的
population n. 人口

The purpose of conservation is to **populate** the area with endangered species.
保育的目的在於讓瀕危物種能在該地區繁衍。

rack
[ræk]
n. 架子；掛物架
v. 使肉體（或精神上）受折磨

For wine collectors, the wine **rack** is probably one of the most important pieces of furniture in the home.
對於葡萄酒收藏家來說，紅酒架很可能是家裡最重要的家具之一。

He used the drug to relieve depression and stress but was **racked** by its side effects.
他使用這種藥物來緩解憂鬱和壓力，但藥物的副作用卻讓他飽受折磨。

❶ Point 重點

rack one's brains 絞盡腦汁
⇨ I **racked** my **brains** all weekend trying to solve a tricky problem.
我整個週末絞盡腦汁，試圖解決一個棘手的問題。

off-the-rack adj.（衣服）現成的
（指衣服是工廠大量製造的成衣，不是客製化的）
⇨ While **off-the-rack** suits are generally cheaper than other suits, they lack the accuracy of tailor-made suits.
雖然成衣西裝一般較為便宜，但它們缺乏訂製西裝的合身度。

聯想單字
bike rack　　n. 腳踏車架
luggage rack　n. 行李置放架

refuge
[ˋrɛfjudʒ]
n. 避難所；庇護

衍 refugee n. 難民

The project exists to support refugees and migrants who are seeking **refuge** from disadvantaged conditions.
這項專案的存在是為了協助那些為逃離惡劣處境而尋求庇護的難民和移民。

❶ Point 重點

seek/take refuge from...
為了逃離／躲避～而尋求庇護（所）
⇨ A dog was **seeking refuge from** the rains in an abandoned house.
一隻狗在一間廢棄的房子裡避雨。

residential
[ˌrɛzə`dɛnʃəl]
adj. 居住的；定居的；住宅的

Any kind of commerce activity in a **residential** area is prohibited.
禁止在住宅區內進行任何形式的商業活動。

❶ Point 重點
residential 的衍生字家族很龐大，而且經常出現在各種考試的字彙題裡，一起來看看吧！

residence n. 住所
in residence = live 居住

reside v. 居住；定居
reside 後面要搭配**介系詞 in**，表示「居住於～（某地）」。

residency n. 居住；定居
residency 指的是「居住在某地的事實」，例如 permanent residency（永久居留權）。

resident n. 居民；住戶 adj. 常駐的
除了名詞的「居民」或「住戶」之外，resident 還可以用來形容「固定會在某處執業的人」，例如 resident doctor（住院醫師）、resident DJ（駐店 DJ）。

slum
[slʌm]
n.（尤指城市中的）貧民窟；髒亂的地方

Growing up in the **slums**, she was aware that many children couldn't go to school because of poverty.
因為自己在貧民窟長大，她明白有很多孩子會因為貧窮而無法上學。

spacious
[ˈspeʃəs]
adj. 寬敞的

衍 spaciousness n. 寬敞
　　spaciously adv. 寬敞地

同 roomy adj. 寬敞的

The Presidential Suite features a **spacious** lounge, sitting area and separate bedroom.
總統套房主打有寬敞的休息室、沙發區和獨立臥室。

storage
[ˈstɔrɪdʒ]
n. 保存；儲藏

衍 store v. 存放；儲藏
　　n. 商店；儲存量；倉庫

The first step to creating more **storage** space in your home is to remove items you don't use.
在家中創造更多儲藏空間的第一步，就是把你用不到的東西丟掉。

❶ Point 重點
in storage 存放著
⇨ On average, over 95% of objects in museums and private collections are **in storage** rather than on display.
平均而言，博物館和私人收藏中有超過 95% 的藏品都會被存放起來而沒有展出。

聯想單字
storeroom	n. 儲藏室
stockroom	n. 儲藏室；倉庫
storehouse	n. 大型貨倉
warehouse	n. 倉庫，貨倉

threshold
[ˋθrɛʃhold]
n. 門檻；界限；起點

You may also face additional taxes if your income exceeds a certain **threshold**.
如果你的收入超過特定門檻，那也許還會面臨要多繳稅的情形。

> **❶ Point 重點**
> **on the threshold of sth** 邁向～，在～的起點
> ⇨ She is **on the threshold of** a major career breakthrough.
> 她正邁向職業生涯的重大突破。

trivial
[ˋtrɪvɪəl]
adj. 微不足道的，瑣碎的；沒有價值的；容易解決的

衍 trivia n. 瑣事；枝微末節
triviality n. 瑣事，小事
trivialize v. 使～顯得不重要

Don't make a mountain out of a molehill; this is just a **trivial** matter.
不要小題大作，這只是一件小事。

vacuum
[ˋvækjʊəm]
n. 真空；缺乏，空白；與世隔絕
v. 用吸塵器清潔

We need a new leader to fill the **vacuum** left by his retirement.
我們需要一位新的領導者來填補他退休後留下的空缺。

Avoid **vacuuming** hot items such as fireplace ashes or even cigarette butts.
不要用吸塵器去吸熱的東西，像是壁爐的灰或甚至菸蒂之類的。

聯想單字	
vacuum cleaner	n. 吸塵器
robot vacuum cleaner	n. 掃地機器人
power vacuum	n. 權力真空

vicinity
[vəˋsɪnətɪ]
n. 鄰近地區；附近

Concentrated in the **vicinity** of Times Square and Grand Central Terminal, these buildings are known for their unique designs.
這些集中在時代廣場和中央車站附近的建築物，因其獨特的設計而聞名。

> **Point 重點**
>
> **in the vicinity of** 在～附近；大概
> ⇨ I'm hoping there are some nice places to eat **in the vicinity of** our hotel.
> 我希望在我們飯店附近有一些不錯的地方能吃飯。
> The average daily commute in the UK is **in the vicinity of** 20 miles.
> 英國人的平均每日通勤距離接近 20 英里。

聯想單字
proximity　n. 接近；鄰近
nearby　　adj. 附近的 adv. 附近
adjacent　adj. 鄰近的；毗連的

villager
[ˋvɪlɪdʒɚ]
n. 村民

衍 village n. 村莊；全體村民

The **villagers** are worried that the construction of a second plant will jeopardize their future.
這些村民擔心興建第二座工廠會對他們的未來造成危害。

warranty
[ˋwɔrəntɪ]
n. 保證書；保固

衍 warrant v. 使有正當理由做～；擔保，保證
　　　　n. 搜查令，逮捕狀

The **warranty** service does not extend to wear, scratches or other signs of poor maintenance of the product.
產品磨損、刮傷或其他因維護不佳而造成的跡象皆不在保固服務範圍內。

❶ Point 重點 ·················
warranty 的後面常會出現 cover，表示保固的涵蓋範圍。
⇨ The **warranty covers** some of your car repairs that may occur during the time specified in your contract.
保固涵蓋某些在您合約所註明的期間內可能會進行的車輛維修。

guarantee vs. **warranty**
guarantee 是對於產品及服務的品質和耐用度，做出承諾或保證，也可以用來表示「保證或承諾將以某特定方式做到某事」。另外，除動詞外，guarantee 也可以做為名詞使用。

warranty 通常是對個別產品提出的書面保證，例如保固卡、保證書等等，上面會記載保固涵蓋的範圍和期限等資訊。warranty 只能做為名詞使用。

主題分類單字 房屋、家具、日常用品、家庭

attic	[ˈætɪk]	n. 閣樓
carton	[ˈkɑrtn̩]	n. 紙盒
cellar	[ˈsɛlɚ]	n. 地窖；酒窖
chapel	[ˈtʃæpl̩]	n. 小禮拜堂
compass	[ˈkʌmpəs]	n. 羅盤；指南針；圓規
condom	[ˈkɑndəm]	n. 保險套
courtyard	[ˈkort͵jɑrd]	n. 庭院；天井
covering	[ˈkʌvərɪŋ]	n. 覆蓋物
crib	[krɪb]	n. 嬰兒床
debris	[dəˈbri]	n. 殘骸；碎片
diaper	[ˈdaɪəpɚ]	n. 尿布
directory	[dəˈrɛktərɪ]	n. 通訊錄；名錄
disintegrate	[dɪsˈɪntəgret]	v. 碎裂；瓦解；崩潰
dismantle	[dɪsˈmæntl̩]	v. 拆卸
doorstep	[ˈdor͵stɛp]	n. 門階
doorway	[ˈdor͵we]	n. 玄關，門口
driveway	[ˈdraɪv͵we]	n. 私人車道
exile	[ˈɛksaɪl]	v. 流放；流亡 n. 流放；流亡；被流放者
firecracker	[ˈfaɪr͵krækɚ]	n. 鞭炮

furnace	[ˈfɝnɪs]	n. 熔爐;暖氣爐
ghetto	[ˈgɛto]	n. 貧民區
heating	[ˈhitɪŋ]	n. 供暖系統,暖氣設備
heir	[ɛr]	n. 繼承人
hometown	[ˈhomˈtaʊn]	n. 故鄉;家鄉
incense	[ˈɪnsɛns]	n.(尤指宗教儀式用的)香 v. 激怒
insecticide	[ɪnˈsɛktəˌsaɪd]	n. 殺蟲劑
jug	[dʒʌg]	n. 壺;罐
kin	[kɪn]	n. 親屬
lifestyle	[ˈlaɪfˌstaɪl]	n. 生活方式
lighting	[ˈlaɪtɪŋ]	n. 照明;照明設備
live-in	[ˌlɪvˈɪn]	adj.(未婚)同居的;住(僱主)家的
maiden	[ˈmedn̩]	adj. 初次的;n. 少女,女孩
mattress	[ˈmætrɪs]	n. 床墊
motherhood	[ˈmʌðɚhʊd]	n. 母親身分
mower	[ˈmoɚ]	n. 除草機
newlywed	[ˈnjulɪˌwɛd]	n. 新婚者(常複數)
offspring	[ˈɔfˌsprɪŋ]	n. 子孫,後代
ornament	[ˈɔrnəmənt]	v. 裝飾;美化 n. 裝飾品;裝飾
pane	[pen]	n.(門窗上的)玻璃片
password	[ˈpæsˌwɝd]	n. 密碼

單字	音標	詞性與中譯
peg	[pɛg]	v. 用釘（或樁）固定 n. 釘；栓
pendulum	[ˋpɛndʒələm]	n. 擺錘；鐘擺；搖擺不定的事態
pesticide	[ˋpɛstɪˌsaɪd]	n. 殺蟲劑
porcelain	[ˋpɔrsəlɪn]	n. 瓷；瓷器
radiator	[ˋredɪˌetɚ]	n. 散熱器
recording	[rɪˋkɔrdɪŋ]	n. 記錄；錄音；錄影；唱片
slate	[slet]	v. 用石板蓋屋頂；抨擊；預定 n. （屋頂的）石板；名單
spouse	[spaʊz]	n. 配偶
stepchild	[ˋstɛpˌtʃaɪld]	n. 繼子；繼女
terrace	[ˋtɛrəs]	n. 露臺；大陽台；梯田
thermos	[ˋθɝməs]	n. 保溫瓶
tile	[taɪl]	v. 鋪瓦片或瓷磚 n. 瓦片；瓷磚
toddle	[ˋtɑdl]	v. （幼童）蹣跚行走
tract	[trækt]	n. 大片土地
upbringing	[ˋʌpˌbrɪŋɪŋ]	n. 養育；教養
wallpaper	[ˋwɔlˌpepɚ]	v. 貼上壁紙 n. 壁紙；電腦桌布
wed	[wɛd]	v. 娶；嫁
widow	[ˋwɪdo]	v. 喪夫；喪妻 n. 寡婦，遺孀

Chapter 03・房屋、家具、日常用品、家庭

Chapter 03 Quiz Time

一、請選出正確的答案。

1. The team will _____ the stadium from the government for NT$1 million per year.

    A. clinch
    B. dwell
    C. lease
    D. populate

2. For those who want to _____ to Australia, you need to apply for and obtain a permanent residence visa.

    A. immigrate
    B. vacuum
    C. lodge
    D. rack

3. Free internet service is available in the _____ of many stations.

    A. commodity
    B. vicinity
    C. threshold
    D. outskirt

二、請根據下列中文句子，填入適當的英文單字。

1. 每年哺乳類、鳥類或甚至是昆蟲都會因為各種原因進行遷徙。

    Mammals, birds and even insects are known to m_____ annually for a variety of reasons.

2. 保固不適用於從其他賣家或第三方所購得的電腦。

   This w_____ does not apply to computers purchased from other sellers or third parties.

3. 在河水潰堤後，數百人被迫撤離家園。

   Hundreds of people were forced to e_____ their homes after the river burst its banks.

4. 我的父母過去總是教導我要好好接待任何我遇到的人。

   My parents always taught me to be h_____ to anyone I met.

5. 這個放待洗衣物的箱子在不使用時可以快速摺成扁平狀收納起來。

   This laundry bin can be quickly folded flat for s_____ when not in use.

Answer
(一)：1. C 2. A 3. B
(二)：1. migrate 2. warranty 3. evacuate 4. hospitable 5. storage

翻譯：
(一)
1. 這支屋齡在五年以上但每月租金 100 萬元的豪華房屋將被租用並販售掉。
2. 相當多居民被州政府命令撤離並被永久居留安置。
3. 許多專車站所附設有旅客的流動廁所隨意可使用。

Chapter 04

交通
交通工具、運輸方式

Ch04.mp3

★核心單字情境對話

Jack : Did you notice the **barricade** on Maple **Boulevard**?

Lisa : Yes, it made my **commute** this morning rough. Two cars **collided** because of it.

Jack : That's terrible! Proper **infrastructure** should ensure the safety of **pedestrians** and drivers.

Lisa : I agree. Hey, our **shipment** is scheduled to arrive tomorrow. We need to make sure there's enough space on the **pavement** for unloading.

Jack : Good point. Let's double check that before it arrives.

Lisa : By the way, have you received the **manifest** yet? We need it to check all the shipment is in place.

Jack : Yes, I'll print it out later and give you a copy.

翻譯

Jack : 妳有注意到 Maple 林蔭大道上放了**路障**嗎?

Lisa : 有,那個路障讓我今天早上的**通勤**變得很麻煩。有兩輛車還因為它而**撞在了一起**。

Jack : 太可怕了!完善的**基礎設施**應該要能保障**行人**和駕駛人的安全。

Lisa : 我也覺得。嘿,我們的**貨**預定明天會到。我們得確保**人行道**上有足夠的空間可以卸貨。

Jack : 妳說得對。我們在貨到之前再確認一次吧。

Lisa : 對了,你收到**貨物明細**了嗎?我們得有它才能確認所有貨都到了。

Jack : 收到了,我晚點會把它印出來,然後給妳一份。

anchor
[ˈæŋkɚ]
n. 錨；賴以支撐的人（或物）；主播
v. 下錨；使固定；主持（廣播節目等）

Yoga is my **anchor** when I am exhausted and anxiety is taking over my life.
當我精疲力盡且被焦慮占據生活時，瑜珈是我的支柱。

We **anchored** the tent stakes to the ground and built a fire.
我們把營釘固定在地上並生了火。

❗ Point 重點
anchor... to... 把～固定住；使穩定
⇨ We have **anchored** ourselves **to** financial stability and responsible fiscal management for a decade.
我們十年來一直都致力於維持金融穩定及負責任的財政管理。

aviation
[ˌevɪˈeʃən]
n. 航空（學）；航空工業

衍 aviator n. 飛行員

For everyone involved in the **aviation** industry, safety is always the top priority.
對於每個從事航空業的人來說，安全始終是重中之重。

❗ Point 重點
常見的「航空相關人員」
ground crew 地勤人員
flight crew 機組人員
flight attendant 空服員
captain 機長
first officer 副機長

聯想單字
aviation industry	n. 航空業
Civil Aviation Administration	n. 民航局
aviation fuel	n. 航空燃料
apron	n. 停機坪
runway	n.（機場的）跑道
terminal	n. 航廈；航空站
airlift	n.（因交通不便而進行的）空運

Chapter 04・交通工具、運輸方式

barricade
[ˈbærəˌked]
n. 障礙物；路障
v. 設下路障

Protesters broke through the **barricades** in front of the Presidential Office Building.
抗議者衝破了總統府前的路障。

The police **barricaded** the street to prevent the demonstrators from marching through the town.
警方在街上設下路障，阻止示威者遊行穿越過整座城鎮。

> **Point 重點**
> **build/make/erect a barricade 設下路障**
> ⇨ Protesters **built barricades** to block police and paralyze traffic.
> 抗議者設下路障以阻擋警察及癱瘓交通。
>
> **barricade vs. barrier**
> **barricade** 指**臨時設置**、**存在時間短**的**實體**障礙物，常見於示威遊行或臨時交通管制時所設的路障；**barrier** 則可指**任何形式**的障礙，既可以是具體的 **road barrier**（路障），也可以是抽象的 **language barrier**（語言障礙）。

boulevard
[ˈbuləˌvɑrd]
n. 林蔭大道

As you walk along the **boulevard**, you will see old olive trees planted about 100 years ago along the way.
在沿著林蔭大道走的時候，你沿途會看到大概在 100 年前種下的老橄欖樹。

> **Point 重點**
> **avenue vs. boulevard**
> avenue 也是「大道」的意思，不過 boulevard 比 avenue 更寬闊，且一般來說路的兩側會有行道樹、中央會有分隔島隔開左右道，整體設計看上去會比 avenue 更氣派、景觀更佳。

carrier
[ˈkærɪɚ]
n. 攜帶用工具；運輸公司；帶原者

衍 carry v. 扛；背；運送；攜帶；支持
carriage n. 四輪馬車；（火車）車廂

We cannot determine which **carrier** will be used for the shipment before the order is placed.
在訂單成立之前，我們無法確定將會由哪一間運輸公司來運送這批貨。

❗ Point 重點
carrier vs. **courier**
carrier 是負責運輸**大型貨物**的公司，例如載運貨櫃的公司，而 **courier** 是處理**小型包裹**的快遞員或快遞公司，如網購宅配的公司。

collide
[kəˈlaɪd]
v.（移動中的物體）猛力碰撞；衝突，牴觸

衍 collision n.（車輛等的）猛力碰撞；衝突，牴觸

The main road through the area is closed after a car and a truck **collided** at the crossroads.
在一輛汽車和卡車在十字路口相撞後，穿過那一區的主要道路就被封閉了。

❗ Point 重點
A collide with B A 與 B 發生碰撞
⇨ The car **collided with** a woman crossing the road.
那輛車撞上了正在過馬路的女子。

聯想單字		
crash	v.（車輛等）撞毀 n. 撞車事故；失事
bump	v. 撞擊；意外撞上
wreck	v. 撞毀 n. 嚴重損毀的交通工具；殘骸
hit	v. 碰撞
hit and run	n. 肇事逃逸

commute
[kəˈmjut]
v. 通勤；變換 n. 通勤

衍 commuter n. 通勤者
commuting n. 通勤的行為

I usually **commute** to work by bicycle unless the weather is really bad.
除非天氣非常糟糕，否則我通常會騎自行車上班。

He recently quit his job at a restaurant which required an hour's bus **commute**.
他最近辭去了他那份必須要花一個小時搭公車通勤的餐廳工作。

Chapter 04・交通工具、運輸方式

❗ Point 重點 ⋯⋯⋯⋯⋯⋯⋯⋯⋯⋯⋯⋯⋯⋯⋯
commute from A to B
（或 **commute between A and B**）
　　　　　　　從 **A** 通勤到 **B**，在 **A** 到 **B** 之間往返
⇨ If he took the job, he would have to **commute from** London **to** Cambridge every day.
如果他接受了那份工作，他就必須每天從倫敦通勤到劍橋了。

compact
[kəm`pækt]
adj. 密實的；小巧的
n. 小型車；粉盒；合約
v. 把～緊緊壓實

The company succeeded in creating a lighter and more **compact** camera.
這間公司成功打造了一款更輕、更小巧的相機。

This is a **compact** car aimed exclusively to women.
這是一款專門以女性為目標的小型車。

These vehicles can carve the path and **compact** the snow.
這些車輛可以開出一條路來並把雪緊緊壓實。

❗ Point 重點 ⋯⋯⋯⋯⋯⋯⋯⋯⋯⋯⋯⋯⋯⋯⋯
其他常見的「汽車類型」
sedan 四門轎車
SUV (Sport Utility Vehicle)（運動）休旅車
RV (Recreational Vehicle) 露營車
van 廂型車
sports car 跑車
convertible 敞篷車

convoy
[`kɑnvɔɪ]
n.（護衛的）艦隊，車隊
v. 護衛，護送

A **convoy** of trucks carrying supplies entered the base.
一隊運送補給品的卡車進入了基地。

Police **convoyed** the president to the White House.
警方護送了總統前往白宮。

> **Point 重點**
> **in convoy**（人）成群結隊；（車）組成車隊
> ⇨ They gathered at the station and then walked **in convoy** to the park.
> 他們在車站集合，然後成群結隊地走向公園。

cruise
[kruz]
n. 航遊；乘船遊覽
v. 航遊；巡航

If you want to take a vacation and visit some new countries along the way, then going on a **cruise** is a no-brainer.
如果你想度個假，並在途中造訪一些沒去過的國家，那麼當然就是去參加郵輪之旅了。

The ship **cruised** along the coast looking for smugglers.
這艘船沿著海岸一邊巡航一邊尋找走私者。

聯想單字		
	cruise ship	n. 大型遊輪
	ferry	n. 渡輪
	sailboat	n. 帆船
	lifeboat	n. 救生艇
	boat	n. 中小型的船
	ship	n. 中大型的船
	vessel	n. 泛指船舶；船艦
	yacht	n. 快艇；遊艇

embargo
[ɪm`bɑrgo]
n. 禁止（或限制）買賣；禁運
v. 對～施行禁運；禁止（買賣等）

If a country imposes an **embargo** on another country, it prohibits trade with that country.
如果一個國家對另一個國家實施禁運，就表示禁止與該國進行貿易。

The European Union is planning to **embargo** Russian oil.
歐盟正計劃對俄羅斯石油實施禁運。

> **Point 重點**
> **put/place/lay/impose an embargo on**
> 　　　　　　　　　　　　　　對～實施禁運
> ⇨ The party reiterated its call for **putting an embargo on** Saudi Arabia.
> 該黨再次呼籲對沙烏地阿拉伯實施禁運。

lift/raise/take off the embargo on 對～解除禁運
⇨ The UN Security Council voted 14-1 to **lift the embargo on** Somalia.
聯合國安理會以 14 比 1 的票數決定解除對索馬利亞的禁運。

> 聯想單字
> resolution　　　　　n. 決議
> sanction　　　　　　n. 制裁
> economic sanction　n. 經濟制裁

embark
[ɪmˋbɑrk]
v. 上（船或飛機）

反 disembark v.（旅途結束後）下（船或飛機）

We **embarked** at the wharf and then headed south along the coast.
我們在碼頭上船，然後沿著海岸向南行駛。

❶ Point 重點
embark on/upon sth 著手做～
⇨ We are **embarking on** a new project with the company to help protect nearly 100,000 acres of forest.
我們正與那間公司一同著手進行一個新專案，以協助保護將近 100,000 英畝的森林。

escort
[ˋɛskɔrt]
v. 護送；押送；陪同
n. 護送；護衛者；護衛隊

Security guards **escorted** the intruder from the field during the friendly soccer game between the two teams.
在兩隊進行足球友誼賽時，保全人員將闖入者從球場帶離。

The actress left court with a police **escort** to help her avoid the crowd of protesters who gathered outside.
那位女演員在警察的護送下離開了法院，以協助她避開聚集在外面的抗議群眾。

❶ Point 重點
escort vs. convoy
escort 是指為了安全考量，由單一個人、車輛，甚至船艦來陪同護送；而 **convoy** 則指由多輛車或多艘船組成的隊伍進行護送，比起 escort 更強調護送隊伍的規模與成群結隊的感覺。

under N. escort 在～的護送下
⇨ The official arrived at the Prime Minister's Office **under police escort** on Monday evening.
這名官員在星期一傍晚由警方護送抵達首相辦公室。

fleet
[flit]
n. 船隊；艦隊；車隊；機群

The **fleet** was defeated in a series of battles and its mission failed.
那支艦隊在一連串的戰役中被擊敗，而任務也失敗了。

submarine	n.	潛艇
aircraft carrier	n.	航空母艦
destroyer	n.	驅逐艦
cruiser	n.	巡洋艦

haul
[hɔl]
v. 拉，拖
n. 一大批，大量

衍 overhaul v.
徹底檢修，大修

Fleets of trucks **haul** thousands of wreaths during the holiday season to honor veterans.
卡車車隊在聖誕節假期期間運送了數千個向退伍軍人致敬用的花圈。

A police officer discovered a **haul** of drugs after stopping a driver who was using his mobile phone while driving.
一名警察在攔下一位邊開車邊使用手機的駕駛後，發現了大量的毒品。

infrastructure
[ˈɪnfrəˌstrʌktʃɚ]
n. 基礎建設

The city performs street improvement projects to maintain its **infrastructure**.
這座城市施行街道改善計畫以維護其基礎建設。

transportation	n.	運輸；運輸工具
construction	n.	建設；建築物
structure	n.	（大型）建築物；結構

intersection
[ˌɪntɚˋsɛkʃən]
n. 交叉路口；十字路口；相交

衍 intersect v. 交叉；與～相交

Turn left at the next **intersection** and continue for one block.
在下一個十字路口左轉，然後繼續走一個街區。

❶ Point 重點
intersection vs. **crossroads**
雖然 intersection 和 crossroads 都有十字路口的意思，但語意和用法仍有所不同。intersection 通常指的是都會區中由兩條以上的道路，交會形成的十字路口；crossroads 則是鄉村地區的十字路口，且帶有「決策點」或「分歧點」的語意，而非專指交通路口。

聯想單字
roundabout	n. 圓環
overpass	n. 高架橋
underpass	n. 地下道
footbridge	n. 天橋

manifest
[ˋmænəˌfɛst]
v. 顯示；表明
adj. 顯而易見的
n. 旅客名單；貨物明細

衍 manifestation n. 顯示；表明
manifestly adv. 明顯地，顯然地

Citizens are **manifesting** their dissatisfaction with the current president through demonstrations and other methods.
市民透過示威等手段表明對現任總統的不滿。

The entire case was dismissed due to a **manifest** lack of legal merit.
這整個案例由於明顯不具法律價值而遭駁回。

Flight attendants will check the information on the passenger **manifest** with the seating plan to confirm that the passenger has been assigned to the correct seat.
空服員會核對座位表與乘客名單資訊，以確認乘客被安排的座位正確。

❶ Point 重點
manifest itself ～表現或顯現出來
⇨ The virus takes one week to **manifest itself**.
這種病毒發病需要一週的時間。

navigation
[ˌnævəˈgeʃən]
n. 導航；造訪網站

衍 navigate v. 導航；確定～的方向；造訪網站
navigator n. 導航員，領航員

The mobile app can send trip plans to the car's **navigation** system.
這個行動應用程式能夠將行程計畫發送到汽車的導航系統上。

❗ Point 重點
navigation vs. **guidance**
navigation（導航）可以想成是我們打開 Google Maps 時看到的**路線規劃**，也就是根據我們目前的位置、周圍可以使用的交通工具等資訊來做出的導航；另一方面，**guidance**（引導）則是透過導航得到最佳路線後所接收到的**實際行動引導**，例如左轉後直走或搭特定路線公車等指示。

paddle
[ˈpædl]
n.（小船的）槳
v. 用槳划船；涉水

The more expensive **paddles** are lighter and stiffer, which means you get more power out of each stroke.
價格較昂貴的槳更輕、更硬，這代表你每次划槳都能發揮出更大的力量。

We slowly **paddled** our canoe through the swift current of the river.
我們在湍急的河流裡划著獨木舟緩慢前行。

❗ Point 重點
paddle your own canoe 自立自強（划你自己的獨木舟）
⇨ When you are of age, you should **paddle your own canoe** and make your own decisions.
等到你成年的時候，你就應該自立自強並自己做決定了。

聯想單字
oar	n. 槳；槳手 v. 划行
canoe	n. 獨木舟 v. 划獨木舟
row	v. 划船

Chapter 04・交通

pavement
[ˋpevmənt]
n. [美] 道路鋪面；[英] 人行道

衍 pave v. 鋪（地面）

It is illegal to drive on the **pavement** and obstruct others.
在人行道上行駛並對他人造成妨礙是違法的。

❶ Point 重點
pavement vs. **sidewalk** vs. **crosswalk**
pavement 在英式英文裡是人行道的意思，在美式英文中則是指道路表面的那層，用柏油或水泥等材質鋪設的「道路鋪面」，而 sidewalk 則是美式英文中的人行道。供行人穿越的「斑馬線」則是 crosswalk，或者也可以說成 pedestrian crossing（行人穿越道）。

聯想單字
footpath	n. 鄉間小徑
skywalk	n. 空橋
jaywalk	v. 違規穿越馬路

pedestrian
[pəˋdɛstrɪən]
n. 行人

A **pedestrian** saw the accident and took down the truck's license plate number.
一名行人看到了這起事故，並記下了卡車的車牌號碼。

聯想單字
passerby	n. 路人
passenger	n. 乘客

pier
[pɪr]
n.（伸向海中的）突堤；碼頭

Due to damage from the typhoon, only a portion of the **pier** is open to the public.
由於這次颱風造成的損壞，只有部分突堤對外開放。

❶ Point 重點
wharf vs. **pier**
wharf 是指「用來裝卸船隻貨物，或供乘客上下船的碼頭」，而 pier 是指「從岸邊向外延伸、架高於水面之上，供乘客上下船的突堤」，有時上面還會建有商店或餐廳等設施。

其他與「海港」相關的單字
dock 碼頭（供船隻停靠上下貨或維修的船塢）
harbor 港灣（讓船隻停靠躲避風浪的大港）
port 港口的通稱（規模比 harbor 更大）

propeller
[prə`pɛlɚ]
n. 螺旋槳

衍 propel v.
　 推進；驅動

This particular **propeller** blade's shape is suitable for that type of powered sailplane.
這款特殊的螺旋槳葉片的形狀適合那一型的動力滑翔機。

聯想單字
engine　　n. 引擎
turbine　　n. 渦輪機
blade　　 n. 槳身；刀片

rein
[ren]
n. 韁繩；保護帶（常複數）

When you pull on the right **rein**, the horse will turn to the right because of the pressure the rein puts on the right corner of its mouth.
當你拉動右邊的韁繩時，馬會因韁繩在其右側嘴角施加的壓力而向右轉。

❶ Point 重點

rein in/back 抑制；約束
⇨ We tried to **rein in** our excitement and nervousness before watching the game.
在看比賽之前，我們努力克制自己的興奮和緊張感。

keep a tight rein on sb/sth 對～嚴加管束
⇨ All departments have been told to **keep a tight rein on** expenditure.
所有部門都已被告知要嚴格管控開支。

take over/up the reins 控制；接管（某組織或國家）
⇨ The company welcomed its new Marketing Manager, Joseph Chen, who **took over the reins** of the department in October.
這間公司迎來了新的行銷經理 Joseph Chen，他在十月接管了該部門。

row
[ro]
v. 划（船等）
n. 一排；划（船等）

A group of alumni, faculty and students teamed up to **row** the dragon boat together.
由一群校友、教職員和學生組成隊伍一起划龍舟。

They were invited to sit in the front **row** of the concert hall to watch the symphony orchestra.
他們受邀坐在演奏廳的前排座位上觀看這支交響樂團的演出。

❶ Point 重點
in a row 接連地；連續地
⇨ Our company has been at the top of the customer satisfaction survey three years **in a row**.
我們公司已經連續三年蟬聯顧客滿意度調查榜首了。

shipment
[`ʃɪpmənt]
n. 運輸的貨物；運輸；裝運

衍 ship v. 運輸，運送
　　 n. 大船
　　 shipping n. 船運，海運

A **shipment** of counterfeit jewelry was seized at the airport.
一批仿冒的珠寶在機場被查扣。

聯想單字		
cargo	n.（大型交通工具裝載的）貨物	
ferry	n.（定期的）渡船，渡輪 v.（定期往返）運送	
freight	n. 貨運；貨物 v. 運送（貨物）	

stall
[stɔl]
n. 攤位；隔間
v. 使陷入停滯；拖慢（某人）；（使引擎）熄火

Most of the food **stalls** at the Christmas market only accept cash.
大部分聖誕市集上的小吃攤都只收現金。

She was concerned that pregnancy and maternity leave would **stall** her career.
她擔心懷孕和產假會使她的職涯發展陷入停滯。

● Point 重點

stall vs. **booth**

雖然 stall 和 booth 都是「攤位」，但 stall 更為簡易，整個攤位可能就只有一張展示桌，甚至連可遮風避雨的棚架都沒有；另一方面，booth 的規劃則較為完善，除了有展示桌，還可能會設有如互動區或展示牆等的各種攤位設施與布置。相較於 stall，booth 更像是一間臨時的簡易商店或展覽空間。

聯想單字		
food stall	n. 小吃攤
market stall	n. 市集攤位
set up a stall	phr. 擺攤

tractor
[ˋtræktɚ]
n. 拖拉機

A local farmer used a **tractor** to pull the car off the railway tracks.
一位當地的農民用拖拉機將那輛車從鐵軌上拉走了。

聯想單字		
power saw	n. 電鋸
bulldozer	n. 推土機
trailer	n. 拖車
crane	n. 吊車

主題分類單字　交通工具、運輸方式相關

astray	[ə`stre]	adv. 迷路；誤入歧途
barge	[bɑrdʒ]	n. 大型平底貨船 v. 笨重緩慢地移動；（魯莽地）猛衝，闖
cockpit	[`kɑk͵pɪt]	n.（飛機、小艇等的）駕駛艙
honk	[hɔŋk]	v. 按喇叭 n. 汽車喇叭聲
limousine	[`lɪmə͵zin]	n. 大型豪華轎車
locomotive	[͵lokə`motɪv]	n. 火車頭 adj. 能移動的；移動的
mileage	[`maɪlɪdʒ]	n. 總里程數；行駛里程
motorist	[`motərɪst]	n. 駕駛人
motorway	[`motɚ͵we]	n. [英] 高速公路
saddle	[`sædḷ]	v. 給（馬背）裝鞍；使負擔 n. 鞍；車座
sled	[slɛd]	v. 搭乘雪橇 n. 雪橇
sleigh	[sle]	v. 駕駛雪橇；用雪橇運輸 n. 雪橇
stern	[stɝn]	n. 船尾 adj. 嚴厲的；苛刻的
tollbooth	[`tol͵buθ]	n. 收費亭
tollway	[`tol͵we]	n. 收費公路

Chapter 04 Quiz Time

一、請選出正確的答案。

1. Before _____ on renovating your home, you should consult a professional first and discuss your project.
    A. colliding
    B. embarking
    C. escorting
    D. commuting

2. One of the amendments aims to enhance _____ safety at intersections.
    A. aviation
    B. pavement
    C. embargo
    D. pedestrian

3. Because our warehouses are in different locations, your order will be delivered in two _____.
    A. shipments
    B. anchors
    C. boulevards
    D. barricades

二、請根據下列中文句子，填入適當的英文單字。

1. 該組織捐了台幣 100 萬元給政府，用於重建被颶風摧毀的基礎建設。

    The organization donated NT$1 million to the government to rebuild i_____ destroyed by the hurricane.

2. 有了語音導航指示，貨運駕駛就再也不用一邊開車一邊不斷查看智慧型手機了。

   With voice n_____ directions, delivery drivers no longer need to constantly check their smartphones while driving.

3. 在學完教練教我們的所有東西之後，我們就划船出海了。

   After learning everything the coach taught us, we p_____ out to sea.

4. 路障封鎖了通往該地區一家大型醫院的路。

   B_____ blocked road access to a major hospital in the area.

5. 每次他的要求沒有被滿足，他就會顯現出暴力傾向。

   Whenever his demands are not met, he m_____ a tendency to become violent.

Chapter 05

外表
身體部位、外貌形容

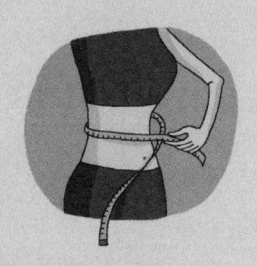

Ch05.mp3

★核心單字情境對話

Emma : Did you see that guy walking **barefoot** in the gym today?
Jessie : Yeah, I noticed him. The one with the **muscular** build and blond hair, right?
Emma : Exactly! He looked pretty **gorgeous**, and did you notice his **posture**?
Jessie : Yeah, it was really **masculine**. He seemed very confident.
Emma : Agreed. I couldn't help but get a **peek** at his **abdomen** when he stretched.
Jessie : His abs were so defined! He must spend a lot of time in the gym.

翻譯

Emma : 妳今天有看到那個**赤腳**走在健身房裡的傢伙嗎？
Jessie : 有啊，我有注意到他。是那個**肌肉結實**的金髮男，對吧？
Emma : 沒錯！他看起來超**帥**，而且妳有注意到他的**姿態**嗎？
Jessie : 有啊，真的很有**男人味**。他看起來非常有自信。
Emma : 我也覺得。我忍不住在他伸展的時候偷**瞄**了一眼他的**肚子**。
Jessie : 他的腹肌超明顯！他一定在健身房裡花了很多時間。

Chapter 05・身體部位、外貌形容　P.087

abdomen
[ˋæbdəmən]
n.（人、動物、昆蟲的）腹（部）

衍 abdominal adj. 腹部的

After the surgery, he experienced discomfort in his **abdomen**, but it gradually subsided as he recovered.
他在手術後感到腹部不適，但不適感隨著他逐漸康復而漸漸消退了。

❶ Point 重點
abdomen 是學術名詞，最常在醫學界使用。如果要表示「肚子」或「腹部」的話，最常見的說法有下面三種。
stomach ⇨ 胃；肚子，腹部（stomach 是 abdomen 裡面的器官）
belly ⇨ 腹部；胃
tummy ⇨ 胃；肚子（小朋友的說法）

artery
[ˋɑrtərɪ]
n. 動脈；（鐵路、公路等的）幹線或要道

衍 arterial adj. 動脈的

The street is the main **artery** of the city from which you can walk to almost all the important places.
這條街是這座城市裡的主要幹道，你從這裡出發，幾乎所有重要的地方都可以走路就到。

聯想單字		
blood vessel	n. 血管
vein	n. 靜脈
capillary	n. 微血管
vascular	adj. 血管的
coronary artery	n. 冠狀動脈

barefoot
[ˋbɛr͵fʊt]
adj. 赤腳的
adv. 赤腳地

衍 bare adj. 赤裸的；無遮蔽的
barely adv. 僅；幾乎沒有

He was barefoot **because** of the sudden and fierce fire.
他那時因為突如其來的猛烈大火而赤著腳。

The supermodel took off her heels and walked **barefoot** at the show after falling over on the runway.
那位超模在伸展台上跌倒後，她就把高跟鞋脫掉，然後赤腳走秀了。

聯想單字		
barehanded	adj. 沒戴手套的；赤手空拳的
bareheaded	adj. 沒戴帽子或頭巾的
barefaced	adj. 厚顏無恥的；明目張膽的

blonde

[blɑnd]
adj. 金色頭髮的
n. 金髮女子（金髮男子是 blond）

The little girl wishes to have **blonde** curls like her favorite doll.
那個小女孩希望擁有像她最喜歡的洋娃娃那般的金色捲髮。

Do you know who the **blonde** is in the movie trailers?
你知道在電影預告裡的那個金髮女子是誰嗎？

❶ Point 重點

染頭髮
dye one's hair
get/have one's hair colored
⇨ 除了染整頭外，也可能會做 highlight（挑染）或 bleach（漂髮）。除金髮外，還有一些髮色擁有特定用字，如 brunette（深褐色）、auburn（紅褐色）、ginger（薑紅）、lilac（淡紫）。

剪頭髮
get a haircut
get/have one's hair cut
⇨ 「我讓我的頭髮被剪了」意思就是「我去剪頭髮了」（不是用 cut my hair），如果剪的不多，只是稍微修一下，會說 trim one's hair（稍微修一下）。

聯想單字		
salon	n.	沙龍；髮廊
stylist	n.	造型師
hairdresser	n.	美髮師

bosom

[ˋbʊzəm]
n.（女人的）胸部，乳房；胸懷

His mother pulled him to her **bosom** and comforted him.
他的母親把他拉到懷裡安慰。

❶ Point 重點
breast vs. **chest** vs. **bosom**
chest 是指整體的**胸腔部位**，**breast** 則是包括**乳房**的部分。**bosom** 和 breast 意思相同，但經常帶有文學性的譬喻，表示「**胸懷**」或「**內心深處**」，例如常見的 **to one's bosom**，除了字面意義的「在～的懷中」之外，也可以表達「**接納**」的意思。

聯想單字		
bosom friend	n. 知己,至交	
clutch/hold to one's bosom	phr. 緊抱在某人的懷中	

crouch
[ˋkraʊtʃ]
v. 蹲伏,蹲縮;蜷縮

The frustrated young woman **crouched** on the floor.
那個沮喪的年輕女子蹲縮在地板上。

聯想單字		
squat	v. 蹲坐;深蹲
crawl	v. 爬行
lie down	phr. 躺下

decent
[ˋdisn̩t]
adj. 正派的;體面的;相當不錯的

衍 decently adv. 正派地;體面地;相當不錯地
decency n. 合宜;得體;正派;體面

I need a **decent** meal with protein, especially if I had a training session before lunch.
我得好好吃一頓有很多蛋白質的正餐,特別是如果我在午餐前還要上訓練課的話。

❶ Point 重點

Are you decent? 你衣服有穿好嗎?
這句話不是在問對方是否是一個正派的人,而是在進去別人的房間或浴室之前,先確認對方是否有把衣服穿好時所使用的問句。

decent vs. descent
請特別注意 decent 的重音在第一音節,而拼字長得非常像的名詞 descent [dɪˋsɛnt](下降;墮落;血緣關係),重音則是在第二音節。雖然兩者的發音完全不同,但因為拼字實在太像,在寫作時常會混淆,所以要小心使用。

dwarf
[dwɔrf]
n. 矮子,侏儒
adj. 矮小的
v. 使～顯得矮小;使～相形見絀

A person of unusually small stature is called a **dwarf**.
身材異常矮小的人被稱為侏儒。

Dwarf fruit trees should be planted in late winter to early spring.
矮生果樹應在冬末春初時種植。

The director predicted that South Korea's film industry would **dwarf** Hollywood.
那位導演預言韓國的電影產業將使好萊塢相形見絀。

❶ Point 重點
如果直接用 dwarf 來稱呼罹患侏儒症的人的話，有些人可能會覺得被冒犯，因此若想委婉一點，可以改用 **person with dwarfism** 或是 **little person** 來表達。此外，在非病理性描述時，也須避免使用 suffering 來表達。

external
[ɪk`stɝnəl]
adj. 外面的；外表的；來自外部的

衍 externals n. 外表；外觀；外在形式
externally adv. 外表地；來自外部地

同 exterior adj. 外面的；外表的；外來的

反 internal adj. 內部的

The company faced **external** challenges from increased competition in the market.
這間公司面臨因市場競爭加劇所帶來的外部挑戰。

❶ Point 重點
字首 ex- 有著 **out（向外）**的意思，擁有相同字首的常見單字還有 exit（出口；離去）、export（出口）、expose（暴露）、express（表達）等等。另一方面，**字首 in-** 則是 **in（向內）**的意思，因此 external 的反義字即是 internal，擁有相同字首的常見單字有 include（包含）、inside（裡面）等等。

feeble
[fibl]
adj. 虛弱無力的；衰弱的

衍 feebly adv. 虛弱地，無力地

The stairs were illuminated by the **feeble** light coming through the windows.
樓梯被從窗戶透進來的微弱光線照亮。

gender
[ˋdʒɛndɚ]
n. 性別

This chart shows the demographics of Facebook users by age and **gender**.
這張圖表呈現了 Facebook 用戶在年齡和性別上的人口統計資料。

❶ Point 重點
sex vs. gender
sex 指的是**生理性別**，如 male（男性）、female（女性）或 intersex（雙性）；**gender** 則是我們在社會上所表現出來的**性別認同**，或稱**社會性別**。也可以想成 sex 是生理、gender 是心理來區分使用。

聯想單字
gender bias	n. 性別偏見
gender discrimination	n. 性別歧視
gender stereotype	n. 性別刻板印象
gender equality	n. 性別平等

gorgeous
[ˋgɔrdʒəs]
adj. 極其漂亮的；令人愉快的

衍 gorgeously adv.
極其漂亮地；令人愉快地
gorgeousness n.
極其漂亮；令人愉快

You can enjoy the **gorgeous** views of the valley from the hotel's infinity pool.
你可以從飯店的無邊際泳池那裡欣賞到山谷的絕美景色。

❶ Point 重點
gorgeous 可以用來形容任何美麗的人或事物，語氣比 beautiful 和 pretty 更加強烈，通常指的是讓人感到非常驚艷、帶有強烈吸引力的美。

「稱讚美人／美景」的其他常用說法
amazing 令人驚豔的
bewitching 令人著迷的
breathtaking 美得令人屏息的
dazzling 光彩奪目的
stunning 美得令人目瞪口呆的

lame
[lem]
adj.（尤指動物）跛腳的；站不住腳的，無說服力的

衍 lamely adv. 站不住腳地，無說服力地
lameness n. 瘸，跛；站不住腳，無說服力

The surgery caused the dog to be **lame** for several days.
這場手術造成這隻狗跛腳跛了幾天。

❶ Point 重點
lame 在口語上有「**很遜**」和「**無聊**」的意思，但這並非正規用法，正式場合較不會使用這種表達方式。
⇨ The party is so **lame**.
這個派對真是無聊。
He cracked a **lame** joke at the party and totally ruined the mood.
他在派對上講了一個爛笑話，完全破壞了氣氛。

> 聯想單字
> lame duck　　n. 跛腳鴨
> （任期屆滿的主政者，如總統、市長等）

masculine
[ˋmæskjəlɪn]
adj. 有男子氣概的，男性化的；陽剛的

同 manly adj. 具有男子氣概的

反 feminine adj. 有女性特質的；陰柔的

She had to cut off her long hair and adopt a more **masculine** hairstyle for the role.
她為了那個角色，不得不剪掉長髮並採用更男性化的髮型。

❶ Point 重點
中文常常會說「很 man」，但英文卻不能直接用 man 這個字，而是要用如下面這種方式來表達。
⇨ He's so **manly**.
他好有男子氣概。
Men with beards look **masculine/manly**.
留鬍子的男人看起來很有男子氣概。

Chapter 05・身體部位、外貌形容　　P.093

muscular
[ˈmʌskjələ]
adj. 肌肉的；肌肉發達的；強壯的

衍 muscle n. 肌肉

You can build **muscular** arms with these simple dumbbell exercises.
你可以用這些簡單的啞鈴訓練來打造肌肉發達的手臂。

● Point 重點
常見的「健身」相關用語
work out 健身（exercise 泛指各種運動或訓練）
treadmill 跑步機
dumbbell 啞鈴
barbell 槓鈴
cardio 有氧運動
weight training 重量訓練

聯想單字
bodybuilding	n. 健美
bodybuilder	n. 健美運動員
muscleman	n. 肌肉發達的男子

nearsighted
[nɪrˈsaɪtɪd]
adj. 近視的

衍 nearsightedly adv. 近視地
nearsightedness n. 近視

同 short-sighted adj. [英] 近視的；目光短淺的，沒有遠見的

反 far-sighted adj. 遠視的；有遠見的，深謀遠慮的

A new study shows that eye drops can help prevent kids from becoming **nearsighted**.
一項新的研究顯示，眼藥水可以有助於避免孩子得到近視。

● Point 重點
與「視力」相關的表達方式

詢問別人近視幾度或眼鏡配幾度
⇒ What's your eyeglasses/contact lens prescription?
你的眼鏡／隱形眼鏡度數是多少？
⇒ What is your glasses/contact lens prescription?
你的視力是多少？
⇒ What is your vision like?
 How good is your vision/eyesight?

回答視力是幾度
⇒ I am nearsighted with 5.0 diopters.
 I have negative 5.0 nearsightedness.
 I am nearsighted with 5.0 diopters.
 我近視 500 度。

※500 度就是 5.0，380 度就是 3.8，以此類推。在唸的時候要將每個數字分開唸（例如 5.0 是 five point zero、3.8 是 three point eight）。

表達自己的近視深淺
⇨ I'm heavily/severely nearsighted.
　我的近視很深。
　I have really poor/bad eyesight.
　我視力真的很差。
　My vision is extremely poor.
　我視力極差。
　I'm slightly/mildly nearsighted.
　我有輕微的近視。

聯想單字
myopia	n. 近視
astigmatism	n. 散光
contact lens	n. 隱形眼鏡

odor
[ˋodɚ]
n.（常指難聞的）氣味；臭味

衍 odorless adj. 無味的，沒有氣味的
odorous adj. 臭的，難聞的

Similar to garlic, the **odor** of onions lasts long after you've eaten them.
與大蒜類似，洋蔥的氣味在你吃完後會持續很久。

❶ Point 重點
smell vs. **scent** vs. **odor**
smell 泛指氣味，一般沒有香臭之分，但依據使用情境，有時會特指難聞或特殊的味道。scent 是濃度若有似無的香氣或動物留下的氣味及體味。odor 的原意雖然中性，但近來常指難聞異味，如果要強調「惡臭」，則可以使用 stench 和 stink 這兩個字。

聯想單字
rotten	adj. 腐爛變質的
stinky	adj. 惡臭的
smelly	adj. 難聞的，臭的

peek
[pik]
v. 窺視，偷看
n.（快速地）看一眼；偷看

同 peep v.（通常指透過小孔）窺視，偷看

The campus guard caught him trying to **peek** at the girls changing in the locker room.
學校警衛抓到他試圖偷看更衣室裡正在換衣服的女孩子。

Shall we take a **peek** at the new bookstore on that street?
我們要不要去看看那條街上新開的書店？

❶ Point 重點
have/take a peek 快速看一眼，看一下
⇒ You can **have a peek** at my blog posts for tips on wedding planning.
你可以看一下我的部落格文章，裡面有婚禮策劃的訣竅。

各種「看」的分辨
see 是「自然看到」，表示進入視線之中。
⇒ Did you **see** the birds flying around?
你有看到那些飛來飛去的鳥嗎？

look 是「專注且刻意去看」，通常看的是靜態人事物。
⇒ I **looked** at my mom's face and smiled at her.
我看著媽媽的臉微笑。

watch 是「長時間特意去看」，通常看的是動態人事物。
⇒ Did you **watch** the World Cup games last night?
你昨晚有看世界盃的比賽嗎？

stare 是「瞪大雙眼盯著看」。
⇒ Why are you **staring** at me?
你為什麼盯著我看？

posture
[ˈpɑstʃɚ]
n. 儀態；姿勢；立場

Choosing the right chair height is crucial to maintaining a healthy sitting **posture**.
選擇適合的椅子高度對於保持健康的坐姿來說至關重要。

❶ Point 重點
posture vs. pose
pose 是名詞也是動詞，指的是「（為拍照或畫肖像而刻意擺出的）姿勢」。如 yoga pose（瑜珈姿勢）、pose

for the camera（拍照姿勢）。另一方面，posture 則是習慣性的姿勢和儀態，不帶有刻意及目的性。

聯想單字		
gesture	n. 手勢
slouch	v. 彎腰駝背；無精打采
stoop	v. 俯身，彎腰
bad/poor posture	phr. 姿勢不良

scent
[sɛnt]
n. 香味；動物的體味；香水

衍 scented adj. 香的，芬芳的

The **scent** of roses is often associated with feelings of relaxation and calmness.
玫瑰的香味常會讓人聯想到放鬆和平靜的感受。

聯想單字		
aroma	n.（食物、飲料的）香味，芳香
fragrance	n. 香氣；香水

spine
[spaɪn]
n. 脊椎；（動物或植物的）刺

衍 spineless adj. 無脊椎的；懦弱的
spine-chiller n. 驚悚片
spine-chilling adj. 令人毛骨悚然的
spine-tingling adj. 緊張刺激的

Failure to maintain good posture can add strain to muscles and put stress on the **spine**.
姿勢不良可能會使肌肉緊繃並對脊椎造成壓力。

聯想單字		
backbone	n. 脊椎骨；骨氣
collarbone	n. 鎖骨
shoulder blade	n. 肩胛骨
cheekbone	n. 顴骨
jawbone	n. 下頜骨

Chapter 05・身體部位、外貌形容　P.097

sprawl
[sprɔl]
v.（懶散地）伸展著四肢坐（或躺）；（建築等）雜亂無序地向外擴展
n.（懶散地）伸展著四肢坐（或躺）的樣子；（建築等）雜亂無序的向外擴展的狀態

衍 sprawled adj. 伸展著四肢坐（或躺）著的
sprawling adj.（尤指城市建築）雜亂無序向外擴展的

We **sprawled** on the beach and breathed in the fresh air.
我們伸展著四肢躺在海灘上，呼吸著新鮮的空氣。

There was a **sprawl** of houses as far as we could see.
我們看得到的地方全都是雜亂無章的房屋。

聯想單字
urban sprawl	n. 都市蔓延
sprawling city	phr. 不斷擴張的城市
sprawling landscape	phr. 綿延不絕的景色

stumble
[ˈstʌmbl̩]
v. 絆倒；跌跌撞撞地走；結巴

衍 stumbling block n. 障礙物；絆腳石

The singer **stumbled** on the stairs during her concert.
這名歌手開演唱會時在樓梯上絆倒了。

❶ Point 重點
stumble into sth 偶然開始（做某事）
➪ Evans **stumbled into** teaching after tutoring a high school student in English.
Evans 在家教過一個高中生英文之後，偶然開始做起了教學工作。

stumble across/on/upon sth/sb
偶然發現；撞見；偶然遇見
➪ When she was cleaning out her drawers, she **stumbled upon** some old family photos.
她在清理抽屜時，偶然發現了一些家裡的老照片。

stumble/trip over words 說話結巴
➪ Sometimes social anxiety can result in **stumbling over** your **words** when talking to other people.
有時社交焦慮會讓你在與他人交談時說話結巴。

stumble vs. tumble
雖然 stumble 和 tumble 都是「摔倒」，但 stumble 是指腳下被某物絆到、失去平衡而摔倒，而 tumble 則是從高處向下滾落而摔倒，因此有時也可以用來指價格的下跌。

聯想單字		
stroll	v. 散步
ramble	v. 漫步；閒晃
stride	v. 大步走
plod	v. 費力行走
pace	v. 來回踱步
march	v. 齊步走；氣勢洶洶地快步走
tramp	v.（尤指長距離且疲憊地）重步行走

sturdy
[ˋstɝdɪ]
adj. 結實的，堅固耐用的；身強體壯的

衍 sturdiness n. 結實；堅固耐用；強壯
sturdily adv. 結實地；堅固耐用地

A **sturdy** tripod is one of the most important pieces of equipment for a photographer.
堅固耐用的三腳架是攝影師最重要的裝備之一。

● Point 重點
無論有無實體，都可以用 sturdy 這個字來形容，常見的搭配詞有 **sturdy construction**（堅固耐用的構造）、**sturdy foundation**（堅固的基礎）等等，都經常在報章雜誌中用到。

聯想單字		
stout	adj. 結實的；壯碩的；堅定的
solid	adj. 結實的；堅固的
durable	adj. 經久耐用的
robust	adj. 強健的；堅固耐用的
tough	adj. 堅韌的；結實的；強壯的

trample
[ˋtræmpl]
v. 踩，踐踏；侵犯（尊嚴等）

They accused the government of **trampling** on the needs and rights of children and teenagers.
他們指控政府侵犯兒童和青少年的需求及權利。

Chapter 05・身體部位、外貌形容　P.099

tread
[trɛd]
v. 踩；踏 n. 腳步聲

Crumbs of cereal had been **trodden** into the carpet.
麥片的碎屑被踩進了地毯之中。

He heard someone's **tread** behind him.
他聽到身後傳來了某人的腳步聲。

❶ Point 重點 ....

tread 做為動詞時的三態變化是 **tread-trod/treaded-trodden**，使用時必須特別注意，下面是一些經常使用的片語，一起來看看該怎麼用吧！

be treading water 原地踏步；裹足不前
⇨ Without any hope of promotion in this company, Mike feels that he **is** just **treading water**.
Mike 在這間公司毫無晉升希望，覺得自己只是在原地踏步。

tread carefully 小心處理，謹慎行事
⇨ We need to **tread carefully** when balancing our future development plans.
我們在協調未來的發展計畫時必須謹慎行事。

tread/step on sb's toes 惹惱或得罪某人
⇨ People sometimes unintentionally **tread on** other's **toes** when trying to complete their own tasks.
人們在試圖完成自己的任務時，有時會無意間得罪了別人。

主題分類單字　身體部位、外貌形容相關

Chapter 05　外表

bodily	[ˋbɑdɪlɪ]	adj. 人體的；身體的
bowel	[ˋbaʊəl]	n. 腸
brow	[braʊ]	n. 眉頭；山頂
calf	[kæf]	n. 小牛；幼崽
complexion	[kəmˋplɛkʃən]	n. 氣色；膚色；一般特徵
dandruff	[ˋdændrəf]	n. 頭皮屑
eyelash	[ˋaɪˏlæʃ]	n. 睫毛
eyelid	[ˋaɪˏlɪd]	n. 眼皮；眼瞼
fatty	[ˋfætɪ]	adj. 富含脂肪的
footstep	[ˋfʊtˏstɛp]	n. 腳步；腳步聲
gnaw	[nɔ]	v. 啃咬；使煩惱
good-looking	[ˋgʊdˋlʊkɪŋ]	adj. 好看的；漂亮的
hairstyle	[ˋhɛrˏstaɪl]	n. 髮型
healthful	[ˋhɛlθfəl]	adj. 有益健康的
hearing	[ˋhɪrɪŋ]	n. 聽力；聽覺；聽證會
navel	[ˋnevl]	n. 肚臍
nostril	[ˋnɑstrɪl]	n. 鼻孔
optical	[ˋɑptɪkl]	adj. 視覺的；視力的；光學的
penis	[ˋpinɪs]	n. 陰莖
rouge	[ruʒ]	n. 胭脂

Chapter 05・身體部位、外貌形容　P.101

shear	[ʃɪr]	v. 剪羊毛；剃光頭髮
skull	[skʌl]	n. 頭蓋骨，顱骨
sniff	[snɪf]	v. 嗅聞；抽鼻子；嗤之以鼻地說 n. 抽鼻子
stature	[`stætʃɚ]	n. 身高，身材
thigh	[θaɪ]	n. 大腿
throb	[θrɑb]	v. 跳動，振動；（身體部位）抽痛
tonic	[`tɑnɪk]	n. 補藥；使人精神振奮的事物
valve	[vælv]	n. 閥門；瓣膜

Chapter 05　Quiz Time

一、　請選出正確的答案。

1. All _____ are capable of pursing any career and achieving success in it.
    A. pines
    B. externals
    C. blondes
    D. genders

2. Earrings, necklaces and rings are all popular items that can complement a _____ style.
    A. masculine
    B. barefoot
    C. muscular
    D. feeble

3. Body _____ occurs when sweat combines with bacteria on the skin.
    A. artery
    B. bosom
    C. odor
    D. tread

二、請根據下列中文句子，填入適當的英文單字。

1. 我在決定要點什麼之前，先看了一眼菜單。

    I took a p_____ at the menu before deciding what to order.

2. 糟糕的姿勢確實會使脊椎的形狀改變並導致身體出問題。

   Poor p_____ can actually change the shape of your spine and lead to physical problems.

3. 根據報導，部分英國人到了 2024 年就無法擁有體面的生活水準了。

   According to reports, a portion of the UK population will not have a d_____ standard of living by 2024.

4. 那位女演員穿著藍色的洋裝參加時裝週，看起來非常漂亮。

   The actress looked g_____ in a blue dress at Fashion Week.

5. 不要只是為了拍照就去踐踏花朵或其他植物。

   Don't t_____ flowers or other plants just to take a picture.

Chapter 06

性格／特質
個性、情緒

Ch06.mp3

★核心單字情境對話

Sam　　：I've been feeling a bit **distressed** lately.
Ashley：What's bothering you?
Sam　　：There's this **arrogant** coworker who constantly tries to **humiliate** me in front of everyone.
Ashley：That sounds awful. Have you tried talking to HR about it?
Sam　　：Not yet. I'm afraid they'll just **disregard** my concerns.
Ashley：Don't be too **skeptical**. Keep talking to HR and your **perseverance** might pay off in the end.
Sam　　：You're right. I need to be more **optimistic** and assertive in dealing with this issue.

翻譯

Sam　　：我最近一直覺得有點**煩躁**。
Ashley：你在煩什麼？
Sam　　：有個**自以為是**的同事老是想要在所有人面前**讓我難看**。
Ashley：聽起來好糟。你有去跟人資講過這件事了嗎？
Sam　　：還沒有。我擔心他們根本**不會在乎**我的煩惱。
Ashley：別太**疑神疑鬼**了。你就一直去跟人資說這件事，到頭來你的**堅持**可能就會發揮效果了。
Sam　　：妳說得對。我得用更**樂觀**和積極的態度來處理這個問題。

Chapter 06・個性、情緒　　P.105

amiable
[`emɪəbl]
adj. 和藹可親的，親切的

衍 amiably adv. 友善地；親切地
amiability n. 友善；親切

The **amiable** old woman always had a kind word for everyone.
那位和藹的老太太對大家說話總是很親切。

annoyance
[ə`nɔɪəns]
n. 煩躁；惱火；令人不快的事

衍 annoy v. 使煩惱
annoyed adj. 生氣的；煩惱的
annoying adj. 討厭的；惱人的
annoyingly adv. 令人討厭地，惹人厭地

The constant noise from the construction site was a source of **annoyance** for the residents nearby.
不斷從工地傳來的噪音讓附近的居民覺得煩躁。

❶ Point 重點
annoyance 通常指的是程度較輕的不悅或煩惱，與 anger 或 disgust 等較強烈的憤怒或不滿有所不同。

be annoyed at (sth) 因某事或某狀況感到煩躁
⇒ He **was annoyed at** the slow service at the restaurant.
他對這間餐廳緩慢的服務速度感到煩躁。

be annoyed with (sb) 對某人感到惱火
⇒ They **were annoyed with** their children for making a mess in the living room.
他們對於把客廳弄得一團糟的孩子們感到惱火。

聯想單字	
irritation	n. 激怒；惱人的事
frustration	n. 挫敗感
disturbance	n. 干擾
nuisance	n. 討厭或麻煩的人事物
bother	n. 讓人煩惱的人事物 v. 煩擾；使困擾

arrogant

[ˈærəgənt]
adj. 傲慢的；
狂妄自大的

衍 arrogance n. 傲慢
　　arrogantly adv.
　　傲慢地；狂妄自大地

反 modest adj. 謙虛的
　　humble adj.
　　謙虛的；卑微的

She refused to apologize and displayed an **arrogant** attitude that she could do no wrong.
她拒絕道歉並以傲慢的態度表示自己不可能做錯事。

❶ Point 重點
除了形容人態度傲慢外，arrogant 也可以用來形容事物或情況。
⇨ The company's **arrogant** disregard for customer complaints led to a loss of business.
該公司對客訴的傲慢無視讓他們損失了生意。

arrogant vs. **prideful**
arrogant 指的是**態度或行為上的自大傲慢**，如輕視他人或表現出高人一等的感覺，帶有負面意味。另一方面，**prideful** 一般表達的是**對自己或自己的成就感到自豪或驕傲**的狀態，字義會因為上下文而有正面或負面的解讀。

聯想單字
overconfident	adj. 過於自信的；自負的
superiority	n. 優越；上級
look down on	phr. 輕視～

carefree

[ˈkɛrˌfri]
adj. 無憂無慮的；
無牽掛的

She lived a **carefree** life, traveling the world without worrying about responsibilities.
她過著無憂無慮的生活，在世界到處旅行而不用擔心責任。

❶ Point 重點
字尾 **-free** 表示與特定事物或狀態「**無關**」或「**不受影響**」。下面是 -free 結尾的常見單字。
（除了 carefree 以外，大部分以 -free 結尾的單字，中間的「-」都不可省略）
⇨ alcohol-free 不含酒精的
　 sugar-free 無糖的
　 chemical-free 無化學添加的
　 stress-free 無壓力的，輕鬆自在的

聯想單字		
happy-go-lucky	adj. 樂天的，無憂無慮的	
optimistic	adj. 樂觀的	
positive	adj. 正面的	
look on the bright side	phr. 正面來說～；幸運的是～	

commend
[kə`mɛnd]
v. 表揚，讚許

衍 commendation n.
表揚，讚許
commendable adj.
值得讚許的
commendably adv.
值得讚許地

反 criticize v. 批評

The teacher **commended** Sarah for her outstanding performance in the school play.
老師表揚了 Sarah 在學校話劇中的出色表現。

❶ Point 重點

commend sb for sth 因某事表揚某人
⇒ The manager **commended** the team **for** their hard work and dedication.
經理表揚了團隊的努力和投入。

commend vs. compliment vs. praise
雖然都是「稱讚」，但傳達的語意和使用情境卻有著細微差異，使用時要特別注意。

commend 會在如**官方或職場**等「正式場合」中使用，通常是**上級單位對下級所屬**的優秀表現表達肯定。

compliment 則多在**社交或輕鬆**的場合中使用，且一般是針對某人的**外表、特質或具體行為**的稱讚。
⇒ She received many **compliments** on her new hairstyle.
她的新髮型得到了很多讚美。

praise 沒有限制使用情境，無論是因為表現優秀、品德高尚或是外表好看，只要是肯定或讚賞就可以用 praise。
⇒ The teacher **praised** the student for his excellent essay.
老師稱讚了這名學生的優秀作文。

聯想單字		
commendation letter	n. 推薦信	
recommend	v. 推薦	
recommendation	n. 推薦；推薦信，介紹信	

compassionate
[kəm`pæʃənet]
adj. 富有同情心的

衍 compassion
　n. 同情，惻隱之心
　compassionately
　adv. 有同情心地

反 indifferent
　adj. 漠不關心的

She showed a **compassionate** attitude towards the homeless and offered food and shelter.
她對這些無家可歸者表示同情，並提供了食物和住處。

❶ Point 重點

feel compassion for 對～感到同情
⇨ When I heard about her difficult situation, I couldn't help but **feel compassion for** her.
當我得知她的艱難處境時，我忍不住開始同情她了。

sympathy vs. empathy vs. compassion
sympathy（同情心）指對他人的困境或痛苦感到同情，但這種同情並非感同身受，而是一種**外在的**、**情感上**所表達的支持或關懷。
empathy（同理心）指對他人所面臨的處境**共情**，能夠**真正理解和感受**對方所經歷的情感狀態，是一種層次更深的共鳴和理解。
compassion（關懷心，憐憫心）比起 sympathy 更多的是對他人處境的憐憫、理解及關心，且**願意採取積極的行動**來幫助或支持受苦的對象。

可以用「先有 sympathy，再產生 empathy，最後發展出 compassion」，也就是 sympathy → empathy → compassion 的順序及層次來理解與分辨。

conscientious
[ˌkɑnʃɪ`ɛnʃəs]
adj. 認真的；盡心盡責的

衍 conscience
　n. 良心；良知
　conscience-stricken
　adj. 於心不安的；良心受譴責的
　conscientiously
　adv. 認真地；盡心盡責地
　conscientiousness
　n. 認真；盡心盡責

This **conscientious** employee always goes above and beyond his duties and has taken up additional responsibilities.
這位盡責的員工總會做超出職責要求的事，且承擔了更多的責任。

❶ Point 重點

有一個長得和 conscientious 很像的字是 **conscious**（**有意識的；清醒的；察覺到的**），但兩者無論是字義還是用法都非常不同。conscientious 強調的是對工作或責任的認真盡責，而 conscious 指的則是對**某事物有所察覺或認知**。若在題目中看到，請一定要特別注意分辨用的是哪一個字！

⇨ She was **conscious** of the fact that she had made a mistake.
她意識到自己確實犯了一個錯。

Chapter 06・個性、情緒　P.109

consent
[kən`sɛnt]
n. 允許；同意
v. 允許；同意

衍 consensus n. 共識

反 dissent v. 不同意

The patient must sign a **consent** form before the doctor can perform the surgery.
患者在手術前必須先簽同意書，醫生才能執行手術。

The participants **consented** to the terms and conditions of the study before enrolling.
在報名參加前，參與者同意了這次研究的規定和條件。

❶ Point 重點
consent vs. **agree**
consent 常是**涉及法律、醫療、商業等方面的正式同意**，需要以口頭或書面來明確表達同意或贊成。
⇨ She gave her **consent** to the use of her artwork in the exhibition.
她同意在展覽中展出她的作品。

agree（同意）的範圍更加廣泛，無論是觀點、主張、計畫或建議，不論表達型式，只要**意見確定取得共識**，便可使用 agree。
⇨ We all **agree** that this is the best course of action.
我們全都同意這是最好的行動方案。

聯想單字
| give consent to | phr. 同意～ |
| obtain consent from | phr. 從～獲得同意 |

cynical
[`sɪnɪkl]
adj. 憤世嫉俗的

衍 cynic n.
憤世嫉俗的人
cynically adv.
憤世嫉俗地
cynicism n.
憤世嫉俗

His **cynical** view of human nature made it difficult for him to trust others.
他對人性憤世嫉俗的看法讓他很難信任別人。

❶ Point 重點
cynical 表達的是一種「對人性、社會或政治等議題，充滿質疑且認為人皆自私自利」的態度，日常生活中較常看到的搭配詞有 **cynical attitude**（憤世嫉俗的態度）、**cynical view**（憤世嫉俗的觀點）、**cynical remark**（憤世嫉俗的言論）等等。

discreet
[dɪˋskrit]
adj. 小心謹慎的

衍 discreetly adv. 小心謹慎地
discretion n. 慎重，謹慎

反 indiscreet adj. 輕率的，不慎重的

He made **discreet** inquiries about the job opening without letting his current employer know.
他在沒讓現任雇主知道的情況下，小心地打聽了那個職缺的消息。

❶ Point 重點

discreet vs. **cautions**
discreet 指的是為了**避免引起過分關注或造成尷尬**，而展現的謹言慎行和自我克制
⇨ She was **discreet** about her relationship with her boss.
她對於自己和老闆之間的關係很小心謹慎。

cautions（謹慎的，慎重的）一般描述的是在**面對潛在風險或不確定性時**，為避免可能的危險或損失，而展現的謹慎態度及行為。
⇨ She is **cautious** about lending money to friends.
她對於借錢給朋友的這件事很慎重。

disregard
[͵dɪsrɪˋgɑrd]
n. 忽視，漠視
v. 忽視，漠視

The company's **disregard** for its employees' rights led to a strike.
這間公司對員工權利的漠視導致了罷工。

It is important to **disregard** negative comments and focus on your goals.
忽視負面評論並專注於自身目標是很重要的。

distress
[dɪˋstrɛs]
n. 悲傷；痛苦；遇險
v. 使煩躁，使焦慮

衍 distressed adj. 煩躁的，焦慮的
distressing adj. 令人苦惱的，令人擔憂的（也可用 distressful）

The news of his sudden death caused her great **distress**.
他驟然去世的消息使她極為悲傷。

The constant noise from the campaign **distressed** the residents.
宣傳活動不斷發出的噪音讓居民們覺得煩躁。

Chapter 06・個性、情緒　P.111

❶ Point 重點
in distress 表示「處於困境、痛苦、擔憂、危險或急需幫助的狀態」，這是經常看到的片語，請一定要好好記住。
⇨ The stranded hikers were **in distress** and needed immediate assistance.
這些去健行的人受困遇險，需要立即援助。

聯想單字
distress call	n. 求救訊號
agony	n.（肉體或精神的）極度痛苦
misery	n. 痛苦，悲慘
suffering	n. 疼痛；折磨
pain	n.（肉體上的）疼痛；（精神上的）痛苦

drawback
[ˋdrɔˏbæk]
n. 缺點；弱勢；不利因素

同 disadvantage n. 缺點；弱勢；不利因素

While the new car model is very efficient, a notable **drawback** is its high maintenance cost.
雖然這款新車的效能非常高，但養護費用高昂是一個明顯的缺點。

聯想單字
setback	n. 挫敗；障礙
hindrance	n. 阻礙，障礙
shortcoming	n. 缺點，短處
defect	n. 缺陷；瑕疵

eloquent
[ˋɛləkwənt]
adj. 能言善道的，有說服力的

衍 eloquence n. 能言善道，有說服力的口才
eloquently adv. 能言善道地，有說服力地

She gave an **eloquent** speech that moved everyone in the audience.
她的演講很有說服力，打動了在場的所有人。

❶ Point 重點
eloquent vs. **fluent**
eloquent 是指能用清楚精練又有力量的方式表達，且**內容通常具有感染力和說服力**，能引起聽眾或讀者的共鳴，常用來形容如演講等口語表達。另一方面，**fluent** 則是形容能以熟練且流暢自然的方式使用某種語言技能，**與表達內容所能造成的影響力無關**。

⇨ He is **fluent** in three languages: English, Spanish, and French.
他能流利使用英語、西班牙語和法語這三種語言。

聯想單字		
silver-tongued	adj.	口才好的，能言善道的
convincing	adj.	令人信服的
persuasive	adj.	具有說服力的
plausible	adj.	貌似可信的

frustration
[ˌfrʌsˋtreʃən]
n.（因無法滿足需求而）沮喪，挫敗感；令人沮喪的事物

衍 frustrate v. 使挫敗，使氣餒；阻撓
frustrated adj. 感到挫敗的，氣餒的
frustrating adj. 令人感到挫敗的；使人氣餒的

She expressed her **frustration** with the broken appliance by calling customer service multiple times.
她打了好幾次電話給客服，表達她對於設備故障的不滿。

hostile
[ˋhɑstl̩]
adj. 不友善的；敵對的；有敵意的

衍 hostility n. 敵意；不友善

The atmosphere in the meeting room was **hostile** due to the recent disagreements.
由於最近的意見分歧，會議室裡的氣氛很不友善。

❶ Point 重點
hostile 後面常搭配介系詞 **to** 或 **towards**。
⇨ He remained very **hostile towards** his former colleagues.
他對前同事仍舊充滿敵意。

Chapter 06．個性、情緒　　P.113

humiliate
[hju`mɪlɪˌet]
v. 羞辱，使丟臉

衍 humiliation n.
恥辱感
humiliated adj.
感到被羞辱的，難堪的

He felt **humiliated** when his mistake was pointed out in the meeting.
當在會議上被指出他的錯誤時，他覺得被羞辱了。

聯想單字	embarrass	v. 使尷尬，使窘迫
	agitate	v. 使坐立不安；使焦慮
	uncomfortable	adj. 令人不自在的；感覺有點尷尬的
	mortify	v. 使非常尷尬；使感到極度羞辱

hypocrisy
[hɪ`pɑkrəsɪ]
n. 虛偽，偽善

衍 hypocrite n.
偽君子，偽善者
hypocritical adj.
虛偽的；偽善的
hypocritically adv.
虛偽地；偽善地

The CEO's lecture on business ethics was dripping with **hypocrisy** considering the numerous scandals his company was involved in.
考量到他公司所涉入的無數醜聞，這位執行長就商業道德發表的演說充滿虛偽。

聯想單字	insincere	adj. 虛偽的；不誠懇的
	insincerity	n. 虛偽，虛情假意
	pretend	v. 做作；假裝
	pretentious	adj. 做作的；自以為是的
	fake	v. 造假 adj. 虛假的；偽造的

hysterical
[hɪs`tɛrɪkl]
adj. 歇斯底里的；
[口] 非常滑稽搞笑的

衍 hysteria n. 歇斯底里
hysterically adv.
歇斯底里地

She became **hysterical** when she found out her dog was missing.
當她發現她的狗不見時，她變得歇斯底里。

❶ Point 重點
hysterical vs. **hilarious**
hysterical 是形容「因**極端情緒**（如憤怒或難過）而表現出異常行為」的狀態，不過在口語上，hysterical 也常用來形容某件事或情境「非常滑稽搞笑」。另一方面，**hilarious** 則只有「非常有趣而讓人想笑」的意思，且**和情緒失控無關**。

聯想單字	uncontrollable	adj. 無法控制的
	manic	adj. 十分興奮的；狂躁不安的
	get worked up	phr. 情緒激動

impulsive
[ɪm`pʌlsɪv]
adj. 衝動的

衍 impulse n. 衝動；突如其來的強烈欲望
impulsiveness n. 衝動
impulsively adv. 衝動地

She made an **impulsive** decision to buy a new car without thinking about her finances.
她沒有考慮自己的財務狀況，就衝動決定要買一輛新車了。

❶ Point 重點
act on impulse 衝動行事
⇨ He often **acts on impulse** without considering the consequences.
他經常不考慮後果就衝動行事。

聯想單字
| impulsive buying | n. 衝動購物 |
| impulse buy | n. 衝動購入的商品 |

indifferent
[ɪn`dɪfərənt]
adj. 不感興趣的；漠不關心的

衍 indifference n. 不感興趣；漠不關心
indifferently adv. 不感興趣地；漠不關心地

The teacher noticed that some students were **indifferent** about the upcoming exams.
這名老師注意到有些學生對於即將到來的考試漠不關心。

❶ Point 重點
be indifferent to 對～漠不關心
⇨ The manager seemed to **be indifferent to** the complaints from his team.
那位經理似乎對於來自他團隊的抱怨漠不關心。

聯想單字
| apathy | n. 冷漠；無感情 |
| nonchalance | n. 漠不關心；毫不在乎 |

Chapter 06・個性、情緒

irritate
[ˈɪrəˌtet]
v. 激怒，使惱火；使疼痛

衍 irritation n. 激怒；惱人的事；疼痛
irritated adj. 被激怒的，惱火的
irritating adj. 惱人的，令人厭煩的
irritatingly adv. 惱人地，令人厭煩地
irritant adj. 令人煩惱的事物；造成麻煩的事物
irritable adj. 易怒的，暴躁的

His habit of tapping his fingers on the table **irritates** me.
他用手指敲桌子的習慣讓我很惱火。

❶ Point 重點
irritate vs. **annoy**
雖然 irritate 和 annoy 表達的都是因某個人事物而引起的不悅，但 **irritate** 更強調**因生理或重複性的行為所造成的持續不適感**，annoy 則涵蓋範圍更廣，可以用來表達單一事件所造成的惱火或煩躁。
⇨ Her constant complaining started to **irritate** everyone in the office.
她的不斷抱怨讓辦公室裡的大家都開始煩躁了起來。
The buzzing of the mosquito in the room was really **annoying**.
蚊子在房間裡的嗡嗡聲真的很煩。

naive
[nɑˈiv]
adj. 天真的；輕信的

衍 naively adv. 天真地；輕信地
naivete n. 天真；輕信

It was **naive** of her to believe he would keep his promise.
她真是天真，相信他會信守諾言。

❶ Point 重點
因為 naive 暗示著一種涉世未深、容易被欺騙或過於信任他人的特質，因此本身經常**帶有輕微的貶義**，使用上須特別留意。

聯想單字		
innocent	adj. 無辜的；天真的
childlike	adj. 孩子般的，純真無邪的

optimistic
[ˌɑptə`mɪstɪk]
adj. 樂觀的

衍 optimism n. 樂觀；樂觀主義
optimist n. 樂觀主義者，樂天派
optimistically adv. 樂觀地

反 pessimistic adj. 悲觀的

She remained **optimistic** even when the situation seemed bleak.
即使情況看來希望渺茫，她仍保持樂觀。

❶ Point 重點
be optimistic about 對～感到樂觀
⇨ The scientists **are optimistic about** finding a cure for the disease.
科學家們對於找到這種疾病的治癒方法感到樂觀。

聯想單字
passionate	adj. 熱情的；熱烈的
hopeful	adj. 懷抱希望的
confident	adj. 具有信心的
positive	adj. 正面的

outrageous
[aʊt`redʒəs]
adj.（因奇怪或異常而）驚人的；無恥的；（道德上）無法接受的

衍 outrage n. 道德上難以接受的事情；駭人聽聞的行為
outraged adj. 氣憤的；憤慨的
outrageously adv. 驚人地；無法接受地

Her **outrageous** sense of fashion always turns heads wherever she goes.
她驚人的時尚感無論去哪裡都會引來他人的目光。

❶ Point 重點
outrageous vs. outraged
形容詞的 outrageous 指的是某件事物或某人的行為極端、脫離常軌，因而讓旁人感到震驚、無法接受，甚至憤慨。另一方面，outraged 是 outrage 的過去分詞，形容某人因某事感到震驚、憤怒或無法接受的情緒反應。

perseverance

[ˌpɝsəˋvɪrəns]

n. 毅力；堅持不懈

衍 persevere v. 鍥而不捨，堅持不懈
perseverant adj. 堅持不懈的，鍥而不捨的

Through hard work and **perseverance**, he transformed his dream of becoming an author into reality.
透過努力和堅持不懈，他將成為作家的夢想變成了現實。

❶ Point 重點

perseverance 的後面可以用介系詞 **in**，表示對於某件事情的堅持不懈，且態度相當有毅力與恆心。

⇨ The student's **perseverance in** mastering the difficult subject earned him praise from his teachers and classmates alike.
這名學生很有毅力地掌握了這門困難的科目，為他贏得了老師和同學的一致讚賞。

perseverance vs. **persistence**

在某些情境下 perseverance 和 persistence 可以互換使用，但這兩個字所傳達的語意並非完全相同，一起來看看實際的運用方法吧！

perseverance 表示「堅持不懈地努力追求長期且困難的目標」，**強調克服困難和堅持不懈的精神。**

⇨ His **perseverance** in overcoming obstacles led to his success in the business world.
他在克服困難方面的毅力讓他得以在商界獲得成功。

persistence（堅持不懈；持續）表示「不斷進行某個行動或追求特定目標」，比起 perseverance 強調的堅持精神，**更加強調行動本身的持續進行。**

⇨ Her **persistence** in practicing the piano every day eventually led to her becoming a skilled musician.
她每天堅持練習鋼琴，最終讓她成為了一名技巧精湛的音樂家。

聯想單字
stout	adj. 結實的，牢固的；不屈不撓的
diligence	n. 勤勉
staunch	adj. 忠實的；堅定的

P.118　國際學村・全民英檢

persistent
[pɚˋsɪstənt]
adj. 持續的；堅持不懈的

衍 persist v. 持續；堅持不懈
persistence n. 持續；堅持不懈
persistently adv. 持續地；堅持不懈地

Despite facing numerous rejections, he remained **persistent** in his job search, sending out resumes every day.
儘管遭到多次拒絕，他仍然每天寄出履歷，持續尋找工作機會。

❶ Point 重點

persist vs. **insist**

persist 和 insist 都是動詞「堅持」的意思，但兩者在用法上有一些微妙的差異，這部分經常成為出題重點，請特別注意。

persist 通常表達的是「**為了達到特定的目標或解決問題，持續不斷地做某事**」，後面常搭配介系詞 **in**。
⇨ He **persisted in** his efforts to find a solution to the problem.
他持續努力尋找問題的解決方法。

insist 一般會用來表達強烈的意願，表示「**堅持某種立場、要求或意見，不接受其他選擇或解釋**」，後面常搭配的介系詞是 **on**。
⇨ She **insisted on** going to the party despite feeling unwell.
儘管身體不舒服，她還是堅持要去參加派對。

聯想單字

resolute	adj. 堅決的，堅定的
committed	adj. 堅定的；盡忠職守的
dedicated	adj. 投入的；盡心盡力的
devoted	adj. 投入的；盡心盡力的

provoke
[prə`vok]
v. 激起，引起（尤指負面反應）；激怒，挑釁

衍 provocative adj. 蓄意挑釁的，煽動的；引發思考的，啟發性的

The politician's speech **provoked** outrage among the public.
這名政客的演講引起了群情激憤。

● Point 重點
provoke sb into V-ing 激怒某人去做某事
⇨ The insult **provoked** John **into** punching the wall.
這種侮辱激怒了 John，讓他一拳打在了牆上。

聯想單字
instigate	v. 促使發生；發起
enrage	v. 使非常憤怒；激怒；觸怒
infuriate	v. 使大怒，激怒

rebellious
[rɪ`bɛljəs]
adj. 反叛的；叛逆的；難以控制的

衍 rebel v. 叛逆；反叛
n. 反抗者，造反者
rebellion n. 反叛；反抗
rebelliously adv. 難以控制地

反 obedient adj. 服從的

The teenager's **rebellious** attitude often led to conflicts with his parents.
這名青少年的叛逆態度時常導致他與父母之間發生衝突。

reckless
[`rɛklɪs]
adj. 魯莽的；輕率的；不顧後果的

衍 recklessly adv. 魯莽地；輕率地
recklessness n. 魯莽；輕率

反 cautious adj. 謹慎的

The company suffered huge losses due to the CEO's **reckless** financial decisions.
這間公司因其執行長魯莽的財務決策而遭受了巨大損失。

● Point 重點
reckless vs. careless
雖然 reckless 和 careless 都可以用來形容草率或不考慮後果的行為，但兩者在語意上仍有一些區別，使用時可以透過上下文來決定要用哪個字。

reckless 通常指的是魯莽且不負責任的行為，且**可能導致嚴重的風險和後果**。
⇨ His **reckless** driving led to a serious accident on the highway.
他的魯莽駕駛導致公路發生了嚴重事故。

careless 一般用來描述粗心或未經充分思考的行為，但**導致的後果可能並不嚴重**。
⇨ Kelly lost her keys because of her **careless** mistake.
Kelly 粗心大意地弄丟了她的鑰匙。

reliability
[rɪˌlaɪəˋbɪlətɪ]
n. 可靠度，可信度

衍 rely v. 依靠，依賴；信賴
reliable adj. 可信賴的；可靠的
reliably adv. 可信賴地；可靠地

The **reliability** of the new software has been praised by many users.
新軟體的可靠度得到了許多用戶的稱讚。

❶ Point 重點
reliable vs. **dependable**
reliable 表達的是「一直以來品質保持穩定和優秀」的語意，更強調**一貫的穩定性和一致性**，常用來描述技術和專業領域。
⇨ The weather forecast is **reliable**.
氣象預報是可靠的。

dependable 則常用來表示在特定情境下某個人事物是可以依賴且值得信任的，比起 reliable 的日常，更強調是**在特定情境下的可靠度**。
⇨ We need a **dependable** contractor for this project.
我們需要一個可靠的承包商來完成這個專案。

ruthless
[ˋruθlɪs]
adj. 殘忍無情的；冷酷的

衍 ruthlessly adv. 殘忍無情地；冷酷地
ruthlessness n. 殘忍無情；冷酷

The coach's **ruthless** training plan pushed the athletes to their limits.
教練無情的訓練計畫將運動員們逼到了極限。

聯想單字

cruel	adj. 殘忍的；殘酷的
cold-blooded	adj. 殘忍的；冷血的
merciless	adj. 殘忍的，冷血無情的

Chapter 06・個性、情緒　P.121

sentimental
[ˌsɛntəˋmɛnt!]
adj. 多愁善感的；感情用事的

衍 sentiment n.
傷感；觀點
sentimentally adv.
多愁善感地；感情用事地
sentimentalist n.
多愁善感的人；感情用事的人

She became **sentimental** when she looked at the old family photos.
她在看著那張家庭舊照時感傷了起來。

❶ Point 重點
sentimental vs. **emotional**
sentimental 往往帶有**懷舊情緒**，並傳達出柔軟感性的意味，但**有時會帶有貶義**，表示感傷的情緒表現太過誇張而沒有必要。
⇒ He kept the old letter for **sentimental** reasons.
他出於情感因素保留了這封舊信。

emotional 的意思是「情緒激動強烈的」或「充滿情感的」，範圍**涵蓋所有強烈的情感表達和反應**，不限於特定情感，**性質亦較中性**，須從上下文來判斷正確語意。
⇒ He gave an **emotional** speech at the wedding.
他在婚禮上的致詞充滿情感。

skeptical
[ˋskɛptɪk!]
adj. 持懷疑態度的

衍 skeptic n.
持懷疑態度的人
skeptically adv.
持懷疑態度地

Many viewers were **skeptical** of the news report due to its lack of sources.
由於缺乏消息來源，許多觀眾對該篇新聞報導持懷疑態度。

❶ Point 重點
skeptical of/about sth 對某事持懷疑態度
⇒ She was **skeptical about** the effectiveness of the new drug.
她對這款新藥的效力持懷疑態度。

skeptical vs. **suspicious**
skeptical 的懷疑帶有探索和探究的意味，強調這種懷疑是**基於理性或邏輯推理**而來，不一定帶有負面語意。
⇒ He's **skeptical** of the new plan until he sees more data.
在看到更多數據之前，他對新方案持懷疑態度。

suspicious（可疑的）暗示存有欺騙或隱藏資訊的可能性，**帶有更強的不信任和猜疑意味**，因此通常具有負面的含義。
⇨ She became **suspicious** when she noticed money missing from her wallet.
在發現皮夾裡的錢不見了的時候，她起了疑心。

superstitious
[ˌsupɚˋstɪʃəs]
adj. 迷信的

衍 superstition n. 迷信
superstitiously adv. 迷信地

Kevin carries a lucky charm with him at all times due to his **superstitious** beliefs.
Kevin 因為自身的迷信信仰，總是隨身帶著幸運符。

❶ Point 重點
be superstitious about 對～迷信
⇨ Many people **are superstitious about** the number 13.
許多人對 13 這個數字很迷信。

聯想單字		
pious	adj. 虔誠的，篤信的
religious	adj. 宗教的
religion	n. 宗教

wretched
[ˋrɛtʃɪd]
adj. 糟糕的；悲慘的

Living in that **wretched** apartment was totally unbearable during the winter months.
冬天住在那間糟糕的公寓裡真是令人完全難以忍受。

聯想單字		
miserable	adj. 悲慘的
mourn	v. 哀悼
woes	n. 災難；不幸（常複數）

Chapter 06・個性、情緒

主題分類單字 個性、情緒

Ch06.mp3

單字	音標	詞性/中譯
absent-minded	[ˈæbsn̩tˈmaɪndɪd]	adj. 心不在焉的；健忘的
absurd	[əbˈsɝd]	adj. 荒謬的；愚蠢的
acclaim	[əˈklem]	v. 為～喝采；稱讚 n. 歡呼；稱讚
accustom	[əˈkʌstəm]	v. 使習慣於
adore	[əˈdor]	v. 崇拜；愛慕；非常喜歡
affectionate	[əˈfɛkʃənɪt]	adj. 充滿愛意的
boredom	[ˈbordəm]	n. 無聊；厭倦
chuckle	[ˈtʃʌkl̩]	v. 輕笑；暗自發笑 n. 輕笑聲
confusing	[kənˈfjuzɪŋ]	adj. 令人困惑的
console	[ˈkɑnsol]	v. 安慰；慰問
cowardly	[ˈkaʊɚdlɪ]	adj. 膽小的；怯懦的
daring	[ˈdɛrɪŋ]	adj. 大膽的；勇於冒險的 n. 勇敢；膽量
despise	[dɪˈspaɪz]	v. 鄙視
disturbing	[dɪˈstɝbɪŋ]	adj. 令人心煩意亂的
encouraging	[ɪnˈkɝɪdʒɪŋ]	adj. 鼓勵性的
friction	[ˈfrɪkʃən]	n. 摩擦；不和
fury	[ˈfjʊrɪ]	n. 狂怒；（天氣等的）猛烈
gloom	[glum]	n. 陰暗；暗處；沮喪的氣氛

greed	[grid]	n. 貪婪
hateful	[ˈhetfəl]	adj. 可恨的；充滿憎恨的
indignant	[ɪnˈdɪgnənt]	adj. 憤怒的；憤慨的
indulge	[ɪnˈdʌldʒ]	v. 沈迷於；滿足（慾望等）；縱容
inhibited	[ɪnˈhɪbɪtɪd]	adj. 拘謹的
lonesome	[ˈlonsəm]	adj. 孤單寂寞的
lure	[lʊr]	v. 誘惑；以誘餌吸引 n. 誘惑物；魅力；誘餌
melancholy	[ˈmɛlənˌkɑlɪ]	adj. 憂鬱的；令人沮喪的 n. 憂鬱；愁思
moody	[ˈmudɪ]	adj. 喜怒無常的；悶悶不樂的
obsession	[əbˈsɛʃən]	n. 執念；念念不忘的人事物
outgoing	[ˈaʊtˌgoɪŋ]	adj. 開朗外向的
pathetic	[pəˈθɛtɪk]	adj. 可悲的
quarrelsome	[ˈkwɔrəlsəm]	adj. 喜歡爭吵的
rejoice	[rɪˈdʒɔɪs]	v. 欣喜；慶祝
reliance	[rɪˈlaɪəns]	n. 信任；依賴
relieved	[rɪˈlivd]	adj. 鬆一口氣的；寬慰的
resent	[rɪˈzɛnt]	v. 怨恨
ridicule	[ˈrɪdɪkjul]	v. 嘲笑；戲弄 n. 嘲笑；戲弄
scorn	[skɔrn]	v. 輕蔑；鄙視 n. 輕蔑；鄙視

Chapter 06 性格／特質

seduce	[sɪ`djus]	v. 誘惑；引誘
self-esteem	[ˌsɛlfə`stim]	n. 自尊
sensation	[sɛn`seʃən]	n. 感覺；知覺；轟動的事物
sensitivity	[ˌsɛnsə`tɪvətɪ]	n.（話題等）敏感；善解人意；體貼
shudder	[`ʃʌdɚ]	v. 發抖；戰慄 n. 發抖；戰慄
sorrowful	[`sarəfəl]	adj. 悲傷的；令人傷心的
stammer	[`stæmɚ]	v. 口吃；結巴地說話 n. 口吃；結巴
startle	[`startl̩]	v. 使驚嚇；使大吃一驚
thrill	[θrɪl]	v. 使興奮；使激動 n. 興奮；激動
unpleasant	[ʌn`plɛzn̩t]	adj. 令人不愉快的
unwilling	[ʌn`wɪlɪŋ]	adj. 不情願的；勉強的

Chapter 06　Quiz Time

一、請選出正確的答案。

1. It is illegal to access someone's personal information without _____.
    A. consent
    B. reliability
    C. annoyance
    D. drawback

2. The committee commended her for her _____ to the project.
    A. frustration
    B. dedication
    C. disregard
    D. hypocrisy

3. The company's _____ approach to cost-cutting led to massive layoffs.
    A. sentimental
    B. optimistic
    C. compassionate
    D. ruthless

二、請根據下列中文句子，填入適當的英文單字。

1. 她在考試期間不斷敲打桌子，對她的同學們造成了困擾。

    Her constant tapping on the desk became an a_____ to her classmates during the exam.

2. 隔壁公寓傳來的巨大音樂聲開始讓鄰居們覺得煩躁了。

   The loud music from the next apartment started to i_____ the neighbors.

3. 他對同事們的傲慢舉止使得他們合作起來效果不佳。

   His a_____ behavior towards his colleagues made it difficult for them to work together effectively.

4. 在家工作的主要缺點之一是缺乏與同事的社交互動。

   One major d_____ of working from home is the lack of social interaction with colleagues.

5. 她透過取笑弟弟的成績來故意激怒他。

   She deliberately p_____ her brother by teasing him about his grades.

Answer
(一)：1. A 2. B 3. D
(二)：1. annoyance 2. irritate 3. arrogant 4. drawback 5. provoked

翻譯：
(一)
1. 未經同意就取用真人的個人資訊是違法的。
2. 委員會正在搜集針對張氏家族的證據。
3. 我們立刻知道那本豪華手錶是假冒的贗品。

Chapter 07

工作
職業、工作地點、職場相關

Ch07.mp3

★核心單字情境對話

Tony : We need to **allocate** resources effectively for our latest **acquisition** and ensure **administrative** tasks are handled smoothly.

Amanda : Absolutely. **Abiding** by the new policies, we'll set a clear **agenda** for the team. I've **authorized** the budget for additional **personnel**.

Tony : That's great. Our success comes from our team's **collaboration** and **innovative** ideas, so I need you to **supervise** the onboarding process.

Amanda : Of course. Our new colleagues have impressive **expertise** and seem very **capable**. I'm confident they will contribute significantly to our **workforce**.

翻譯

Tony : 我們得為最新的**收購**案有效**分配**資源，並確保**行政**工作都有順利進行。

Amanda : 沒錯。我們會在**遵守**新政策的情況下，為團隊制定一個明確的**工作進度安排**。我已經**批准**了預算來增加**人手**。

Tony : 太棒了。團隊**合作**和**創新**思維是我們成功的原因，所以我需要妳來**管理**入職程序。

Amanda : 沒問題。我們的新同事擁有令人印象深刻的**專業知識**，而且看起來非常**能幹**。我有信心他們會成為我們的一大助力。

abide
[əˋbaɪd]
v. 忍受；遵守

She couldn't **abide** the loud noise coming from the construction site.
她無法忍受來自工地的巨大噪音。

❗ Point 重點
當 abide 用來表示**遵守法律或規則**時，後面會接介系詞 **by**。
⇨ Visitors are required to **abide by** the local regulations during their stay.
遊客在停留期間必須遵守當地法規。

acquisition
[͵ækwəˋzɪʃən]
n. 收購；獲得；養成

衍 acquire v. 收購；獲得；養成

The company announced the **acquisition** of a smaller startup in the tech industry.
這間公司宣布收購科技業內一間規模較小的新創公司。

❗ Point 重點
acquisition 常被用來描述「**獲得或養成某物（如知識、技能、財產）的過程或行為**」，如 **corporate acquisition**（收購公司），報章雜誌上常見的其他搭配詞還有 **language acquisition**（養成語言能力）、**acquisition of knowledge**（獲得知識）等等。

聯想單字	
merger	n. 合併
M&A (mergers and acquisitions)	n. 併購
merge	v. 合併

administrative
[ədˋmɪnə͵stretɪv]
adj. 管理的；行政的

衍 administration n. 行政；管理
administratively adv. 行政上地
administer v. 掌管；管理
administrator n. 管理人員，行政人員

Sherry handles **administrative** tasks such as scheduling meetings and managing emails.
Sherry 會處理如會議排程及電子郵件管理等的行政工作。

聯想單字	
administrative law	n. 行政法
administrative staff	n. 行政人員
minister	n. 部長，大臣
ministry	n.（政府的）部

agenda
[əˋdʒɛndə]
n.（會議等的）議程；
待辦事項

The meeting **agenda** includes discussing the budget for the upcoming year.
這場會議的議程包括討論來年的預算。

❶ Point 重點
set the agenda 制定議程
⇨ As the CEO, it's important for me to **set the agenda** for our quarterly board meetings.
身為執行長，制定每季的董事會會議議程，對我來說很重要。

hidden agenda 隱祕的動機，不可告人的目的
⇨ His generous offer seemed genuine, but everyone wondered if there was a **hidden agenda** behind it.
他的大方提議似乎很真誠，但所有人都在想背後是不是有什麼不可告人的目的。

allocate
[ˋæləˌket]
v. 分配；分派

衍 allocation n. 分配；分派

The funds were **allocated** to different departments based on their needs and priorities.
這些資金是根據不同部門的需求和優先順序來分配的。

❶ Point 重點
allocate vs. **distribute**
allocate 常指**根據目標需求或計畫安排**來分配資源（如金錢、時間、人力、空間等）給特定對象。
⇨ They **allocated** enough time for each stage of the project.
他們分配了足夠的時間給此專案的各個階段。

distribute 通常指將某物或資源分配給多個對象（如群眾、複數組織或地點等），著重於**一對多**的「**分散發放**」或「**分散配給**」。
⇨ The charity organization **distributes** food to families in need.
這個慈善組織將食物分發給有需要的家庭。

聯想單字		
assign	v. 分派；指派
appoint	v. 指派

Chapter 07・職業、工作地點、職場相關

attribute
[ˈætrəˌbjut]
n. 特性;特質;屬性
v. 把～歸因於

衍 attribution n.
歸因;歸屬

His leadership **attributes** include decisiveness and empathy.
果斷和同理心是他領導特質的一部分。

Zack **attributes** his success to hard work and perseverance.
Zack 認為自己的成功是來自努力和毅力。

❶ Point 重點
attribute to 歸因於
⇨ The success of the project can be **attributed to** careful planning and teamwork.
這項專案會成功可以歸因於謹慎的規劃及團隊合作。

聯想單字		
contribute	v. 貢獻	
distribute	v. 分發;分配	
tribute	n. 貢品;頌詞	

authorize
[ˈɔθəˌraɪz]
v. 授權;批准

衍 authorized adj.
獲得授權的;經過批准的
authorization n.
授權;批准
authority n. 權力;當局;權威人士

The supervisor **authorized** the purchase of new computers for the office.
這名主管批准為辦公室購買新的電腦。

❶ Point 重點
authorize sb to do sth 授權某人可以做某事
⇨ The board only **authorizes** the heads of departments **to** access sensitive company information.
董事會僅授權各部門主管存取公司的敏感資料。

聯想單字		
the authorities concerned	phr. 有關當局
figure of authority	phr. 權威人士
central/local authority	phr. 中央／地方當局

bonus
[ˋbonəs]
n. 獎金；紅利；額外的好處

Employees receive an annual **bonus** based on company profits and individual performance.
員工會根據公司獲利和個人表現獲得年度獎金。

聯想單字
year-end bonus	n. 年終獎金
performance bonus	n. 績效獎金
salary	n. 月薪
wage	n. 工資；報酬
commission	n. 佣金
payday	n. 發薪日

capability
[͵kepəˋbɪlətɪ]
n. 能力；才能

衍 capable adj. 有能力的；能幹的

His leadership **capabilities** were evident in how he handled the crisis.
他處理危機的方式清楚展現了他的領導能力。

❶ Point 重點

ability vs. **capability** vs. **capacity**

ability 指的是某人或某物能夠完成特定任務或活動的「能力」或「技能」。
⇨ She has the **ability** to speak five languages fluently.
她有能力流利地說五種語言。

capability 是指某人或某物能夠達到某個目標的「能力範圍」或「潛力」。
⇨ The company is investing in research and development to expand its technological **capabilities** in artificial intelligence.
這間公司正投入研發，希望擴展他們在人工智慧上的技術能力。

capacity 一般會用來指「空間、時間或技能上能夠處理的量」，也就是「容量」、「量能」或「產能」，亦有「處理能力」的意思。
⇨ The stadium has a seating **capacity** of 50,000 people.
這個體育館可以坐 5 萬人。

collaboration
[kəˌlæbəˈreʃən]
n. 合作

衍 collaborate v. 合作
collaborative adj. 合作的
collaboratively adv. 合作地

The project's success was attributed to the close **collaboration** among different departments.
這項專案的成功原因在於不同部門之間的密切合作。

❶ Point 重點
collaboration vs. cooperation
雖然 collaboration 和 cooperation 都是指人或組織之間的合作行為，不過兩者在用法和語意上都有些微的不同，實際運用時必須透過上下文來決定該使用哪一個字。

collaboration 強調為達成某個共同目標或任務，投注心血、共同努力、分享資源且密切的合作，**常用於開發新產品或完成創意作品等特定情境之中。**
⇨ The **collaboration** between the two companies resulted in a successful product launch.
這兩家公司的合作讓產品得以成功上市。

cooperation 指的是基於「互惠、相互支持或共同利益」的合作，一般並不深入，僅是善意協助的程度，但視使用情境不同，也有可能指較深入的協同合作，**多用在完成一般工作目標或日常任務的情境之中。**
⇨ **Cooperation** among members is important for the ceremony.
成員之間的合作對於這次典禮來說很重要。

聯想單字
teamwork	n.	團隊合作
coordination	n.	協調；調節
coordinator	n.	協調人員，統籌人員

competent

[`kɑmpətənt]
adj. 有能力的；能幹的；稱職的

衍 competence n. 能力；才能
competently adv. 能幹地

反 incompetent adj. 無能力的；不能勝任的

Crystal is a **competent** manager who knows how to lead her team effectively.
Crystal 是一位能幹且知道如何有效帶領團隊的經理。

❶ Point 重點

competent vs. **able** vs. **capable**
competent 強調對「**某一領域的熟練度和可靠度**」都足以完成工作或任務的能力。
⇨ She is a **competent** lawyer who handles complex cases with ease.
她是一位能幹的律師，能夠輕鬆應對複雜的案件。

able 泛指**現在所具備、能夠完成某件事情的能力**，用法廣泛。
⇨ She is **able** to solve complex mathematical problems quickly and accurately.
她能夠快速準確地解決複雜的數學習題。

capable 相較於 able，更強調達成某目標所需的「**特定才能**」或「**潛力**」。
⇨ Despite his young age, he is quite **capable** of making important decisions.
儘管他很年輕，但他相當有能做出重要決定的能力。

counsel

[`kaʊnsl]
n. 建議；勸告；律師
v. 建議，勸告

衍 counselor n. 顧問
counseling n. 諮詢；輔導

He sought **counsel** from his lawyer before signing the contract.
他在簽署這份合約之前，先徵求了他律師的建議。

She **counseled** the team members on how to improve communication within the group.
她為團隊成員提供了如何改善團體內部溝通的建議。

❶ Point 重點

keep your own counsel 不表露自己的意見
⇨ It's often wise to **keep your own counsel** until you have all the facts.
在你掌握所有事實之前，不表露自己的意見通常是明智的。

counsel vs. **advise**
counsel 指**專業上的建議或指導**，常見於法律、心理健康、重大決策或其他專業領域。
⇒ The therapist **counseled** her patient on managing anxiety.
這名治療師為她的病人提供處理焦慮的建議。

advise 指一般性的建議或意見，任何領域或情境均可使用。
⇒ The doctor **advised** him to get more exercise and eat a balanced diet.
醫生建議他多運動和均衡飲食。

> 聯想單字
> legal counsel　　n. 法律顧問；法律建議
> external counsel　n. 外部律師

counterpart
[ˋkaʊntɚˌpɑrt]
n.（與不同地方或組織的人或物）作用相同者，相對應者

The company's European **counterpart** handles sales in that region.
這間公司的歐洲同行掌握了那個區域的銷售。

endeavor
[ɪnˋdɛvɚ]
v. 努力；奮力
n. 嘗試；努力

They **endeavored** to find a solution to the problem before the deadline.
他們努力在截止日期之前找到那個問題的解決方案。

Success in business often requires a great deal of **endeavor** and persistence.
生意成功通常需要大量的努力和堅持。

❶ Point 重點
make an endeavor 做出努力
⇒ She **made** every **endeavor** to complete the project ahead of schedule.
她竭盡全力提前完成這項專案。

endeavor to do sth 努力做某事
⇨ As a teacher, she **endeavors to** inspire her students to pursue their dreams.
做為一名教師，她努力啟發她的學生追求他們自己的夢想。

entrepreneur
[ˌɑntrəprəˋnɝ]
n. 企業家，創業者

衍 enterprise n. 企業
entrepreneurship n. 創業能力；創業精神

Steve Jobs is often regarded as an iconic **entrepreneur** who revolutionized the tech industry.
Steve Jobs 常被認為是一位徹底改變了科技業的標誌性企業家。

聯想單字
startup	n. 新創企業
venture	n. 冒險；投機事業 v. 冒險從事；大膽行事
venture capital	n. 創業投資，風險投資

expertise
[ˌɛkspɚˋtiz]
n. 專門技能（知識）；專長

衍 expert n. 專家
adj. 專門的；內行的

We need someone with legal **expertise** to advise us on this matter.
我們需要具備法律專業的人來就此事給我們建議。

❶ Point 重點
expertise in 專精於～
⇨ The company is known for its **expertise in** healthcare sectors.
這間公司以專精於醫療保健領域而聞名。

expertise vs. **skill** vs. **technique**
expertise 專指在特定領域內**累積所養成**的深厚專業知識和經驗。
⇨ His **expertise** in family and parenting issues is well-known worldwide.
他在家庭和育兒議題上的專業舉世聞名。

skill 是指可以**透過訓練及練習來獲得**、用來完成特定工作或任務所需的技能。
⇨ She has excellent communication **skills**, which help her in her job.
她具有對她工作有幫助的出色溝通技能。

technique 指用來完成特定任務、工作項目或藝術作品所需的**方法、技巧或技術**。
⇨ The artist used a unique painting **technique** to create this masterpiece.
這位藝術家使用了一種獨特的作畫技巧來創作出這幅傑作。

聯想單字		
proficiency	n. 熟練；精通
profession	n.（專門）職業
professional	adj. 職業的

harassment
[hə`ræsmənt]
n. 騷擾

衍 harass v. 騷擾；打擾
　　harasser n. 騷擾他人的人

Sexual **harassment** in the workplace is illegal and should not be tolerated.
職場性騷擾違法且不應容忍。

inaugurate
[ɪn`ɔgjə͵ret]
v. 使正式就職，為～舉行就職典禮；正式啟用；開始

衍 inauguration n. 就職；就職典禮；正式啟用
　　inaugural adj. 就職的

The company plans to **inaugurate** its new headquarters with a ribbon-cutting ceremony.
該公司計劃為其新總部舉行剪綵啟用儀式。

聯想單字		
inaugural address	n. 就職演說
inauguration ceremony	n. 就職典禮
commencement	n. 開始；畢業典禮

innovative
[`ɪnoˌvetɪv]
adj. 創新的

衍 innovate v. 創新
innovation n. 創新
innovator n. 創新者

The designer won awards for her **innovative** designs in fashion.
這位設計師因其創新的時尚設計而獲獎。

聯想單字
creative	adj. 有創意的
critical	adj. 批判性的；挑剔的
cliché	n. 陳腔濫調
routine	n. 例行公事

pension
[`pɛnʃən]
n. 養老金；退休金

衍 pensioner n. 領養老金者，退休人員

After retiring from the company, he received a monthly **pension** to support his living expenses.
從公司退休後，他領取每月退休金來支撐生活開銷。

聯想單字
allowance	n. 津貼；零用金
subsidy	n. 補助金，津貼
scholarship	n. 獎學金

personnel
[ˌpɝsn̩`ɛl]
n.（總稱）人員，員工；人事部門

The company hired new **personnel** to handle the increased workload.
該公司聘請了新員工來處理增加的工作量。

❶ Point 重點
personnel 通常做為**集合名詞**使用，表示一個組織、機構或公司中的所有員工或管理全部員工的人事部門。雖然 personnel 是集合名詞，不可數且沒有複數形，但受其字義多指複數人員所影響，通常搭配複數動詞使用，不過若強調 personnel 為一個整體單位（也就是「人事部門」），則可能會與單數動詞搭配使用，但這種表達方式較不常見，一般仍多與複數動詞搭配使用，如 All personnel **are** asked to join the union.（所有員工都被要求加入公會。）另一方面，若想**指單一特定人員**，應使用 **an employee** 或 **a staff member**，不可使用 personnel。

聯想單字
staff	n.（全體）職員，（全體）工作人員
crew	n. 全體機組員；全體船員
human resources	n. 人力資源

prosecutor
[ˈprɑsɪˌkjutɚ]
n. 檢察官；公訴人

衍 prosecute v.
起訴；檢舉
prosecution n.
起訴；檢舉；訴訟

The **prosecutor** presented strong evidence against the defendant in court.
檢察官在法庭上出示了對被告不利的有力證據。

removal
[rɪˈmuvl]
n. 移開；去除

衍 remove v. 移開；去除

The **removal** of the old furniture was scheduled for next Monday.
把舊家具清掉的時間排定在下週一。

retirement
[rɪˈtaɪrmənt]
n. 退休；退役；退休生活

衍 retire v. 退休；退役
retiree n. 退休人員

After thirty years of service, she finally announced her **retirement** from the company.
她在公司服務三十年後，終於宣布退休了。

聯想單字
retirement plan	n. 退休（財務）計畫，退休方案
veteran	n. 經驗老到的人；退伍軍人
contractor	n. 約聘人員；承包商

specialize
[ˈspɛʃəlˌaɪz]
v. 專攻；專門從事

衍 specialized adj.
專門的；專科的
specialty n. 專業；專長；特產
specialist n. 專家；專業人員；專科醫生
specialization n.
專門化；專業化

She **specializes** in corporate law, handling mergers and acquisitions for multinational companies.
她專攻公司法，為跨國公司處理併購事宜。

❶ Point 重點
specialize 後面常搭配介系詞 **in**，表示專攻某個領域或專門從事某業務內容。
⇨ The college offers programs where students can **specialize in** digital marketing.
該學院提供可以專攻數位行銷的學程給學生。

superiority
[sə͵pɪrɪ`ɔrətɪ]
n. 優勢；優等；優越感

衍 superior adj. 較高等的；好過其他的 n. 上司，長官

反 inferiority n. 劣勢；劣等；自卑感

The company prides itself on the **superiority** of its customer service.
該公司以其卓越的顧客服務而自豪。

聯想單字
inferior	adj. 較差的；下級的 n. 部下，下屬
equality	n.（地位等）平等
status	n.（社會）地位；（社群媒體上的）近況

supervise
[`supɚ͵vaɪz]
v. 監督；指導

衍 supervision n. 監督；指導
supervisor n. 主管；監督者
supervisory adj. 監督的；指導的

It is important for parents to **supervise** their children's internet use.
家長對於孩子在網路使用上的監督相當重要。

❶ Point 重點

supervise vs. **monitor** vs. **oversee**
這三個單字都涉及到**監督、控管或指導**的語意，然而這三者在使用方法及語意上仍有些微差異，必須透過上下文來判斷使用。

supervise 著重於**上對下**的直接指導和管理，通常是針對**日常事項或工作**的實際監督。
⇨ The teacher will **supervise** the students during the exam to ensure there is no cheating.
這位老師會在測驗期間監督學生，確保沒有存在作弊行為。

monitor 指針對**特定目標**持續觀察及檢查，以收集相關資訊或維持有效控制。
⇨ The government agency **monitors** air quality in urban areas.
這個政府機構會監控都會區的空氣品質。

Chapter 07・職業、工作地點、職場相關　　P.141

oversee 是整體或全面性的負責和控管，通常會在表達**領導階級或高階管理層**，針對**某事務或活動的整體進展**進行監督管理時使用。
⇨ The project manager **oversees** the construction of the new office building.
這位專案經理會監督新辦公大樓的興建。

terminate
[ˈtɜmə‚net]
v. 停止，終止

衍 termination n.
停止；終止
terminal adj.
晚期的；末期的

The landlord **terminated** the lease agreement after the tenant failed to pay rent.
房東在房客付不出租金後終止了租賃契約。

❶ Point 重點
terminate 常在法律、商業契約、就職任用等各種正式語境中使用。
⇨ terminate a contract 終止契約
terminate services 終止服務
terminate an employment relationship
結束聘僱關係

unemployment
[͵ʌnɪmˈplɔɪmənt]
n. 失業（狀態）；失業人數

衍 unemployed adj.
失業的；待業的

同 joblessness n.
失業狀態

She has been struggling with **unemployment** since she graduated last year.
她從去年畢業到現在都一直受失業所苦。

聯想單字		
unemployment rate	n. 失業率
layoff	n. 解雇
occupation	n. 職業；工作；（軍隊等的）占領
furlough	n. 無薪假

vacancy
[ˋvekənsɪ]
n. (職位) 空缺；空處；空位

衍 vacant adj. 空的；未被占用的

There is a job **vacancy** for a graphic designer at our company.
我們公司有一個平面設計師的職缺。

| (job) opening | n. 職缺 |
| hotel vacancy | n. 飯店空房 |

vocation
[voˋkeʃən]
n. (具有使命感的) 職業，工作；使命感

衍 vocational adj. (教育課程或培訓) 職業的；業務的

He found his true **vocation** as a chef after years of working in various jobs.
在多年來做過各種工作之後，他發現自己的天職是擔任廚師。

❶ Point 重點
vocation 指的不是單純用來餬口的職業，而是能為從事者**帶來心靈滿足和成就及使命感**的特定工作內容或職業。除此之外，英文裡還有一個跟 vocation 長得非常像的 vacation（假期，休假），無論是在拼字或發音上都非常相似，但意義完全不同，使用時要小心不要混淆喔！

| vocational school | n. 高職 |
| vocational training | n. 職業訓練 |

workforce
[ˋwɝk͵fɔrs]
n. 勞動力；勞動人口

The company plans to expand its **workforce** by hiring more engineers next year.
該公司計劃明年透過僱用更多工程師來擴充人力。

❶ Point 重點
workforce 是集合名詞，因此在句子中一般會與**單數動詞**搭配使用，如 the workforce **is** growing（勞動人口正在成長）。

workforce vs. **manpower**
workforce 和 manpower 都是指一個組織、公司或社會中擁有的勞動力資源，但兩者並非完全相同，因此須透過上下文來判斷使用。

workforce 是正在某個公司、行業或國家中工作或能夠工作的具體人口群體，也就是**在單一群體中存在的全部人力資源**。
⇨ The company's **workforce** includes engineers, technicians, and administrative staff.
這間公司的工作人員有工程師、技術人員和行政人員。

manpower 的重點在於勞動力供給，也就是整體勞動力資源供給量，更常見於政府報告或軍事行動上，用以描述**整體能夠供應的勞動人口數量及可用性**。
⇨ The country needs to increase its **manpower** in the healthcare sector.
該國必須提升投入醫護產業的人力。

聯想單字		
labor	n. 勞工；勞動 v.（艱苦）勞動；努力做	
labor force	n. 勞動力	

主題分類單字 職業、工作地點、職場相關

Chapter 07 工作

Ch07.mp3

advisory	[əd`vaɪzərɪ]	adj. 顧問的；諮詢的 n. 報告；公告
aide	[ed]	n. 助手
astronomer	[ə`strɑnəmɚ]	n. 天文學家
attorney	[ə`tɝnɪ]	n. 律師
autograph	[`ɔtə͵græf]	v. 親筆簽名 n.（尤指名人的）親筆簽名
automation	[͵ɔtə`meʃən]	n. 自動化
barbershop	[`bɑrbɚ͵ʃɑp]	n. 理髮店
blacksmith	[`blæk͵smɪθ]	n. 鐵匠
briefing	[`brifɪŋ]	n. 簡報；簡要介紹
cashier	[kæ`ʃɪr]	n. 出納員；收銀員
chairperson	[`tʃɛr͵pɝsn̩]	n. 主席
computerize	[kəm`pjutə͵raɪz]	v. 使電腦化；用電腦處理
contractor	[`kɑntræktɚ]	n. 約聘人員；承包商
counselor	[`kaʊnslɚ]	n. 顧問
courier	[`kʊrɪɚ]	n. 快遞員；快遞服務，快遞公司
dealer	[`dilɚ]	n. 業者；交易商
disciplinary	[`dɪsəplɪn͵ɛrɪ]	adj. 紀律的；懲戒的
dismissal	[dɪs`mɪsl̩]	n. 解僱；開除；認為～不重要
displace	[dɪs`ples]	v. 迫使～離開常位（或原位）

Chapter 07．職業、工作地點、職場相關　P.145

distributor	[dɪˋstrɪbjətɚ]	n. 分配者；分銷商
expulsion	[ɪkˋspʌlʃən]	n. 驅逐；開除
framework	[ˋfremˏwɝk]	n. 架構；組織
hacker	[ˋhækɚ]	n. 駭客
logo	[ˋlɔgo]	n. 商標；標誌
mastery	[ˋmæstərɪ]	n. 支配，完全控制；精通，熟練
merchandise	[ˋmɝtʃənˏdaɪz]	v. 推銷，促銷 n. 商品；貨物
nanny	[ˋnænɪ]	n. 保姆
outsider	[ˋaʊtˋsaɪdɚ]	n. 外人；局外人
oversee	[ˋovɚˋsi]	v. 監管；監督
overwork	[ˋovɚˋwɝk]	v. 使工作過度；使過勞 n. 過勞
part-time	[ˋpɑrtˋtaɪm]	adj. 部分時間的；兼職的 adv. 部分時間地；兼職地
playwright	[ˋpleˏraɪt]	n. 劇作家
potter	[ˋpɑtɚ]	n. 陶藝家
presidency	[ˋprɛzədənsɪ]	n. 總統職務（或任期）
psychiatrist	[saɪˋkaɪətrɪst]	n. 精神科醫師
qualifier	[ˋkwɑləˏfaɪɚ]	n. 合格者，入圍者
retired	[rɪˋtaɪrd]	adj. 退休的
sculptor	[ˋskʌlptɚ]	n. 雕刻家
senate	[ˋsɛnɪt]	n. 參議院

senator	[ˈsɛnətɚ]	n. 參議員
shareholder	[ˈʃɛrˌholdɚ]	n. 股東
staple	[ˈstepl̩]	n. 釘書針；主要產品；日常必需品 adj. 基本的；主要的 v. 用釘書針釘住
striker	[ˈstraɪkɚ]	n. 罷工者
submit	[səbˈmɪt]	v. 提交；呈遞；使服從
surveillance	[sɚˈveləns]	n. 看守；監視；監督
syndicate	[ˈsɪndɪkɪt]	n. 企業聯合組織；聯盟
teller	[ˈtɛlɚ]	n. 銀行出納人員
termination	[ˌtɝməˈneʃən]	n. 結束，終止
therapist	[ˈθɛrəpɪst]	n. 治療師
utilize	[ˈjutl̩ˌaɪz]	v. 利用
veteran	[ˈvɛtərən]	n. 富有經驗的人；退役軍人
veterinarian	[ˌvɛtərəˈnɛrɪən]	n. 獸醫
vocational	[voˈkeʃənl̩]	adj. 職業的
workman	[ˈwɝkmən]	n. 工匠；工人
workplace	[ˈwɝkˌples]	n. 工作場所

Chapter 07　Quiz Time

一、請選出正確的答案。

1. The company decided to _____ his employment due to budget cuts.
   A. specialize
   B. terminate
   C. abide
   D. allocate

2. _____ allowed him to pursue his hobbies and spend more time with his family.
   A. Vacancy
   B. Harassment
   C. Retirement
   D. Vocation

3. Each team member was _____ specific tasks to complete by the end of the week.
   A. allocated
   B. inaugurated
   C. authorized
   D. endeavored

二、請根據下列中文句子，填入適當的英文單字。

1. 新的軟體大大提升了我們電腦系統的功能。

   The new software greatly enhances the c_____ of our computer systems.

2. 家長應隨時看管在外面玩的孩子們。

   Parents should always s_____ their children while they are playing outside.

3. 老師和家長們密切合作，為學生在家庭和學校中的學習提供支持。

   Teachers and parents have established a strong c_____ to support student learning at home and in school.

4. 他在電腦程式設計方面的專業，使他能夠有效率地解決複雜的軟體問題。

   His e_____ in computer programming enabled him to solve complex software issues efficiently.

5. 為了騰出空間蓋新的大樓，這棵樹必須移除。

   The r_____ of the tree was necessary to make space for the new building.

Answer
（一）：1. B 2. C 3. A
（二）：1. capabilities 2. supervise 3. collaboration 4. expertise 5. removal

翻譯：
（一）
1. 由於預算限制，這間公司決定裁員。
2. 這些休閒活動能夠滿足自己的個性，也能花更多的時間與家人相處。
3. 每個團隊成員都充分配合了重要週末之前完成的待辦任務。

Chapter 08

休閒娛樂

興趣、嗜好、運動、購物相關

Ch08.mp3

★核心單字情境對話

Mia : Have you seen the **advertisement** for that luxurious **villa** in Bali?
Jake : Yes, I have! It looks absolutely **lavish**. I'm planning to book there.
Mia : The **villa** seems so **versatile** and is also perfect for hosting a small party.
Jake : I'm already **anticipating** the stunning views and the private pool.
Mia : I'm **ecstatic** just thinking about it! Let's go ahead and book it before it's too late.
Jake : Great idea! I'll do it right away. I'm sure we'll be more than **satisfied** with our choice.

翻譯

Mia : 你有看到那棟峇里島豪華**別墅**的**廣告**嗎？
Jake : 有啊，我有看到！看起來超級**奢華**。我打算要訂那裡。
Mia : 那棟**別墅**看起來**用途很廣**，而且也很適合拿來辦小型派對。
Jake : 我已經在**期待**令人驚豔的景色和私人泳池了。
Mia : 我光是用想的就覺得**超級開心**！我們趕快去訂吧，免得來不及。
Jake : 好主意！我馬上訂。我覺得我們一定會對自己的選擇非常**滿意的**。

accustom
[ə`kʌstəm]
v. 使習慣（於）

衍 accustomed adj.
習慣的；一如往常的

It took me a while to **accustom** myself to the new work environment.
我花了一段時間才適應新的工作環境。

❶ Point 重點
accustom 通常與介系詞 **to** 搭配使用，例如 **accustom oneself to sth**，且常用**反身代名詞**（myself, yourself, himself, herself, ourselves, themselves）來強調是**自己使自己習慣於某事**。
⇨ She **accustomed herself to** the early morning routine.
她讓自己習慣早起的生活作息。

become accustomed to 逐漸習慣於
⇨ They quickly **became accustomed to** the new rules.
他們很快就習慣了新規則。

除了 become accustomed to，也可以用 **make a habit of** 來表達「**養成習慣**」。
⇨ I want to **make a habit of** exercising every morning.
我想養成每天早上運動的習慣。

聯想單字
| custom | n. 習俗；習慣 |
| customary | adj. 慣常的；傳統的 |

Chapter 08 休閒娛樂

Chapter 08．興趣、嗜好、運動、購物相關　P.151

addicted
[əˋdɪktɪd]
adj. 上癮的；入迷的

衍 addiction n. 上癮
addict n.（尤指對有害之物）成癮的人，入迷的人
addictive adj. 使人上癮的；使人入迷的
addictiveness n. 上癮（性），成癮（性）

Many people are **addicted** to social media and spend hours scrolling through their feeds.
很多人對社群媒體成癮，會花費數小時瀏覽動態消息。

⦿ Point 重點
addicted 通常與介系詞 **to** 搭配使用，如 **addicted to sth**（對某物上癮）。
⇨ She is **addicted to** shopping and spends all her money on clothes.
她購物成癮，把她所有的錢都花在買衣服上了。

聯想單字		
obsessed	adj.	著迷的；念念不忘的
absorbed	adj.	全神貫注的
mesmerize	v.	（用催眠術）迷惑；迷住
hooked	adj.	入迷的，上癮的

advertisement
[͵ædvɚˋtaɪzmənt]
n. 廣告

衍 advertise v. 打廣告；宣傳
advertiser n. 刊登廣告者，廣告客戶
advertising n. 廣告（業）

The company spent millions on a new **advertisement** campaign.
這間公司在新的廣告宣傳活動上花了數百萬元。

⦿ Point 重點
在口語或非正式的寫作中，advertisement 經常會縮寫成 **ad**。

anticipate
[ænˋtɪsəˏpet]
v. 預期，期望；預料

衍 anticipation n. 期望；盼望

We **anticipate** that the new product will be very popular among young adults.
我們預期這款新產品將大受年輕人歡迎。

⦿ Point 重點
anticipate 後面經常接**名詞**、**V-ing** 或 **that** 子句。
⇨ The students **anticipate receiving** their exam results next week.
這些學生預期下週會收到他們的測驗結果。

anticipate vs. expect

雖然 anticipate 和 expect 的中文字義都是「預期」，但兩者在用法和語意都不盡相同，使用時須透過上下文來判斷該使用哪一個字。

anticipate 是預期會發生某事，並**為此做好準備**；另一方面，**expect** 雖然也是預期或相信會發生某事，但通常**不會因此而提前準備或付出努力**以迎接這件事的發生。

一起來透過例句比較箇中差異吧！

⇨ The company **anticipated** a surge in demand and increased their inventory.
這間公司預期需求會激增，因此增加了庫存量。
（帶有「對此預期提前做準備」的意思）

⇨ The company **expects** sales to increase by 10% next quarter.
這間公司預期下一季的銷售額會增加 10%。
（沒有「對此預期提前做準備或付出努力」的意思）

> 聯想單字
> foresee　v. 遇見；預知；預料
> predict　v. 預測；預料

arena
[ə`rinə]
n. (體育競賽或表演用的) 場地，競技場；競爭舞台

The new sports **arena** can hold up to 20,000 spectators.
新的體育場館可容納多達兩萬名的觀眾。

❶ Point 重點
下面是其他常見的各種場館說法和簡單的分辨方式。

stadium 體育館
⇨ 通常是露天開放式的大型體育場館，設有座位區和跑道或球場等設施。

gym 體育館；健身房
⇨ 室內的多功能體育場館，通常用作進行體操、桌球、羽球和其他室內運動的場地。

court 球場，賽場
⇨ 在室內或戶外的平面賽場，通常用作進行球類運動的場地，例如網球、籃球或排球等。

field 運動場
⇨ 露天開放且通常有草坪的運動場，常用作進行如足球、田徑等戶外運動的場地。

dome 巨蛋；穹頂
⇨ 圓頂的大型場館，常用於舉辦大型室內體育活動。

athletics
[æθˋlɛtɪks]
n. 體育運動；[英] 田徑運動

衍 athlete n. 運動員；擅長運動的人
athletic adj. 強壯的；擅長運動的
athleticism n.（競技運動中的）技術，能力

Athletics events, such as the 100 meters, javelin throw, and high jump, are physically demanding.
如 100 公尺賽跑、標槍和跳高等體育運動，都對身體素質的要求很高。

聯想單字
sportsman　　　n. 運動員；體育運動愛好者；擅長體育運動者
sportsmanship　n. 運動家精神

broadcasting
[ˋbrɔdˌkæstɪŋ]
n.（電視或電台節目的）播出

衍 broadcast v. 播送（電視或電台節目）；廣播
broadcaster n. 播音員；播報員

The **broadcasting** of the live concert reached millions of viewers worldwide.
全球收看這場現場演唱會播出的觀眾達到了數百萬。

❶ Point 重點
近年興起的 Podcast 字源即是來自 iPod 和 broadcast 的結合。Podcast 就像是沒有畫面的 YouTube 節目，或是可以訂閱並隨時隨地收聽的廣播節目；broadcast 則是指現場直播的傳統廣播節目。

P.154　國際學村・全民英檢

carnival
[ˈkɑrnəvl]
n. 嘉年華；園遊會

The local **carnival** featured rides, games, and delicious food from various vendors.
當地嘉年華的主打特色是遊樂設施、遊戲和各種攤販提供的美食。

聯想單字		
parade	n. 遊行
gala	n. 慶典，盛會
festival	n. 節日；節
carnival rides	n. 遊樂設施（＝amusement rides）

casino
[kəˈsino]
n. 賭場

The **casino** has become a popular destination for tourists seeking entertainment and excitement.
這個賭場已經成為遊客尋求娛樂和刺激的熱門地點。

聯想單字		
gambling	n. 賭博
jackpot	n. 頭獎
slot machine	n. 吃角子老虎機
blackjack	n. 21 點
roulette	n. 輪盤
bet	v. 打賭；賭博 n. 賭注

celebrity
[səˈlɛbrətɪ]
n. 名人，明星；名流

Many fans seek autographs and selfies with their favorite **celebrities**.
許多粉絲希望能拿到他們最喜歡的名人的親筆簽名並一起自拍。

聯想單字		
public figure	n. 公眾人物
influencer	n. 網紅
content creator	n. 內容創作者
subscriber	n. 訂閱者
live stream	n. 直播
algorithm	n. 演算法
go viral	phr. 瘋傳；爆紅

check-in
[ˈtʃɛk͵ɪn]
n. 報到櫃台；報到

The **check-in** at the hotel took longer than expected because there was a long line of guests and only one staff member at the front desk.
飯店的入住手續花了比預期更久的時間，因為排隊的客人很多，但前台卻只有一位員工在處理。

● Point 重點
「報到」的名詞是 **check-in**，中間有連字號；動詞片語則是 **check in**，反義詞是表示**退房**或**結帳離開**的 **check out**。

聯想單字		
registration	n. 登記；註冊
customs	n. 海關
go through	phr. 通過
security inspection	n. 安檢

ecstatic
[ɛkˈstætɪk]
adj. 欣喜若狂的

衍 ecstasy n. 狂喜；搖頭丸
ecstatically adv. 狂喜地

He felt **ecstatic** about the surprise birthday party his friends had organized for him.
他對朋友們為他籌辦了驚喜生日派對感到非常開心。

● Point 重點
ecstatic about/at/over 對～感到非常開心
⇨ Tina was **ecstatic at** the announcement of her friend's engagement.
Tina 對朋友宣布訂婚的消息感到非常開心。

聯想單字		
elated	adj. 興高采烈的
overjoyed	adj. 極度高興的

exposition
[͵ɛkspəˈzɪʃən]
n. 展覽會；博覽會；詳盡的解釋

The **exposition** featured the latest advancements in technology and attracted many industry professionals.
這場博覽會主打最新的先進科技，吸引了眾多業界專業人士參加。

● Point 重點
exposition vs. **exhibition**
exposition 常簡稱為 **expo**，通常規模較大且內容主題涵

蓋的領域更加多元，如世界博覽會。另一方面，可使用 exhibition（展覽；展示）來指稱的範圍較廣泛，無論是小規模展出還是大型展覽活動，都可以使用 exhibition。

聯想單字
fair	n. 市集
organizer	n. 組織者；籌辦者
venue	n. 會場；（事件或活動等的）舉行地點

haunt
[hɔnt]
v. 使經常苦惱，不斷困擾；（鬼魂等）經常出沒
n. 常去的地方

衍 haunted adj. 煩惱的，焦慮不安的；（鬼魂等）經常出沒的
haunting adj. 難以忘懷的，縈繞心頭的

The memory of the accident continued to **haunt** him for years.
那次事故的記憶多年來不斷困擾著他。

This restaurant is a popular **haunt** for local artists.
這家餐廳是當地藝術家經常出沒的熱門地點。

聯想單字
linger	v. 逗留；徘徊不去
hangout	n. 經常去的地方

lavish
[ˋlævɪʃ]
adj. 奢華的；慷慨大方的
v. 揮霍

衍 lavishly adv. 慷慨大方地；奢華地
lavishness n. 慷慨；奢華

The mansion features **lavish** interiors with custom-designed furniture.
這座宅邸主打配有訂製家具的奢華內部裝潢。

He **lavished** his time and money on his new project.
他揮霍大把時間和金錢在他的新專案上。

❗ Point 重點
lavish sth on sb/sth 為～揮霍～，為～提供大量的～
⇨ The billionaire **lavished** expensive gifts **on** his wife for their anniversary.
為慶祝他們的週年紀念日，那位億萬富翁大手筆地送妻子昂貴的禮物。

lavish vs. **generous**

lavish 和 generous 的字義都可以譯成「大方」，但兩者無論是字義還是用法都不盡相同，使用時必須透過上下文來判斷應該要用哪一個字。

lavish 通常指的是大量奢侈的投入或支出，甚至**可能會到異常或不必要的地步**。**generous** 的重點在於**行為動機出自善意和無私的理由**，除物質金錢外，付出的也有可能是愛心或關注等，**通常用於正面形容**。

聯想單字		
splurge	v. 亂花錢；揮霍	
extravagant	adj. 奢侈的；不切實際的	

outing
[ˋaʊtɪŋ]
n. 短程旅遊，遠足

The school organized an educational **outing** to the science museum for the students.
這間學校為學生籌辦了一次去科學博物館的校外教學。

聯想單字		
hiking	n.（在鄉間的）長程徒步旅行，健行
camping	n. 露營
picnic	n. 野餐
mountaineering	n. 登山

pastime
[ˋpæsˌtaɪm]
n. 消遣，娛樂

Knitting is a relaxing **pastime** that she enjoys during the winter months.
編織是她在冬天很愛做的一項輕鬆消遣。

聯想單字		
relaxation	n. 放鬆；消遣；休閒活動
leisure	n. 閒暇；休閒
amusement	n. 樂趣；娛樂活動
entertainment	n. 娛樂；娛樂表演
recreation	n. 娛樂；消遣

peddler
[ˋpɛdlɚ]
[英] **pedlar**
n. 小販

衍 peddle v. 兜售；散播

The **peddler** walked through the busy streets, selling fresh fruits and vegetables.
那名小販走過繁忙的街道，兜售著新鮮的水果和蔬菜。

❶ Point 重點
peddler vs. **vendor**
peddler 是沿街叫賣的小販，通常指以步行等方式，一邊不斷移動、一邊兜售商品的人。**vendor** 則可能擁有固定的攤位或攤車，銷售期間不一定會移動或主動推銷，除固定攤位外，亦可指定點的流動攤販。

retailer
[rɪˋtelɚ]
n. 零售商；零售店

衍 retail n. 零售，零賣
v. 零售，零賣

The **retailer** launched a special promotion to attract more customers during the holiday season.
這間零售業者推出了特別促銷活動，以在聖誕連假期間吸引更多顧客。

聯想單字		
	merchant	n. 商人
	dealer	n. 經銷商；商人
	trader	n. 交易商；商人
	wholesaler	n. 批發商
	manufacturer	n. 製造商
	producer	n. 生產者；製作人
	supplier	n. 供應商
	outlet	n. 通路；暢貨店

roam
[rom]
v.（漫無目的地）閒逛（於）；漫步（於）

衍 roamer n.（尤指沒有目的）四處遊蕩的人
roaming n.（手機）漫遊

He likes to **roam** the countryside on weekends, enjoying the peace and quiet.
他週末喜歡在鄉間漫步，享受寧靜。

聯想單字		
	wander	v. 漫步；閒逛；遊蕩
	ramble	v.（尤指在鄉間）漫步，漫遊
	stride	v. 大跨步快走
	sprint	v. 衝刺

Chapter 08・興趣、嗜好、運動、購物相關

satisfied
[ˈsætɪsfaɪd]
adj. 滿足的；滿意的

衍 satisfy v. 使滿足，使滿意
satisfying adj. 令人滿意的，使人滿足的
satisfaction n. 滿足，滿意

反 dissatisfied adj. 不滿的，不滿意的

Stanley was **satisfied** with the quick response from customer support.
Stanley 對於顧客支援的快速回應感到滿意。

❶ Point 重點
satisfied 的後面常與接介系詞 **with** 搭配使用，表示「**對～感到滿意**」。
⇨ The customers were very **satisfied with** the service at the restaurant.
這名顧客對於這間餐廳的服務感到非常滿意。

聯想單字
content	adj. 知足的；心滿意足的
pleased	adj. 高興的；滿意的
delighted	adj. 高興的，快樂的

suite
[swit]
n.（尤指飯店的）套房；一套家具

The hotel offered us a luxurious **suite** with a stunning view of the ocean.
這間飯店為我們提供了一間有著令人驚艷海景的豪華套房。

❶ Point 重點
各種「房型」的說法

single room 單人房	triple room 三人房
double room 雙人房	quad room 四人房
twin room 雙床房	junior suite 小型套房
queen room 大床房	executive suite 行政套房
king room 特大床房	presidential suite 總統套房

實用的訂房相關英文表達方式

make a reservation 預訂
⇨ I would like to **make a reservation** for a double room.
我想預訂一間雙人房。

book a room 訂房
⇨ Can I **book a room** for three nights?
我可以訂一間房間住三晚嗎？

availability 空房情況
⇨ Do you have any **availability** for next weekend?
你們下週末有空房嗎？

temptation
[tɛmpˋtɛʃən]
n. 引誘；誘惑

衍 tempt v. 引誘，誘惑
tempting adj. 誘人的，吸引人的

The store's big sale was a **temptation** that many shoppers couldn't resist.
這間店的大促銷對於很多購物者來說是難以抗拒的誘惑。

❶ Point 重點
英文裡有一個跟 tempt 長得很像的 attempt，**attempt 可以當動詞和名詞**，意思是為完成困難任務而「**努力**」或「**嘗試**」，小心不要搞混了喔！

聯想單字		
desire	v.（尤指強烈地）渴望，希望 n. 慾望，渴望
longing	n. 渴望，嚮往
lure	n. 誘惑力，誘惑；誘餌 v. 引誘，誘惑

tournament
[ˋtɝnəmənt]
n. 錦標賽

The tennis **tournament** attracted players from all over the world.
這場網球錦標賽吸引了來自世界各地的選手。

❶ Point 重點
competition vs. **contest** vs. **game** vs. **match** vs. **tournament**
competition 是最廣義的競賽，涵蓋任何形式的競爭活動。**contest** 指個人或團隊之間在技能、知識或創意上的競爭，並透過評判決定優劣以贏得獎項。**game** 可以用來指娛樂或體育性的活動，特別重視遵守遊戲規則和輸贏。**match** 通常是指體育競賽，尤其強調兩兩公平對決。**tournament** 指的是一系列的淘汰賽，參賽者在每輪賽事中不斷淘汰對手，直到決出最終獲勝者。

聯想單字		
knockout	n. [英] 淘汰賽
round robin	n. 循環賽
playoff	n. 加時賽，延長賽
quarter-final	n. 八強賽
semifinal	n. 準決賽
final	n. 決賽

triumphant
[traɪˋʌmfənt]
adj. 取得巨大成功的；得意洋洋的

衍 triumph n. 巨大成功；勝利；狂喜
v. 取得巨大成功；勝利
triumphantly adv. 得意洋洋地

As the marathon runner crossed the finish line first, a **triumphant** cheer erupted from the crowd.
當那位馬拉松選手第一個通過終點線時，人群中爆發出了勝利的歡呼聲。

trophy
[ˋtrofɪ]
n. 獎盃；戰利品

She proudly displayed her tennis **trophy** on the bookshelf.
她自豪地在書架上展示她的網球獎盃。

❶ Point 重點
trophy vs. **prize**
trophy 通常指的是象徵某個獎項或榮譽的**實體獎盃或獎章**；另一方面，**prize** 泛指任何可以**做為獎勵的物品**，如金錢、獎狀或獎品等。

versatile
[ˋvɝsətl]
adj. 多種用途的；萬用的；多才多藝的

衍 versatility n. 有多種用途，多功能性；多才多藝

A Swiss army knife is a **versatile** tool that includes a variety of useful functions.
瑞士刀是一種多功能的工具，具有各式各樣有用的功能。

As a **versatile** athlete, she competes in track and field, swimming, and gymnastics.
身為一位多才多藝的運動員，她會參加田徑、游泳和體操的比賽。

❶ Point 重點
versatile 可以用來表示一個人同時具備多種才華，能夠隨情境靈活運用其才能，若用 versatile 來形容物品或工具，則表示其具備多種用途或功能。

victorious
[vɪk`torɪəs]
adj. 勝利的，獲勝的；成功的

衍 victory n. 勝利，獲勝；成功
victor n. 勝利者
victorious adj. 勝利的，獲勝的；成功的
victoriously adv. 勝利地，獲勝地；成功地

Their strategy proved to be effective, leading them to a **victorious** outcome.
事實證明他們的策略有效，讓他們最終獲得了勝利。

villa
[`vɪlə]
n. 別墅

The family spent their summer holidays in a beautiful **villa** by the sea.
這一家人在一棟靠海的美麗別墅中度過了暑假。

聯想單字
terrace	n. 露臺；陽台
pavilion	n.（庭園中的）涼亭
patio	n. 天井；露臺
resort	n. 渡假村

vogue
[vog]
n. 流行；風尚；流行的人事物

The current **vogue** for organic food reflects a growing awareness of health and environmental issues.
目前有機食品的流行反映出人們對於健康和環境議題意識的提升。

❶ Point 重點
in vogue 流行
⇨ Bell-bottom jeans were **in vogue** during the 1970s.
喇叭褲在 1970 年代蔚為流行。

out of vogue 過時
⇨ That style of dress is completely **out of vogue** now.
那種洋裝款式現在完全過時了。

vogue vs. **trend** vs. **fashion**
雖然 vogue、trend 和 fashion 都可以用時尚或潮流的概念來理解，但三者在用法和語意上仍有些微的差異，使用時須透過上下文來判斷用字。

vogue 是指某特定時期或時空背景下，**一時流行**的人事物；**trend** 強調的是在**一段較長時間裡**，整體社會隨著時間流逝而**逐漸發展生成的變化趨勢**，這種趨勢不一定和時尚產業有關，**各領域的發展變化走向都可以用 trend**；另一方面，**fashion** 特別強調時尚產業及相關文化上的流行，例如服裝或造型等領域，並可泛指「流行的風格」。

> 聯想單字
> chic　　　adj. 時髦的；雅致的
> modish　　adj. 流行的，時髦的

zeal
[zil]
n. 熱忱，熱情

衍 zealous adj.
　　熱情的；狂熱的

She approached the project with **zeal**, working late into the night to meet the deadline.
她帶著熱情投入這項專案，為了趕上最後截止期限而工作到深夜。

❗ Point 重點
zeal vs. **passion**
zeal 和 passion 都是指針對某個事物或活動的強烈熱情或熱忱，不過 **zeal** 更強調針對某個目標、理想或事業，展現積極的態度和熱情，**投入具體行動且不吝於付出或犧牲**，以期達成目標；另一方面，**passion** 更加**強調情感上的強烈喜好及投入**，比起 zeal，passion 的運用範圍更加廣泛，泛指心中對任何事物抱持強烈愛好所產生的情感及隨之而來的行動力。

主題分類單字 興趣、嗜好、運動、購物相關

Ch08.mp3

Chapter 08 休閒娛樂

birdie	[ˈbɝdɪ]	v.（高爾夫球）博蒂 n. 小鳥；（高爾夫球）博蒂
blues	[bluz]	n. 藍調
booking	[ˈbʊkɪŋ]	n.（座位或票券的）預訂
boxer	[ˈbɑksɚ]	n. 拳擊手
boxing	[ˈbɑksɪŋ]	n. 拳擊；拳術
carol	[ˈkærəl]	v. 歡快地唱歌；唱頌歌 n. 歡快的歌；聖誕頌歌
cello	[ˈtʃɛlo]	n. 大提琴
choir	[kwaɪr]	n.（教堂的）唱詩班；合唱團
chord	[kɔrd]	n.（音樂的）和絃，和音；弦
closure	[ˈkloʒɚ]	n. 關閉；打烊；結束；終止
dart	[dɑrt]	v. 飛奔 n. 飛鏢；鏢；快速的動作
fad	[fæd]	n. 一時的流行
fiddle	[ˈfɪdl]	v. 拉小提琴；偽造；騙取； （隨意）撥弄 n. 小提琴；（用手做的精細）難事； 欺詐
goalkeeper	[ˈgolˌkipɚ]	n. 守門員
gymnasium	[dʒɪmˈnezɪəm]	n. 體育館；健身房
harmonica	[hɑrˈmɑnɪkə]	n. 口琴

hockey	[ˈhɑkɪ]	n. 曲棍球
inning	[ˈɪnɪŋ]	n.（棒球的）局，回合
lottery	[ˈlɑtərɪ]	n. 彩券；抽獎；碰運氣的事
nightclub	[ˈnaɪt͵klʌb]	n. 夜總會，夜店
peddle	[ˈpɛdl]	v. 兜售；散播（謠言等）
putt	[pʌt]	v.（高爾夫球中）輕擊球，推球入洞 n.（高爾夫球中）輕輕擊球
rugby	[ˈrʌgbɪ]	n. 英式橄欖球
runner-up	[ˈrʌnɚˈʌp]	n. 第二名，亞軍
sporting	[ˈsportɪŋ]	adj. 體育運動的
tango	[ˈtæŋgo]	n. 探戈舞；探戈舞曲
ultraviolet	[͵ʌltrəˈvaɪəlɪt]	adj. 紫外線的
viewer	[ˈvjuɚ]	n. 觀看者；觀眾
visa	[ˈvizə]	n. 簽證

Chapter 08 Quiz Time

一、　請選出正確的答案。

1. The magazine featured an exclusive interview with a famous _____.

    A. pastime
    B. arena
    C. exposition
    D. celebrity

2. He became _____ to video games and started neglecting his studies.

    A. addicted
    B. lavish
    C. zeal
    D. triumphant

3. She is a _____ musician who plays several instruments.

    A. ecstatic
    B. satisfied
    C. versatile
    D. outing

二、請根據下列中文句子，填入適當的英文單字。

1. 出版商在一年一度的書籍博覽會上展出了他們最新上市的書。

    Publishers displayed their latest releases at the annual book e_____.

2. 電子商務的興起對傳統零售商造成了重大影響。

   The rise of e-commerce has significantly impacted traditional r_____.

3. 對於熱愛甜食的人來說，住在烘焙坊旁邊就會不斷受到誘惑。

   Living next to a bakery is a constant t_____ for someone who loves sweets.

4. 在搬到城市裡後，他不得不去習慣都會生活中的喧囂和快節奏。

   After moving to the city, he had to a_____ himself to the noise and fast pace of urban life.

5. 這名老師對於她學生的進步感到滿意。

   The teacher was s_____ with the progress her students had made.

Chapter 09

教育
學校、學科、知識學習相關

★核心單字情境對話

Ryan : Hey, Olivia! How did the **seminar** go today?
Olivia : It was great! The speaker provided some valuable **insights** into effective **teamwork**.
Ryan : Did they **specify** any techniques for improving communication?
Olivia : Absolutely. They discussed **corresponding** strategies to keep everyone with different **standpoints** aligned.
Ryan : I guess you were taking a lot of notes during the session. Is there any chance that I can borrow the notes? I'm also really interested in how to resolve **contentions** in group.
Olivia : Sure, I'll **compile** my notes and make a copy for you.
Ryan : That would be nice, thanks!

翻譯

Ryan : 嘿，Olivia！今天的**研討會**進行得怎麼樣？
Olivia : 很棒啊！這個講者針對有效的**團隊合作**提供了一些寶貴的**見解**。
Ryan : 這些見解裡有**具體說到**些什麼可以改善溝通的技巧嗎？
Olivia : 當然有。這些見解裡有討論到能讓站在不同**立場**的大家達成共識的**相應**策略。
Ryan : 我想妳在研討會上一定做了很多筆記。我可不可以跟妳借筆記呢？我也很想知道怎麼解決團隊裡的**紛爭**。
Olivia : 沒問題，我會把筆記**整理好**之後複製一份給你。
Ryan : 太好了，謝謝！

abstraction
[æbˋstrækʃən]
n. 抽象

衍 abstract adj.
抽象的;空洞的
n. 摘要;抽象畫
abstractly adv.
抽象地

反 realism n. 寫實;
真實性;務實

The artist's work is known for its **abstraction**, focusing more on form and color rather than realistic details.
這位藝術家的作品以抽象聞名,比起逼真的細節,更注重形式和色彩。

abundance
[əˋbʌndəns]
n. 大量;充足;豐富

衍 abundant adj.
大量的;充足的;
豐富的
abundantly adv.
豐盛地;非常地

The garden was filled with an **abundance** of flowers in every color.
這座花園裡滿是各種顏色的花朵。

聯想單字
ample	adj. 大量的;充足的,充裕的
plentiful	adj. 豐富的,充足的,多的
sufficient	adj. 充足的

assimilate
[əˋsɪmḷ͵et]
v. 融入;(使)同化;
消化吸收(食物、知識等)

衍 assimilation n.
融入;同化;消化吸收
assimilable adj.
可同化的;易學好懂的

It took time for the immigrant family to **assimilate** into the new culture.
這個移民家庭花了一段時間來融入新文化。

❶ Point 重點
assimilate vs. **absorb** vs. **integrate**
assimilate 指徹底消化吸收後內化,特別常用在文化知識層面,或者表達「融入某個群體或文化之中」,這個字特別強調將接收到的新資訊或文化「**經過消化後吸收並內化**」的這個過程。

absorb 一般用來表示吸收某物質、資訊或知識,**通常不涉及文化層面的融入或同化**。

integrate 指將某物或某人與更大的一個整體結合,使其成為整體的一部分。通常用於描述**將不同元素與一個系統或群體結合並融為一體**。

聯想單字		
forced assimilation	n. 強制同化
linguistic assimilation	n. 語言同化
cultural assimilation	n. 文化同化
process of assimilation	phr. 同化過程

compile
[kəm`paɪl]
v. 彙整；編纂；匯集

衍 compilation n. 彙整；編纂；匯集（物）
compiler n. 編纂者

She spent hours **compiling** a list of all the references used in her research paper.
她花了好幾個小時將她研究報告中所用的所有參考文獻彙整成一張列表。

❶ Point 重點
compile vs. **gather** vs. **collect**
compile 強調**有多個不同的資訊來源**，並將收集到的資訊**進行系統化的整理和彙編**，常用於與編輯或創作相關的領域。

gather 強調將分散的東西聚集在一起，描述的是**聚集這個行為本身**，後續不一定會對聚集物進行整理或編輯。

collect 強調**有目的、有計畫地收集物品或資訊**，這種收集通常**較有系統或經長期規劃**，但不一定會對收集的成果進行後續處置，因為收集本身就是目的。

component
[kəm`ponənt]
n. 組成部分；成分；零件

Each **component** of the software needs to be tested individually before integration.
在整合之前，組成軟體的各部分都必須經過獨立檢測。

❶ Point 重點
component vs. **constitute**
component 是專門用來描述一個整體中**組成成分的名詞**，指的是組成一個系統、機器、設備或概念中的一個成分。

constitute 是強調**構成過程的動詞**，指的是構成或組成某個整體的動作，而不是具體的組成成分。

其他「構成」的說法
⇨ be composed of 由～組成
　consist of 由～組成
　be made of 由～製成

聯想單字

element	n. 元素
electronic component	n. 電子元件
essential	adj. 必要的；本質上的
key	adj. 關鍵的

comprehend
[ˌkɑmprɪˋhɛnd]
v. 充分理解；領悟

衍 comprehension n.
　理解力
　comprehensible
　adj. 可理解的，易於理解的
　comprehensive adj.
　全面的；綜合的；詳盡的

The book is difficult to **comprehend** due to its advanced vocabulary.
這本書因為用字較難而很難充分理解。

❶ Point 重點

comprehend vs. **understand** vs. **grasp**
comprehend 強調**深入和全面性**，表達對於某複雜事物的意義或內容的全盤理解或領會。

understand 是**表達最廣的用字**，涵蓋了各種程度的理解。

grasp 強調對於**某個細節或概念有清晰明確的掌握**，通常用來表達對於複雜技術或難解理論中的具體步驟、重要技術或關鍵核心論述的理解。

conceive
[kənˋsiv]
v. 設想出，構想出；懷孕

衍 conceivable adj.
　可以想像得到的；可以相信的

They **conceived** a plan to improve the company's efficiency.
他們想出了一個計畫來改善公司的效率。

concentrated
[ˈkɑnsənˌtretɪd]
adj. 專心的；全神貫注的；全力以赴的；濃縮的

衍 concentrate v. 專注；全神貫注；集中；使濃縮
concentration n. 專注；集中；濃度

To pass the exam, he needed to study with a **concentrated** focus for several hours.
為了通過考試，他必須全神貫注的專心讀幾個小時的書。

❶ Point 重點
「專心」的其他常見表達方式
⇨ concentrate on 專注於～
　pay attention to 注意～
　absorb in 全神貫注於～，沉浸於～
　dedicated to 致力於～
　devoted to 奉獻於～；致力於～

contention
[kənˈtɛnʃən]
n. 爭論；紛爭；論點；主張

衍 contend v. 競爭；聲稱

Their heated **contention** was on display during the debate.
他們在辯論過程中發生了激烈的爭論。

❶ Point 重點
contend vs. compete
雖然 contend 和 compete 都是某種形式的**對抗**，但兩者在語意和用法上並不相同，使用時必須透過上下文來判斷該用哪個字。

contend 強調因意見不同而進行的爭論或辯論，或指透過爭論或辯論來取得某個成果，因此常用於**在爭論中據理力爭或爭取達成某個結果的情境**之中。

compete 指的是正面對抗或比拚、一較高下以爭取對自己有利的結果，一般用於**參與正式的比賽或競賽的情境**之中。

contradiction
[ˌkɑntrə`dɪkʃən]
n. 矛盾

衍 contradict v. 反駁；
與～相矛盾
contradictory adj.
對立的；相互矛盾
的

There is a clear **contradiction** between his words and actions.
他的言行之間存在明顯矛盾。

❶ Point 重點

contradict vs. **contrary**
contradict 是指**一個觀點與其他觀點或事實發生矛盾的動詞**。**contrary** 則是表達事物之間呈現對立或相反狀態的名詞，此外，contrary 也可以做為**形容詞**，表示「相反的」或「完全不同的」，如 **contrary viewpoint**（相反的觀點）。

聯想單字		
discrepancy	n. 不一致，出入，差異
paradox	n. 悖論；自相矛盾的情況

controversial
[ˌkɑntrə`vɝʃəl]
adj. 有爭議的；引起爭議的

衍 controversy n.
爭議；爭論

The book was **controversial** due to its critique of government policies.
這本書因其對政府政策的評論而引起爭議。

❶ Point 重點

controversial vs. **debatable**
controversial 和 debatable 都涉及**引起爭議和正反辯論**的概念，但兩者在語意和用法上並不相同，使用時須透過上下文來判斷該用哪個字。

controversial 一般描述的是**本就經常引發激烈議論或引起主觀立場對立的人事物**，通常涉及社會、種族、性別、政治等高敏感議題。

debatable 一般則會用來描述**尚未有定論或仍有待討論的事物**，強調其結論的不確定性或仍保有可討論的空間，表示「**具爭議的；可爭論的**」，但不一定會引發強烈的議論或對立情勢。

聯想單字		
debate	n. 辯論 v. 辯論
dispute	n. 爭論；爭執，糾紛 v. 對～有異議
conflict	n. 衝突；分歧；戰爭 v. 發生抵觸；發生矛盾；衝突

corresponding
[͵kɔrɪˋspɑndɪŋ]
adj. 相似的；相對應的；對等的

衍 correspond n.
相稱；相當
correspondence n.
關聯；信函；通信聯繫
correspondent n.
通信人；特派記者

In this diagram, each color represents a **corresponding** category.
在這個圖表中，每個顏色都對應了一個分類。

❶ Point 重點
corresponding to 與～相應
⇨ Her responsibilities were adjusted **corresponding to** her new role in the company.
她的職責已隨著她在公司的新職務進行了相對應的調整。

dedicated
[ˋdɛdə͵ketɪd]
adj. 盡心盡力的，盡職盡責的；專門的

She is **dedicated** to her research and spends long hours in the lab.
她對她的研究盡心盡力，且花了很多時間待在實驗室裡。

❶ Point 重點
dedicated to N./V-ing 致力於～
⇨ She is **dedicated to** improving the education system.
她致力於改善教育體系。

下面是另外兩個與 dedicated to N/V-ing 相似、常用來表示「某人在某事上投入很多心力」的意思，這些表達方式在各種試題中經常出現，請好好記住正確的用法及語意。

committed to V-ing 致力於～，投入於～
⇨ Eason is **committed to** improving his skills in every possible way.
Eason 致力於盡一切可能讓自己的技術得以提升。

devote sth to sth/sb 致力於～，把～奉獻給～
⇨ He **devoted** his entire life **to** the army.
他把他的一生奉獻給了軍隊。

deduct

[dɪˋdʌkt]
v. 減；扣除

衍 deduction n. 減法；扣除（額）；（根據已知事實所作的）推論
deductible adj. 可扣除的；可減免的

The amount will be automatically **deducted** from your bank account.
這筆款項將自動從你的銀行帳戶中扣除。

❶ Point 重點

deduct vs. **subtract** vs. **reduce**
deduct 指的是**從一個總數或一筆金額中扣除一部分**，通常會在財務、會計或稅務等正式語境中使用。**subtract** 會用在**數學計算**上，表示從一個數字或數量中減去另一個數字或數量。**reduce** 的應用範圍更廣，不僅可以表示**數字上的減少**，也可以用在表達**品質、程度等方面的下降**，通常帶有逐步或隨著時間進展而下降的語意。

聯想單字
deduce	v. 推斷，推論
infer	v. 推斷，推論
derive	v. 得出，導出

distract

[dɪˋstrækt]
v. 使分心，使轉移注意力，干擾

衍 distraction n. 分散注意力的東西；心煩意亂；娛樂消遣
distracting adj. 分散注意力的
distractingly adv. 讓人分心地；擾人地

The teacher was concerned that the students were easily **distracted** during the lesson.
這名老師對於學生在上課時容易分心的事感到擔心。

❶ Point 重點

distract from 使～分心
⇒ The loud noise from the construction site **distracted** me **from** my work.
工地的巨大噪音使我無法專心工作。

跟 distract 相反的表達方式

attract 吸引；引起（注意或興趣等）
⇒ The girl was **attracted** to the cute balloons sold by the vendor.
這個女孩被小販在賣的可愛氣球吸引了。

pay attention to 專注於～，注意～
⇒ It's important to **pay attention to** the instructions given by the teacher.
注意老師所給的指示是很重要的。

be attentive to 對～保持專注，對～關注
⇨ The nurse **was** very **attentive to** the needs of the patients.
這名護理師對於病人的需求非常關注。

> 聯想單字
> disturb　　v. 打斷；干擾
> interrupt　v. 打斷（別人說話）；中斷

enlighten
[ɪn`laɪtən]
v. 啟發；開導；闡釋

衍 enlightening adj. 使人獲得啟發的；具有啟發性的
enlightenment n. 領悟；啟發；開導

Eve was **enlightened** by the documentary about climate change.
Eve 被這支與氣候變遷有關的紀錄片啟發了。

❶ Point 重點
enlighten 是「使他人變得更有知識、思想更進步」或「請求他人解釋或進一步說明」的意思，**常在討論學術、教育、哲學等主題**的情境中使用。

enlighten sb on sth 向某人解釋或進一步說明某事
⇨ Can you **enlighten** me **on** the process of applying for a visa?
你能向我解釋一下簽證的申請流程嗎？

ethical
[`ɛθɪkl]
adj. 道德的；倫理的

衍 ethic n. 行為準則，倫理；道德規範
ethically adv. 符合道德地；合乎倫理地

反 unethical adj. 不道德的，不合乎道德標準的

The debate about animal testing raises significant **ethical** concerns.
關於動物實驗的爭論引起了重大倫理疑慮。

❶ Point 重點
英文裡還有一個和 ethical 在發音及拼字上相似，但字義完全不同的 ethnic，兩者經常會同時出現在字彙題的選項裡，請務必好好分辨。

ethical 是表示「與道德原則或倫理相關的」，常在**判斷行為、決策或行事風格是否合乎道德標準**的情境中使用。另一方面，**ethnic** 的意思則是「**民族的；種族的**」，通常會在**與種族或文化背景有關**的主題中使用。

聯想單字		
moral	adj.	道德的；品行端正的
integrity	n.	正直；誠實
honest	adj.	誠實可信的

faculty

[ˋfæklti]

n. 全體教職員；身體機能；才能

The **faculty** at the university is known for their expertise in various fields.
這所大學的教職員以其在各領域中的專業知識聞名。

❶ Point 重點
當 faculty 是不可數名詞（沒有複數形）時，通常指的是「全體教職員」，但當使用 faculty 來表達一個人的「**才能**」或「**天賦**」時，faculty 便是**可數名詞**，擁有複數形 **faculties**。

faculty vs. **staff** vs. **faculty member**
faculty 通常指的是高等教育，如大專院校等的**全體教職員**，但也可以表示**特定學院或系所**，例如 Faculty of Medicine（醫學院）。

staff 指的是在組織或機構中工作的**全體員工**，如行政、技術、後勤等等，換句話說，staff 涵蓋的是所有類型的員工。
⇨ All the **staff** should wear their uniforms for the company retreat held next month.
所有員工在參加下個月舉辦的公司旅遊時都應穿著制服。

faculty member 則是某一**特定教職員**，強調這位教職員是這個 faculty 的一部分。
⇨ Every **faculty member** is expected to participate in the conference.
所有教職員都應參加這次會議。

genetics
[dʒəˋnɛtɪks]
n. 遺傳學

衍 genetic adj. 基因的
genetically adv. 遺傳地
gene n. 基因
genome n. 基因組

Genetics plays a crucial role in understanding diseases like cancer and diabetes.
遺傳學在了解如癌症和糖尿病等疾病上扮演著重要的角色。

❗ Point 重點
雖然 genetics 擁有複數字尾 s，但其實是**不可數名詞**，因此前面不能加上 a，且要視為單數使用，請一定要注意。

聯想單字
genetic engineering	n. 基因工程
biology	n. 生物學
chromosome	n. 染色體

genre
[ˋʒɑnrə]
n.（尤指藝術的）風格，類型，體裁

The film blends elements of different **genres**, including drama and comedy.
這部電影融合了劇情和喜劇等不同類型的元素。

❗ Point 重點
genre 原本是法文字，所以發音和拼寫方式都和一般的英文單字不太一樣，請特別留意。

聯想單字
film genre	n. 電影類型
literary genre	n. 文學類型
genre fiction	n. 類型小說

ideology
[͵aɪdɪˋɑlədʒɪ]
n. 思想（體系），意識形態

衍 ideological adj. 思想體系上的，意識形態上的
ideologically adv. 從意識形態的角度來看

The political party's **ideology** focuses on promoting social equality and economic justice.
這個政黨的意識形態著重於促進社會平等及經濟正義。

❗ Point 重點
ideology vs. **belief**
ideology 是**一整套系統化的思想體系**，涵蓋範圍及影響層面都非常廣泛，對廣大群體或社會的行為原則及政策走向都會造成顯著影響。另一方面，**belief** 通常指的是**個人或小群體的「信仰；信念」**，也就是較為個人化的看法或觀點，涵蓋範圍相對狹窄。

insight
[ˋɪnˌsaɪt]
n. 洞察力；深入見解

衍 insightful adj.
　　有洞察力的；見解深刻的

After analyzing the data, the scientist gained new **insights** into the behavior of the virus.
在分析過資料後，科學家對於這種病毒的行為有了新的深入見解。

❶ Point 重點
insight into 對～的深入見解
⇨ The book offers **insight into** the cultural practices of ancient civilizations.
這本書提供了對於古文明文化風俗的深入見解。

literacy
[ˋlɪtərəsɪ]
n. 識字，讀寫能力；（對某領域的）知識

衍 literate adj.
　　識字的；掌握（某領域）知識的
　　literal adj. 字面的
　　literally adv. 確實；逐字翻譯地；僅僅
　　literature n. 文學；文學作品

反 illiteracy n. 文盲；（對某領域的）缺乏了解

Improving **literacy** rates is crucial for the development of any nation.
改善識字率對於任何國家的發展都至關重要。

聯想單字	
literacy rate	n. 識字率
financial literacy	n. 金融素養
legible	adj.（字跡等）清楚易讀的；易辨認的
illegible	adj.（字跡等）難以辨認的

novice
[ˋnɑvɪs]
n. 新手，初學者

同 beginner n. 新手，初學者

反 veteran n. 經驗豐富的人，老手；老兵，退伍軍人

As a **novice** in the field, James made several mistakes but learned quickly.
身為這個領域裡的新手，James 犯了幾個錯誤，但他學得很快。

❶ Point 重點

novice at sth 在某事物上是新手
⇨ He's just a **novice at** cooking, so he often needs help from more experienced chefs.
他在烹飪上只是個新手，所以經常需要更有經驗的廚師們幫忙。

聯想單字		
newbie	n. 新手	
rookie	n. 新手；新生；菜鳥	
newcomer	n. 新來的人；新手	
novice/rookie driver	n. 新手駕駛	

questionnaire
[͵kwɛstʃənˋɛr]
n. 問卷

The company sent out a **questionnaire** to gather feedback from its customers.
這間公司發出了一份問卷來收集顧客的回饋意見。

❶ Point 重點

fill out a questionnaire 填寫問卷
⇨ The participants were asked to **fill out a questionnaire** after the workshop.
參加者被要求在工作坊結束後填寫一份問卷。

questionnaire vs. survey
questionnaire 是**整個調查程序中的一部分**，專指用來收集資訊的問卷。強調的是實體或電子問卷這個調查工具的本身。

survey 是**指稱更廣泛的整體調查程序**，在過程中會使用問卷（或其他工具）來收集資訊，但不僅僅只是指問卷本身。另外，當 survey 做為名詞使用時，重音落在第一音節，讀作 [ˋsɝve]，當動詞時重音則落在第二音節，讀作 [səˋve]，請特別注意。

Chapter 09・學校、學科、知識學習相關　P.181

聯想單字		
poll	n. 民意調查 v. 對～進行民意調查	
vote	v. 投票；表決 n. 選票；投票	

quotation
[kwo`teʃən]
n. 引言，引文；報價

衍 quote v. 引用，引述；舉出；報價
quota n. 定額，限額，配額

The professor began the lecture with a famous **quotation** from Shakespeare.
這位教授以莎士比亞的一句名言來做為課程引言。

聯想單字		
quotation marks	n. 引號	
quotation list	n. 報價單	
misquote	v. 錯誤引用	

rhetoric
[`rɛtərɪk]
n. 煽動性言論；修辭（學）；浮誇之詞

衍 rhetorical adj. 詞藻華麗的；浮誇的；修辭的
rhetorically adv. 善用言辭地；反問地

The politician's speech was filled with empty **rhetoric** but lacked real substance.
這名政客的演說充滿空洞的浮誇之詞，卻缺乏實質內容。

❶ Point 重點
rhetoric 是**不可數名詞**，因此**沒有複數形**，使用時請特別注意。另外，雖然這個字原本指的是修辭學，但現在多半用來指「以對他人造成影響為目的，用華麗詞藻包裝、缺乏實質內容的空洞言論」，通常**帶有負面含義**。

聯想單字		
rhetorical question	n. 反詰句	
oratory	n. 演講才能；雄辯	
eloquent	adj. 雄辯滔滔的，有說服力的	
expressive	adj. 富有表現力的	

seminar
[`sɛmə͵nɑr]
n. 研討會；專題討論會

The **seminar** provided valuable insights into the latest research techniques.
這場研討會針對最新研究技術提供了寶貴見解。

> ❶ Point 重點
> **seminar** vs. **workshop** vs. **conference** vs. **lecture** vs. **forum**
> **seminar** 通常是**針對某個主題進行深入討論**的小型會議，一般常會翻譯成**專題研討會**。另一方面，相較於 seminar，**workshop** **更重視實際操作或技能培訓**，會上可能會有實際操作或練習的環節，一般叫做**工作坊**或**實作課程**。**conference** 則是**大型會議**，通常一次 conference 的議程會**包括多場演講和小組討論等內容**。**lecture**（講座）通常是由教授或專業人士主講，向台下聽眾進行**一對多的單向知識傳授**，參與者主要是聽取資訊，互動較少。
> **forum** 是一種公開討論特定議題的平台，也就是「**論壇**」，討論時會聚焦於某個特定主題，特別**注重多方意見的交流和觀點碰撞**。

specify
[ˋspɛsə͵faɪ]
v. 具體說明；明確指出

衍 specific adj. 特定的；具體明確的
specifically adv. 特意，專門地；具體明確地
specification n. 規格；標準；詳細說明

Can you **specify** which model you want to purchase?
你能具體說明你想買的是哪個型號嗎？

聯想單字		
identify	v. 確定；識別
define	v. 定義
designate	v. 指定；委派
indicate	v. 指出；表明

squad
[skwɑd]
n. 小隊；特別行動組

The police **squad** was dispatched to handle the emergency situation.
警方特別小組被派去處理緊急情況。

> ❶ Point 重點
> squad 跟 team 或 group 不一樣，通常指由數人組成的固定小組，專門負責特定的任務或工作，特別常見於執法單位或體育相關活動之中。

standpoint
[ˋstændˌpɔɪnt]
n. 觀點，立場

Understanding different **standpoints** helps in resolving conflicts more effectively.
了解不同的立場有助於更有效地解決衝突。

❶ Point 重點
表達「觀點、立場或意見」的常見字詞

viewpoint 或 point of view
➪ 表示個人或群體對某事的觀點或看法。

perspective
➪ 受到特定經驗或背景知識所影響，針對某事提出的看法或觀點。

opinion
➪ 表示個人主觀的偏好、看法或意見，有時缺乏客觀性。

position
➪ 在正式討論、辯論或表態時常用，表示對某議題所持的態度或立場。

attitude
➪ 表示個人對特定事物或情境的感受、心態或態度。

「表達意見」的常用片語
➪ In my opinion, 依我看，
As far as I'm concerned, 就我而言，
From my perspective, 從我的角度來看，
It seems to me that... 我覺得～
My view is that... 我的觀點是～

symbolic
[sɪm`bɑlɪk]
adj. 代表的，象徵的

衍 symbol n. 標誌，象徵
symbolize v. 象徵，代表

The colors in the painting have a **symbolic** meaning related to the artist's emotions.
這幅畫中的色彩有著與這位藝術家情感相關的象徵意義。

teamwork
[`tim`wɝk]
n. 團隊合作

The team's success was due to their strong **teamwork**.
這個團隊會成功，是因為他們的團隊合作十分出色。

聯想單字		
collaboration	n. 合作
cooperation	n. 合作
synergy	n. 協同作用；合力
team building	phr. 團隊建立

transcript
[`træn͵skrɪpt]
n. 文字記錄；抄本

衍 transcribe v. 抄錄；記錄下；轉錄；改編
transcription n. 文字記錄；抄寫

Instead of a full **transcript**, he provided a brief summary.
他沒有提供完整的文字記錄，而是提供了簡短的摘要。

主題分類單字 — 學校、學科、知識學習相關

單字	音標	詞性/中文
aesthetics	[εs`θεtɪks]	n. 美學
analogy	[ə`nælədʒɪ]	n. 相似；比擬；類推
appendix	[ə`pεndɪks]	n. 附錄，附件；盲腸
apprehension	[ˌæprɪ`hεnʃən]	n. 理解；領悟；憂慮，擔心；逮捕
archive	[`arkaɪv]	v. 把～歸檔 n. 檔案館；文檔；紀錄
assignment	[ə`saɪnmənt]	n.（分派的）任務，工作；作業
assumption	[ə`sʌmpʃən]	n. 假設；擔任
astronomy	[əs`trɑnəmɪ]	n. 天文學
attendance	[ə`tεndəns]	n. 出席；出席人數
attendant	[ə`tεndənt]	adj. 出席的；伴隨的 n. 出席者；隨員、服務人員
bibliography	[ˌbɪblɪ`ɑgrəfɪ]	n. 參考書目
biochemistry	[`baɪo`kεmɪstrɪ]	n. 生物化學
biological	[ˌbaɪə`lɑdʒɪkl]	adj. 生物的；生物學的
clarity	[`klærətɪ]	n. 清楚；明白易懂
comma	[`kɑmə]	n. 逗號
commentary	[`kɑmənˌtεrɪ]	n.（時事）評論；評註
complexity	[kəm`plεksətɪ]	n. 複雜（性）；錯綜複雜
concise	[kən`saɪs]	adj. 簡明的；言簡意賅的
copyright	[`kɑpɪˌraɪt]	n. 版權；著作權

correction	[kəˋrɛkʃən]	n. 訂正，修正
creativity	[͵krieˋtɪvətɪ]	n. 創造力，創意
creator	[krɪˋetɚ]	n. 創造者；創作者
criterion	[kraɪˋtɪrɪən]	n.（判斷的）標準，準則
curriculum	[kəˋrɪkjələm]	n. 學校的全部課程
encyclopedia	[ɪn͵saɪkləˋpidɪə]	n. 百科全書
equation	[ɪˋkweʃən]	n. 方程式；等式
ethics	[ˋɛθɪks]	n. 倫理學，道德學；行為準則
examinee	[ɪg͵zæməˋni]	n. 應試者；受檢查者
excerpt	[ɪkˋsɝpt]	v. 摘錄；引用 n. 摘錄；引用
exemplify	[ɪgˋzɛmplə͵faɪ]	v. 做為～的模範；舉例說明
feminist	[ˋfɛmənɪst]	adj. 和女權主義有關的 n. 女權運動者
grammatical	[grəˋmætɪkl̩]	adj. 文法的；合乎文法的
ideological	[͵aɪdɪəˋlɑdʒɪkl̩]	adj. 意識形態上的
index	[ˋɪndɛks]	v. 把～編入索引 n. 索引；指數
journalism	[ˋdʒɝnl̩͵ɪzm]	n. 新聞業；新聞工作
notion	[ˋnoʃən]	n. 概念；想法；打算，意圖
poetic	[poˋɛtɪk]	adj. 詩的，詩歌的；充滿詩意的
rhetorical	[rɪˋtɔrɪkl̩]	adj. 修辭學的；詞藻華麗的
rhythmic	[ˋrɪðmɪk]	adj. 有節奏的；有韻律的

socialize	[ˈsoʃəˌlaɪz]	v. 交際；使社會化
sophomore	[ˈsɑfəmor]	n.（大學或高中的）二年級學生
stanza	[ˈstænzə]	n. 詩的一節
syllabus	[ˈsɪləbəs]	n. 教學大綱，課程大綱
symbolism	[ˈsɪmbḷˌɪzəm]	n. 象徵性
synonymous	[sɪˈnɑnəməs]	adj. 同義的
systematical	[ˌsɪstəˈmætɪkḷ]	adj. 有系統的；有條理的
terminology	[ˌtɝməˈnɑlədʒɪ]	n.（總稱）術語，專門用語
thesis	[ˈθisɪs]	n. 命題；論點；畢業論文
tuition	[tjuˈɪʃən]	n. 學費
undergraduate	[ˌʌndɚˈgrædʒʊɪt]	n. 大學生

Chapter 09 Quiz Time

一、請選出正確的答案。

1. The researcher provided deep _____ into the causes of climate change.
   A. standpoint
   B. teamwork
   C. insights
   D. genre

2. Please complete the _____ and return it to the front desk.
   A. seminar
   B. literacy
   C. questionnaire
   D. abstraction

3. The team had a _____ discussion to address all the issues before the deadline.
   A. concentrated
   B. rhetoric
   C. corresponding
   D. symbolic

二、請根據下列中文句子，填入適當的英文單字。

1. 削減該計畫資金的決定極具爭議性。

   The decision to cut funding for the program was highly c_____.

2. 他沒有完全領悟到自己行為所代表的意涵。

   He did not fully c_____ the implications of his actions.

3. 她是一位盡心盡力、照顧病人不怕辛苦的護理師。

   She is a d_____ nurse who works tirelessly to care for her patients.

4. 這間大學計劃舉辦一場與人工智慧有關的研討會。

   The university plans to hold a s_____ on artificial intelligence.

5. 一邊要健康生活,一邊卻一直吃垃圾食物,真是矛盾。

   Living a healthy lifestyle while constantly eating junk food is a c_____.

Chapter 10

自然

動物、昆蟲、環境、
景色、天氣、自然現象

Ch10.mp3

★核心單字情境對話

Barry : Look at this **picturesque** view! The rolling hills are so **scenic**.

Melisa : Absolutely! But did you notice the **barren** land near the river?

Barry : Yes, the farmers need to **nurture** the soil better. If they don't, the crops **wither**.

Melisa : I heard they want to introduce more **mainstream** planting methods. That way, the **livestock** can thrive, too.

Barry : But the weather is way more **treacherous** now, **devastating** droughts and floods happen all the time, and all the hard work can easily **evaporate** after a **catastrophe** hits.

Melisa : Yeah, it is really difficult for farmers to recover from such **disastrous** damage.

翻譯

Barry : 看看這**美得像畫的**景色！山丘連綿起伏的**景色**真是**漂亮**。

Melisa : 真的！但你有注意到河邊那塊**荒**地嗎？

Barry : 有啊，那些農夫們得努力**讓**土壤更**肥沃**一點了。如果他們沒做到，農作物就會**枯掉**。

Melisa : 我聽說他們想要引進更**主流**的栽種技術。這樣做的話，**牲畜**也能一起成長茁壯了。

Barry : 不過現在的天氣要比以前**凶險**多了，老是發生**嚴重的**旱災和水災，結果所有的辛勤努力，都可能在受災後一下子就**付諸流水**了。

Melisa : 是啊，農夫們要從這樣**災難性的**損害中復原真的很難。

agricultural
[ˌægrɪˈkʌltʃərəl]
adj. 農業的

衍 agriculture n. 農業；農藝

The country's economy is heavily dependent on its **agricultural** sector.
這個國家的經濟高度依賴其農業部門。

聯想單字
farming	n. 務農
rural	adj. 鄉村的
agricultural product	n. 農產品
produce	n. 農產品

barren
[ˈbærən]
adj. 貧瘠的；不孕的；無成果的

同 infertile adj. 貧瘠的；不能生育的

反 fertile adj. 肥沃的

The land remained **barren** despite several irrigation attempts.
儘管試著灌溉了幾次，這片地仍舊貧瘠。

聯想單字
wasteland	n.（都市中的）荒地；（精神上的）荒原
wilderness	n. 荒無人煙的地區；荒野

boundary
[ˈbaʊndrɪ]
n. 分界線；邊界；界線

衍 boundless adj. 無限的；無邊際的

The river forms a natural **boundary** between the two countries.
這條河形成了兩國之間的天然邊界。

❶ Point 重點
push the boundaries 突破限制
⇨ The artist's latest work **pushes the boundaries** of traditional painting techniques.
這位藝術家的最新作品突破了傳統繪畫技巧的限制。

聯想單字
territory	n. 領土
border	n. 邊界
frontier	n. 邊境

catastrophe
[kə`tæstrəfɪ]
n. 大災難；大災禍；困境

衍 catastrophic adj.
極差的，災難性的

The earthquake was a major **catastrophe** that affected thousands of lives.
這場地震是一次對數千人的生命造成影響的重大災難。

聯想單字
tragedy	n. 悲劇；不幸
debacle	n.（計劃不周而）徹底失敗
misfortune	n. 不幸
setback	n. 挫折；失敗

clutch
[klʌtʃ]
v. 緊抓，緊握

She managed to **clutch** her purse tightly as she walked through the crowd.
她設法在走過人群時緊緊抓住了自己的包包。

❗ Point 重點

clutch at sth 努力緊抓
⇨ As the roller coaster plunged down, she instinctively **clutched at** the safety bar in front of her.
當雲霄飛車急速下墜時，她本能地努力緊抓她面前的安全桿。

clutch/grasp at straws
（為了脫離困境）抓救命稻草，病急亂投醫
⇨ After losing his job, he started **clutching at straws**, applying for positions he wasn't even qualified for.
他在失業後開始病急亂投醫，應徵一些自己根本做不來的工作。

clutch vs. **hold** vs. **grip**
clutch 常用在「**緊張不安**」或「**害怕失去**」的情境之中，表示在情急之下用力握住或緊抓某物。

hold 這個字的用法廣泛，可以表示**任何形式的「握」**，此外也可以表達「**保持當下狀態**」的意思。

grip 特別強調使用**大且穩定的力道**來用力握住或牢牢控制住某物。

Chapter 10・動物、昆蟲、環境、景色、天氣、自然現象　　P.193

聯想單字

clutch bag	n.（無帶）手拿包
seize	v. 抓住；奪取
grab	v. 抓取；奪取 n. 抓住；搶奪
snatch	v. 奪得；抓住 n. 奪取；搶奪；片段
grip	v. 緊握（夾或咬）；掌控；理解 n. 控制；緊握

contaminant
[kən`tæmənənt]
n. 汙染物

衍 contaminate v. 汙染
contamination n. 汙染；玷汙

The factory was fined for releasing harmful **contaminants** into the river.
這間工廠因排放有害污染物到河裡而被罰款。

❗ Point 重點

contaminant vs. **pollutant**
contaminant 是指任何會使物質（如水、土壤或食品）**品質下降**的外來物質（自然生成或人為製造都可以），但品質下降**不代表一定具有毒性或會造成危害**。另一方面，**pollutant**（汙染物）一定會造成危害或負面影響，這個字經常在**自然環境或科學相關領域**中使用，且多半是**因人類活動而產生**。

聯想單字

taint	v. 汙染；玷汙
poison	v. 毒害；汙染 n. 毒藥；毒
harm	v. 傷害

devastating
[`dɛvəsˌtetɪŋ]
adj. 毀滅性的，破壞性極大的；令人震驚的

衍 devastate v. 摧毀；毀滅；使極為震驚
devastated adj. 被徹底摧毀的；毀滅的；極度震驚的
devastatingly adv. 毀滅性地；強烈地
devastation n. 毀滅性，極大的破壞

The earthquake had a **devastating** impact on the small village.
這場地震對這個小村莊造成了毀滅性的影響。

聯想單字

destructive	adj. 破壞性的；有害的
ruinous	adj. 毀滅性的；災難性的
havoc	n. 浩劫；大混亂
wreak havoc on sth	phr. 對某事物造成嚴重破壞
mayhem	n. 混亂狀態

developed
[dɪˋvɛləpt]
adj. 發達的；先進的

衍 develop v.（使）發展；（使）成長；開發
development n. 成長；發展；開發
developing adj. 發展中的；成長中的

反 underdeveloped adj.（尤指國家）不發達的

Japan is considered one of the most **developed** countries in the world.
日本被認為是世界上最發達的國家之一。

❶ Point 重點
developed country 是「**已開發國家**」的意思，指在經濟結構或社會制度運作上都具有一定發展水準的國家，**developing country** 則是「**發展中國家**」，指尚在建立完善制度的國家。

另一方面，developed 的前面如果搭配 well，就會變成形容詞 **well-developed**，意思是「**發展良好的；完善的**」。
⇨ The city has a **well-developed** public transportation system that makes commuting easy.
這座城市擁有完善的大眾運輸系統，讓通勤變得很簡單。

聯想單字		
advanced		adj. 先進的
sustainable development		n. 永續發展
R&D（= research and development）		n. 研究與開發

disastrous
[dɪzˋæstrəs]
adj. 極其糟糕的；災難性的

衍 disaster n. 災難
disastrously adv. 災難性地

The hurricane caused **disastrous** damage to the coastal towns, leaving many homeless.
這個颶風對沿海城鎮造成了災難性的破壞，使許多人無家可歸。

drizzle
[ˋdrɪzl]
n. 毛毛雨；（灑落的）少量液體
v. 下毛毛雨；灑落（少量液體）

衍 drizzly adv. 下毛毛雨的

The sky was overcast, and a light **drizzle** began to fall.
天空布滿烏雲，然後開始下起了毛毛細雨。

The chef **drizzled** some vinegar on the salad.
主廚在沙拉上淋了一些醋。

❶ Point 重點

各種「雨勢」的說法

misty
⇨ 霧氣夾雜著細小的水滴，通常是非常輕微的雨勢。

drizzle
⇨ 輕微的小雨，通常指細密的毛毛雨。

sprinkle
⇨ 指輕微且短暫的小雨，降雨強度在毛毛雨和陣雨之間。

shower
⇨ 陣雨，通常強度較小，且來得快、去得也快。

light rain
⇨ 比陣雨持續的時間更長，但雨勢不大，不撐傘也不會到濕透的地步。

heavy rain
⇨ 可以明顯感覺得到雨勢，雨勢大到必須撐傘。

pouring
⇨ 滂沱大雨，雨勢強烈到連撐傘也會淋濕的程度。

downpour
⇨ 指短時間內的大量降雨，通常非常突然且強烈，如午後雷陣雨。

erupt
[ɪˋrʌpt]
v.（火山）爆發，噴發；突然發生；（情感等）爆發

衍 eruption n. 突然發生；（情感等）爆發
eruptive adj. 噴發的；爆發性的

Protests **erupted** across the country following the controversial election results.
全國各地在爭議性的選舉結果出爐後爆發了抗議。

❶ Point 重點
除了火山之外，erupt 還可以用來形容情感或事件的突然爆發，例如醜聞、事故、災害、憤怒、笑意、愛戀等等，帶有突如其來且難以控制的語意。

erupt into laughter 爆發笑聲
⇨ The audience **erupted into laughter** at the comedian's joke.
這位喜劇演員的笑話讓觀眾大爆笑。

聯想單字	explosion	n. 爆炸
	volcano	n. 火山
	lava	n. 熔岩；火山岩

evaporate
[ɪˋvæpəˌret]
v.（尤指透過加熱）（使）揮發，蒸發；消失

衍 evaporation n. 蒸發；消失

The water in the pot began to **evaporate** a lot after boiling for a long time.
鍋中的水在沸騰好一段時間後開始大量蒸發了。

❶ Point 重點
evaporate vs. **disappear**
evaporate 強調的是逐漸消失或消散的**過程**；然而，**disappear** 更重視的是消失的**結果**，無論瞬間還是逐漸，只要最終的結果是消失，便可以使用 disappear。

雖然 evaporate 一般用於自然科學領域，描述物理狀態上的變化，但也可用來指**情感或興趣等事物的消失**。
⇨ His confidence **evaporated** after hearing the harsh criticism.
他的信心在聽到嚴厲的批評後消失了。

聯想單字	condense	v.（使）凝固；（使）凝結
	solidify	v.（使）固化
	vapor	n. 蒸氣；霧氣

famine
[ˋfæmɪn]
n. 饑荒；饑荒時期

衍 famish v. 極度飢餓；使挨餓
famished adj. 非常飢餓的

Millions of people faced starvation due to the prolonged **famine**.
數百萬人因長期饑荒而陷入飢餓。

聯想單字	malnutrition	n. 營養不良
	starvation	n.（常會造成死亡的）飢餓；挨餓
	hunger	n. 飢餓

Chapter 10・動物、昆蟲、環境、景色、天氣、自然現象

fertility
[fɝˋtɪlətɪ]
n.（土地的）肥沃度；
（動植物的）繁殖能力

衍 fertile adj. 肥沃的；
（動植物）可繁殖的
fertilization n.
施肥；受精
fertilize v. 施肥；
使受精
fertilizer n. 肥料

反 infertility n. 不育；
不孕

The **fertility** of the soil in this region is ideal for growing crops.
這個地區的土壤肥沃度非常適合種植農作物。

聯想單字		
fertility rate	n. 生育率
birth rate	n. 出生率
give birth to	phr. 生產
reproduce	v. 繁殖；生育；複製
sterile	adj.（生物）不育的；（土地）貧瘠的

hedge
[hɛdʒ]
n.（樹）籬笆；障礙（物）；保護（或控制）手段
v. 嚴格限制；迴避問題；避險

The farmer planted a **hedge** to separate his land from his neighbor's.
這名農夫種了一道樹籬，將他的土地與鄰居的土地分隔開來。

To minimize losses, the investor decided to **hedge** by buying options.
為了把損失降到最低，這名投資人決定利用購買選擇權來避險。

❶ Point 重點
hedge 後面可接介系詞 **against**（對抗）或 **with**（用以）來表示要避開的風險或損失。
⇨ They **hedged against** potential losses with various strategies.
他們運用各種策略來避免可能的損失。

聯想單字		
hedge fund	n. 避險基金
insure	v. 為～投保；確保
risk-averse	adj. 風險迴避的

livestock
[ˈlaɪvˌstɑk]
n. 牲畜；家畜

The recent outbreak of disease among **livestock** has raised concerns about food safety.
近期在家畜之間爆發的疾病引發了對食品安全的疑慮。

❶ Point 重點
livestock vs. **poultry**
livestock 指的是為**經濟目的**（生產肉品、乳製品等農產品）所飼養的動物，如牛、羊或豬等。

poultry（家禽）指的是用於**生產肉類和蛋等產品的鳥類**，如雞、鴨、鵝等。

livestock 是**不可數名詞**，因此**不會搭配冠詞 a/the**，但可以用 **a herd of livestock**（一群牲畜）來表示數量。
⇨ There is **a herd of livestock** grazing in the field.
田野之中有一群牲畜正在吃草。

mainstream
[ˈmenˌstrim]
n.（河流或思想的）主流
adj. 主流的

The **mainstream** of public opinion often influences government policies.
主流公眾意見經常會影響政府政策。

She prefers listening to **mainstream** music rather than independent artists.
她偏好聽主流而非獨立藝人的音樂。

❶ Point 重點
go mainstream 流行起來，成為主流
⇨ The innovative app finally **went mainstream** after a successful marketing campaign.
這個創新的應用程式在成功的行銷宣傳活動後終於流行了起來。

聯想單字	
mainstream media	n. 主流媒體
mainstream culture	n. 主流文化
alternative	adj. 替代的；兩者擇一的 n. 替代選項

mining
[ˋmaɪnɪŋ]
n. 採礦；礦業

衍 mine n. 礦；地雷；水雷 v. 開採（礦物）；布雷於～
miner n. 礦工
landmine n. 地雷

Environmentalists are concerned about the impact of **mining** on local ecosystems.
環保人士擔心採礦對當地生態系統的影響。

❶ Point 重點
mining 常用作不可數名詞，表示「採礦的這個行為」。
⇒ **Mining** is essential for providing raw materials.
採礦對於原物料的供應至關重要。

聯想單字
mining industry	n. 礦業
mineral	n. 礦物
iron ore	n. 鐵礦砂
coal mine	n. 煤礦
rare earth	n. 稀土

nurture
[ˋnɝtʃɚ]
v. 養育，培育；懷有
n. 教育，養成；後天培育

The organization is dedicated to **nurturing** the skills of young athletes through training programs.
這個組織致力於透過培訓計畫培養年輕運動員的技能。

The **nurture** of young talent is essential for the future of any industry.
年輕人才的養成對於任何產業的未來都至關重要。

❶ Point 重點
nurture vs. **cultivate** vs. **nourish**
nurture 是「照顧和培育，使其成長壯大」的意思，對象可以是人或事物（例如某個計畫或風氣等等），**強調付出情感支持和關懷**，常用於與個人成長相關的情境之中。

cultivate（培養）原本指的是農業上的耕種和培養，但後來也能用來表達「發展或培養某種技能、態度或關係」，**特別強調有意識的養成某項技能或知識**。

nourish（滋養；養育）指的是**提供生存所需的食物及養分**，讓某人或某事物能充滿養分的健康成長，也可以用來比喻情感上的支持或鼓勵。

offshore
[`ɔfʃor]
adj. 近海的；離岸的；境外的
adv. 離岸；在近海
v. 離岸經營

衍 offshoring n.（為降低成本的）境外經商

反 onshore adj. 向岸上的，向陸地的；陸上的

Offshore wind farms are becoming a popular source of renewable energy.
離岸風電場逐漸變成受歡迎的可再生能源來源。

The boat is sailing **offshore**.
那艘船正在向海上航行。

Many companies have been **offshoring** their businesses for decades.
許多公司數十年來都在將他們的業務移往海外。

聯想單字		
offshore wind power	n. 離岸風力（發電）
offshore company	n. 境外公司

perennial
[pəˋrɛnɪəl]
adj. 長期存在的；多年生的；不斷發生的
n. 多年生植物

衍 perennially adv. 長期地；常年地；不斷發生地

These flowers are **perennial** and will bloom every year without needing to be replanted.
這些花是多年生的，不用重新栽種就會每年開花。

Roses are one of the most common **perennials** in traditional gardens.
玫瑰是傳統花園中最常見的多年生植物之一。

聯想單字		
perpetual	adj. 永久的，永恆的
everlasting	adj. 永久的，永恆的
standing	adj. 永久的，長期的；常設的 n. 聲望；地位

picturesque
[ˌpɪktʃəˋrɛsk]
adj. 景色如畫的

衍 picturesquely adv. 景色如畫地
picturesqueness n. 景色如畫

The small village was so **picturesque** that it looked like something out of a fairy tale.
這個小村莊景色如畫到看起來就像是會出現在童話故事裡似的。

Chapter 10・動物、昆蟲、環境、景色、天氣、自然現象

❶ Point 重點
「稱讚景色宜人」的常見說法
⇨ awe-inspiring 令人敬畏的，令人驚嘆的
breathtaking 令人屏息的，美得驚人的
impressive 令人印象深刻的，壯觀的
magnificent 壯麗的，宏偉的
majestic 雄偉的，莊嚴的
stunning 令人驚嘆的

prey
[pre]
n. 獵物；犧牲者
v. 捕食；掠奪

反 predator n.
狩獵者，掠食者；
尾隨作案者

The weaker animals often become **prey** to predators.
較弱小的動物常常成為掠食者的獵物。

Hawks **prey** on small mammals like mice and rabbits.
老鷹會捕食像老鼠和兔子這樣的小型哺乳類動物。

❶ Point 重點
prey 是**不可數名詞**，所以**沒有複數形**，使用上須特別留意。下面是一些常用的 prey 相關片語，這些片語在文章中經常出現，一起來看看吧！

be/fall prey to sth 成為～的犧牲者；受到～之害
⇨ He **fell prey to** a scam and lost a lot of money.
他被詐騙所害，損失了一大筆錢。

be easy prey 易成為～的目標，易被～欺騙（或利用）
⇨ Tourists unfamiliar with the city **are** often **easy prey** for pickpockets.
不熟悉這座城市的遊客常是扒手眼中好下手的目標。

prey on sb's mind 使耿耿於懷，使難以釋懷
⇨ The mistake Hank made during the presentation **preyed on his mind** for days.
Hank 在簡報時犯的錯讓他耿耿於懷了好幾天。

聯想單字		
hunt	v. 狩獵	
hunter	n. 獵人，狩獵者	
victim	n. 受害者，獵物	

reproduce
[͵rɪprəˋdjus]
v. 複製；重演；生殖

衍 reproduction n.
繁殖；生育；
複製品
reproducible adj.
能再生的；能再製造的；能再現的

The printer can accurately **reproduce** the colors of the original photograph.
這台印表機可以精準複製原版相片的顏色。

❶ Point 重點

reproduce vs. **duplicate** vs. **replicate**

雖然 reproduce、duplicate 和 replicate 都帶有「**重複**」或「**複製**」的語意，但三者並非同義字，使用時須透過上下文來判斷該用哪個字。

reproduce 不強調必須與要複製的原物百分之百相同，而 **duplicate** 卻強調「**精確且完整地複製原物**」，特別常用在如文件或圖像等物理性質的對象上。另一方面，**replicate** 強調的是「**在相同條件下重複或複製**」，多用於需要驗證實驗結果是否一致的科學或技術領域。

聯想單字		
mimic	v.（為搞笑）模仿（特定某人）n. 善於模仿的人	
duplicate	v. 複製 adj. 複製的；完全一樣的 n. 複製品；副本	
replicate	v. 重複；複製；自我複製	

scenic
[ˋsinɪk]
adj. 景色優美的

衍 scene n. 場景；情景
scenery n. 風景，景色

The **scenic** view of the mountains took my breath away.
優美的群山景色讓我屏息。

聯想單字		
landscape	n. 風景，景色	
view	n. 景色；視野	
attraction	n.（觀光）景點；吸引人的事物	

Chapter 10・動物、昆蟲、環境、景色、天氣、自然現象　P.203

spectacular

[spɛk`tækjələ]
adj. 壯觀的，壯麗的；令人驚嘆的；驚人的，巨大的

衍 spectacularly adv. 壯麗地，壯觀地，令人驚嘆地；非常
spectacle n. 不尋常的事；出乎意料的情況；壯觀場面

The Grand Canyon offers a **spectacular** view that attracts millions of visitors each year.
大峽谷的壯觀景色每年都會吸引數百萬名遊客。

聯想單字
gorgeous	adj. 華麗的；極好的
marvelous	adj. 令人驚歎的；非凡的
astonishing	adj. 令人驚訝的；驚人的

territorial

[ˌtɛrə`tɔrɪəl]
adj. 領土的；領地的；土地的

衍 territory n. 領土；領地；勢力範圍

The **territorial** integrity of the country was compromised by the ongoing conflict.
該國的領土完整因衝突持續而蒙受損害。

聯想單字
sovereignty	n. 主權
sovereign state	n. 主權國家
regime	n. 政體；政權

treacherous

[`trɛtʃərəs]
adj.（陸地或大海）極端危險的，凶險的；（人）不可靠的；背信棄義的

衍 treachery n. 背叛，背信棄義

The **treacherous** terrain made hiking extremely dangerous.
凶險的地形使健行變得極其危險。

❶ Point 重點
treacherous 除了用來形容環境惡劣外，也可以用來形容人，表示一個人乍看之下值得信任，但其實充滿謊言和背叛。
⇒ Jessica discovered that her **treacherous** friend had been spreading rumors behind her back.
Jessica 發現她那個背信棄義的朋友一直在她背後散布謠言。

聯想單字
hazard	n. 危險物 v. 冒險；使遭受危險
hazardous	adj. 危險的；有害的
perilous	adj. 險惡的
risky	adj. 危險的；冒險的

wither
[ˈwɪðɚ]
v.（使）枯萎，（使）乾枯；萎縮；衰弱

衍 withered adj. 枯萎的；乾枯的
withering adj.（目光或評論等）令人難堪的，尖酸刻薄的

反 bloom v. 開花；綻放；繁榮

The flowers began to **wither** after a week without water.
這些花在缺水一週後開始枯萎了。

❶ Point 重點
wither 除了指植物枯萎以外，也可以用來形容「人或事物逐漸消失或衰退」。
⇨ Olivia's confidence began to **wither** after repeated failures.
在反覆失敗後，Olivia 的信心開始逐漸消失。

聯想單字		
wilt	v.（植物）枯萎，凋謝；（人）變得萎靡不振
decay	v. 腐蝕；（使）衰敗，（使）衰弱

Chapter 10 · 動物、昆蟲、環境、景色、天氣、自然現象

主題分類單字

動物、昆蟲、環境、景色、天氣、自然現象

Ch10.mp3

單字	音標	詞性/中譯
bleak	[blik]	adj. 荒涼的；慘澹無望的
cactus	[ˋkæktəs]	n. 仙人掌
carnation	[karˋneʃən]	n. 康乃馨；淡紅色
Celsius	[ˋsɛlsɪəs]	n. 攝氏溫度 adj. 攝氏的
chimpanzee	[͵tʃɪmpænˋzi]	n. 黑猩猩
coastal	[ˋkostl̩]	adj. 海岸的；沿海的
coastline	[ˋkost͵laɪn]	n. 海岸線
comet	[ˋkamɪt]	n. 彗星
corrode	[kəˋrod]	v. 侵蝕；損害
crocodile	[ˋkrakə͵daɪl]	n. 鱷魚
daybreak	[ˋde͵brek]	n. 黎明；破曉
ecology	[ɪˋkalədʒɪ]	n.（特定區域的）生態學；生態
equator	[ɪˋkwetɚ]	n. 赤道
erode	[ɪˋrod]	v. 腐蝕；侵蝕；磨損
evaporation	[ɪ͵væpəˋreʃən]	n. 蒸發；消失
evergreen	[ˋɛvɚ͵grin]	adj. 常綠的；常青的 n. 常綠植物
Fahrenheit	[ˋfærən͵haɪt]	n. 華氏溫度 adj. 華氏的
fishery	[ˋfɪʃərɪ]	n. 漁業
frontier	[frʌnˋtɪr]	n. 邊境

glacier	[ˋgleʃɚ]	n. 冰河
gorge	[gɔrdʒ]	n. 峽谷；狼吞虎嚥
gorilla	[gəˋrɪlə]	n. 大猩猩
grassy	[ˋgræsɪ]	adj. 長滿綠草的，綠草如茵的
hemisphere	[ˋhɛməsˏfɪr]	n.（地球的）半球；半球體
herb	[hɝb]	n.（料理用或藥用的）草本植物
hillside	[ˋhɪlˏsaɪd]	n. 山腰，山坡
hover	[ˋhʌvɚ]	v. 盤旋；徘徊
ivy	[ˋaɪvɪ]	n. 常春藤
lava	[ˋlɑvə]	n.（火山噴發的）岩漿；火山岩
lizard	[ˋlɪzɚd]	n. 蜥蜴
lotus	[ˋlotəs]	n. 蓮花
mammal	[ˋmæml]	n. 哺乳動物
mellow	[ˋmɛlo]	adj. 柔和的；芳醇的；放鬆的 v. 變柔和；成熟；（使）放鬆
mermaid	[ˋmɝˏmed]	n. 美人魚
nightingale	[ˋnaɪtɪŋˏgel]	n. 夜鶯
octopus	[ˋɑktəpəs]	n. 章魚
ostrich	[ˋɑstrɪtʃ]	n. 駝鳥；有駝鳥心態的人
peacock	[ˋpikɑk]	n. 孔雀；愛炫耀的人
peck	[pɛk]	v. 啄；輕吻 n. 啄；啄痕；輕吻
peninsula	[pəˋnɪnsələ]	n. 半島

perch	[pɝtʃ]	v.（在高處）棲息；座落 n.（鳥的）棲息處；（高處的）休息處
petroleum	[pə`trolɪəm]	n. 石油
realm	[rɛlm]	n. 國土；領域；範圍
reef	[rif]	n. 礁；暗礁
reptile	[`rɛptaɪl]	n. 爬蟲類
rocky	[`rɑkɪ]	adj. 岩石的；多岩石的；崎嶇難行的
rustle	[`rʌsl̩]	v. 使（紙或樹葉等）沙沙作響 n. 沙沙作響
scarecrow	[`skɛrˏkro]	n. 稻草人；威嚇物
silkworm	[`sɪlkˏwɝm]	n. 蠶
specimen	[`spɛsəmən]	n. 樣本；標本
strait	[stret]	n. 海峽
swamp	[swɑmp]	n. 沼澤 v. 淹沒；使應接不暇
tempest	[`tɛmpɪst]	n. 暴風雨；風暴，騷動
terrestrial	[tə`rɛstrɪəl]	adj. 地球的；陸地上的；陸生的
thermometer	[θɚ`mɑmətɚ]	n. 溫度計；體溫計
thunderous	[`θʌndərəs]	adj. 雷鳴般的
torrent	[`tɔrənt]	n. 洪流；狂潮；迸發
tropic	[`trɑpɪk]	n. 回歸線
vegetation	[ˏvɛdʒə`teʃən]	n. 植被；草木
vine	[vaɪn]	n. 藤蔓植物；葡萄藤
woodpecker	[`wʊdˏpɛkɚ]	n. 啄木鳥

Chapter 10 Quiz Time

一、請選出正確的答案。

1. Artists often try to _____ famous paintings using different techniques.
   A. drizzle
   B. clutch
   C. prey
   D. reproduce

2. She _____ in anger when she found out about the betrayal.
   A. erupted
   B. hedged
   C. evaporated
   D. nurtured

3. The program aims to _____ creativity in young artists.
   A. wither
   B. nurture
   C. mining
   D. developed

二、請根據下列中文句子，填入適當的英文單字。

1. 現在有許多農民改用有機的方法來飼養牲畜。

   Many farmers are now switching to organic methods for raising their
   l_____.

2. 這場戰爭的毀滅性消息讓舉國震驚。

   The d_____ news of the war left the nation in shock.

3. 隨著產業外移，這座城鎮的經濟開始衰退了。

   The town's economy started to w_____ as industries moved away.

4. 他比較喜歡看非主流的書，而不是流行的暢銷書。

   He prefers to read books that are outside the m_____ rather than popular bestsellers.

5. 在努力多年後，他們的付出似乎一無所獲。

   After years of hard work, their efforts seemed b_____ and fruitless.

Answer:
(一)：1. D 2. A 3. B
(二)：1. livestock 2. devastating 3. wither 4. mainstream 5. barren

翻譯：
(一)
1. 藝術家繼承家族事業以其以來的回收技巧來重新展示名畫作。
2. 他的發現讓我們大吃一驚了。
3. 這項專案的項目建立者將邀請市轄藝術家的家飾業。

P.210　國際學村・全民英檢

Chapter 11

健康
疾病、醫院、傷病處理、感受

Ch11.mp3

★核心單字情境對話

Nancy : I've been dealing with this terrible **acne** breakout lately.
Dora : Maybe you should get it **diagnosed**. You don't want it to leave **scars**.
Nancy : To add insult to injury, I even **sprained** my ankle yesterday, and now I have a huge **bruise** and can barely walk!
Dora : Oh no! It sounds like you are a bit **vulnerable** lately.
Nancy : Tell me about it! I feel like I'm **plagued** by bad luck. It's **tormenting** me!
Dora : I think it's not the bad luck, but your **fatigue** and all the **side effects** caused by it. You've worked overtime for weeks.
Nancy : Maybe you're right. I've read an article discussing the bad impacts caused by **chronic** stress. I can really use a vacation now!

翻譯

Nancy : 我最近一直在對付這可怕的大爆**痘**。
Dora : 也許妳應該去**給醫生看**一下。妳應該不想要留**疤**吧。
Nancy : 雪上加霜的是,我昨天還**扭到**了腳踝,結果我現在**瘀青**了一大塊,而且幾乎沒辦法走路!
Dora : 噢不!聽起來妳最近有點**脆弱**啊。
Nancy : 真的!我覺得我好像厄運**纏身**。根本就是在**折磨**我!
Dora : 我覺得跟厄運沒關係,而是妳的**疲勞**和疲勞造成的那些**副作用**。妳已經加班好幾個禮拜了。
Nancy : 也許妳是對的。我有看過報導說**慢性**壓力會造成不良影響。我現在真的很需要度假!

abortion
[əˋbɔrʃən]
n. 墮胎，人工流產；失敗

衍 abort v. 中止；夭折；墮胎，人工流產

In some countries, access to safe **abortion** services is still limited.
在一些國家裡，能夠安全執行墮胎的管道仍然有限。

聯想單字		
	miscarriage	n. 流產
	pregnancy	n. 懷孕
	fetus	n. 胚胎；胎兒

acne
[ˋæknɪ]
n. 痤瘡，粉刺，青春痘

She has struggled with **acne** since her teenage years.
她從青少年時期開始就一直在對抗青春痘問題。

❶ Point 重點
acne 是**不可數名詞**，因此**沒有複數形**，可以用 **a lot of acne** 或 **severe acne** 來表示「痘痘很多」或「痘痘很嚴重」。

聯想單字		
	pimple	n. 小痘痘；粉刺
	blackhead	n. 黑頭粉刺
	rash	n. 疹子
	freckle	n. 雀斑
	dermatologist	n. 皮膚科醫生

allergic
[əˋlɝdʒɪk]
adj. 對～過敏的；對～極其反感的

衍 allergy n. 過敏
allergenic adj. 致敏的
allergen n. 過敏原

I'm **allergic** to peanuts, so I always avoid foods that contain peanuts.
我對花生過敏，所以我總是避免含有花生的食物。

❶ Point 重點
be allergic to＋N. 對某事物過敏或極度厭惡
⇒ They're **allergic to** unfair criticism and tend to avoid confrontations.
他們極度厭惡不公平的評論，因此傾向於避免發生衝突。

聯想單字		
	asthma	n. 氣喘
	immune	adj. 免疫的
	respiratory	adj. 呼吸的
	respiration	n. 呼吸

bout
[baʊt]
n.（疾病的）發作；
（拳擊）比賽

After a short **bout** of flu, he quickly recovered and went back to work.
在短暫染上一次流感後，他很快就康復並重回工作崗位了。

❶ Point 重點
bout 指的通常是「一段時間內的某種行為」或「某病痛的一次發作」，特別強調**一次性或短時間**，後面常搭配介系詞 **of**，如 **a bout of illness**（一場病）、**a bout of laughter**（一陣大笑）。此外，bout 也可以用來指一**場競賽**，尤其常用在拳擊比賽上。

bruise
[bruz]
n. 碰傷；瘀傷
v. 出現傷痕；碰傷

After he fell, Lucas noticed a large **bruise** forming on his knee.
在跌倒後，Lucas 發現他的膝蓋上出現了一大片瘀青。

The apples **bruise** easily if they're not handled carefully.
如果沒有小心搬運的話，這些蘋果很容易就會碰傷。

❶ Point 重點
當作動詞使用時，除了身體上的瘀傷，bruise 還能用來比喻「**情感或信心上的受挫**」。

bruise sb's ego 傷了～的自尊
⇨ Not being invited to the event **bruised Luna's ego**, making her question her place in her social circle.
沒有被邀請參加活動的這件事，讓 Luna 覺得自尊心很受傷，也開始質疑起自己在社交圈裡的位置。

聯想單字		
wound	n. 傷口
scratch	n. 擦傷；刮傷
cut	n. 割傷

capsule
[ˋkæpsl]
n. 膠囊；太空艙

The doctor prescribed a **capsule** to be taken twice daily.
醫生開了一種每日服用兩次的膠囊。

❶ Point 重點
常見的藥物形式分類
pill 藥丸　　　　　ointment 藥膏
tablet 藥片　　　　cream 乳膏
syrup 糖漿　　　　patch 貼片

聯想單字
capsule toy　　　n. 轉蛋
coffee capsule　 n. 膠囊咖啡
capsule inn　　　n. 膠囊旅館

challenged
[ˋtʃælɪndʒd]
adj.（生理或精神狀況）有障礙的；殘障的（委婉說法）

衍 challenging adj.
　富有挑戰性的
　challenge n. 挑戰
　v. 挑戰

She was physically **challenged** but never let it stop her from pursuing her dreams.
雖然她身體有缺陷，但她從不讓這點阻止她追求夢想。

❶ Point 重點
目前社會傾向於以更具包容和多樣性的方式來稱呼身心障礙人士。因此常以 challenged 來描述積極面對身心障礙挑戰的人，如 **physically/intellectually/mentally challenged**（身障／智障／精障）。

其他稱呼方式

disabled
➪ 較為傳統的稱呼，指身體或心理功能有損。雖然現在仍廣泛使用，但部分人認為 **disabled** 所傳達的語氣較為負面和消極。

differently-abled
➪ 強調每個人都擁有不同的能力，一般認為是更為積極的替代說法。

people with disabilities
➪ 把重點放在人而不是其身心障礙上的表達方式，也是目前經常使用的稱呼方式，一般認為語氣上較為中立及尊重。

chronic
[ˋkrɑnɪk]
adj.（尤指疾病或不好的事物）慢性的，長期的

衍 chronically adv.
（尤指疾病或不好的事物）慢性地，長期地

反 acute adj.
（病痛）急性的

He was diagnosed with a **chronic** lung condition that requires regular check-ups.
他被診斷出患有一種慢性肺部疾病，必須定期檢查。

❶ Point 重點
在健康和醫療領域中，chronic 經常與名詞形成搭配詞，表示該名詞是「慢性的」或「長期的」。
⇨ chronic disease/condition 慢性病
　chronic stress 慢性壓力
　chronic pain 慢性疼痛
　chronic headache 慢性頭痛

deadly
[ˋdɛdlɪ]
adj. 致命的，致死的

The **deadly** virus spread quickly through the population and caused widespread panic.
這種致命病毒透過人群迅速傳播，造成很多人的恐慌。

❶ Point 重點
與 dead 相關的字詞及使用方式

dead
形容詞，指不再活著的、已經死亡的或失去生命的。
⇨ The flowers are **dead** because they didn't get enough water.
這些花因為水不夠而死掉了。

die
動詞，指生命的結束或死亡。
⇨ The plant will **die** if it doesn't receive sunlight.
植物得不到陽光就會死掉。

dying
形容詞，指處於即將死亡、熄滅或結束的狀態之中。
⇨ He is **dying** from a rare disease.
他因為一種罕見疾病而快死了。

death
名詞，表示生命的結束，死亡的狀態或過程。
⇨ The news of her **death** shocked everyone.
她去世的消息震驚了所有人。

deficiency

[dɪˋfɪʃənsɪ]
n. 不足，缺乏，缺少

衍 deficient adj.
缺乏的；不足的
deficiently adv.
缺乏地；不充分地

Iron **deficiency** is common among young women and can cause anemia.
缺鐵對於年輕女性來說很常見，可能會導致貧血。

❶ Point 重點
「不足」的其他常見片語
⇨ be short of... 缺少～，不足～
  lack of... 缺乏～，缺少～（多用作名詞片語）
  run out of... ～用完，耗盡～
  in need of... 需要～，急需～
  be scarce in... ～稀缺，～不足
  be deficient in... ～不足（某種必需品或特質，常用於正式語境）

聯想單字
insufficiency	n. 不夠；不足
inadequacy	n. 不完善；不適當
shortage	n. 缺乏；缺少
lack	n. 缺乏 v. 缺乏

demise

[dɪˋmaɪz]
n. 倒閉；垮台；死亡，逝世

After the leader's **demise**, the organization faced a period of uncertainty.
在領袖去世後，這個組織面臨了一段不確定的時期。

❶ Point 重點
demise 表現出來的語氣很正經，因此多半用於較正式的情境之中，尤其常用來描述「**原本被認為很強大的某人或某事物的去世、終結或失敗**」。

demise of＋N. 某事物的消亡或終結
⇨ The unexpected **demise of** the popular television show disappointed many fans.
那個人氣電視節目的意外結束，令許多粉絲感到失望。

聯想單字
downfall	n. 衰敗；倒台
termination	n. 終止；停止
cease	v. 停止，中止

diagnose

[ˈdaɪəgnoz]
v. 診斷（病症）

衍 diagnosis n. 診斷
　 diagnostic adj. 診斷的；用於判斷的

反 misdiagnose v. 誤診

He was **diagnosed** with diabetes when he was only twenty-five.
他在只有 25 歲時就被診斷出了糖尿病。

❶ Point 重點
be diagnosed with＋疾病／問題
用來描述「被診斷出有某種疾病或問題狀況」的表達方式。

⇨ He **was diagnosed with** high blood pressure during a routine check-up.
他在例行的健康檢查中被診斷出了高血壓。

也可以用「疾病／問題」做為主詞並改用**介系詞 as**，表示「被診斷為～」。

⇨ The condition **was diagnosed as** severe.
這個病症被診斷為嚴重。

disable

[dɪsˈebl]
v. 使傷殘，使喪失能力；使發生故障，使無法正常工作

衍 disability n. 殘障，缺陷，失能

反 enable v. 使能夠；使可能

The accident **disabled** him from walking for several months.
那場意外使他有幾個月無法走路。

❶ Point 重點
disable 不只能表示人類在生理上的失能，還可用來表達**「技術或設備的失能、故障或停用」**。

⇨ **disable** the alarm 停用警報器
　 disable a user account 停用使用者帳戶
　 disable a function 停用功能

disable sb from V-ing 使某人無法做某事
⇨ The injury **disabled** her **from** playing sports.
這次受傷使她無法進行體育活動。

聯想單字		
cripple	v. 使受傷致殘	
handicap	n. 殘疾，缺陷；障礙，阻礙 v. 阻礙	
sabotage	v.（人為）故意破壞	

fatigue
[fə`tig]
n. 疲憊，勞累

衍 fatigued adj. 勞累的；疲倦的

Fatigue from the long journey made Louis want to rest immediately.
長途旅行的疲勞讓 Louis 想立即休息。

❶ Point 重點
fatigue vs. **tiredness**
fatigue 是一種深入身體和心靈、持續不斷的身心疲勞感，且通常**無法透過短暫的休息來完全消除**。此外，比起日常生活情境，fatigue 更常用在與醫學相關的專業領域之中。

⇨ The long hours of study brought on a deep sense of **fatigue** that couldn't be relieved by a short nap.
長時間學習帶來了無法透過小睡一下來緩解的深層疲憊感。

tiredness 指短期的疲累或倦怠感，通常只要**經過休息或睡眠便可大幅緩解**。在一般日常生活情境中比較常用到這個字。

⇨ After a long day at work, he felt a wave of **tiredness**.
在工作忙碌一整天後，他感到了一陣疲倦。

聯想單字
exhaustion	n. 精疲力竭
burnout	n. 身心俱疲
chronic fatigue	n. 慢性疲勞
worn out	adj. 不能再用的；耗盡的；筋疲力盡的
burn out	phr. 消耗殆盡；累垮

frail
[frel]
adj. (體質) 虛弱的；脆弱的；易受損

衍 fragility n. 脆弱
　fragile adj. 脆弱的

After her illness, she became too **frail** to walk without assistance.
在生病之後，她變得虛弱到無法在沒人幫忙的情況下走路。

❶ Point 重點

表達「虛弱」的常見字彙

weak
⇨ 身體或心理層面的強度不足，缺乏力量或能量。

infirm
⇨ 尤指因年邁或病痛而導致的長期性身體體質虛弱，需要特別照顧。

feeble
⇨ 常指身體力氣或精神狀態上的缺乏能量、虛弱無力。

delicate
⇨ 因為嬌嫩細緻、結構精細，所以脆弱而易受傷害。

hospitalize
[`hɑspɪtḷ͵aɪz]
v. 送～住院治療

衍 hospitalization n. 住院治療

After the car accident, Hank was quickly **hospitalized** for emergency treatment.
在車禍後，Hank 被迅速送入醫院進行緊急治療。

❶ Point 重點

英文裡有一個字跟 hospitalize 長得很像，就是名詞的 **hospitality**（熱情款待或接待他人的行為），這個字經常出現在與**餐旅業**相關的情境之中。
⇨ The hotel is known for its excellent **hospitality** and service.
這間飯店以優秀的待客之道和服務聞名。

那要怎麼區分這兩個字呢？
hospitalize 可以與 hospital（醫院）聯想在一起，可以想像某人因為生病而需要「hospital 醫院＋ -ize 化（動詞字尾）」→「hospitalize 住進醫院裡」。
hospitality 則可以與 host（主人）串聯，想像主人家熱情款待，準備食物及舒適環境的樣子（因此是名詞字尾 -ity）。

Chapter 11．疾病、醫院、傷病處理、感受　　P.219

infectious

[ɪnˋfɛkʃəs]
adj.（疾病）傳染性的；有傳染力的；有影響力的

衍 infect v.（疾病）傳染，感染
infective adj. 傳染的，感染的
infection n. 感染
infected adj. 受感染的

The flu is highly **infectious**, spreading easily from person to person.
流感具有高度傳染性，很容易人傳人。

❶ Point 重點

infect sb with sth 讓某人感染某種疾病
⇒ She accidentally **infected** her classmates **with** a cold after returning from vacation.
她在度假回來後，不小心把感冒傳染給了她的同學們。

聯想單字

infectious disease	phr. 傳染病
epidemic	n.（疾病的）流行，傳染
	adj. 流行的；肆虐的
pandemic	adj.（疾病）大規模流行的
	n. 瘟疫，大規模流行疾病
contagion	n. 接觸傳染；（情緒等）感染，擴散
transmissible	adj.（疾病等）可傳播的

lethal

[ˋliθəl]
adj. 致命的；極其危險的

衍 lethally adv. 致命地；極其危險地

The snake's bite can be **lethal** to humans if not treated quickly.
如果不快點治療，被蛇咬可能會致命。

❶ Point 重點

與「致命」相關的常考字彙

lethal
⇒ 強調致命性，常用於醫學或法律情境之中，如描述能夠導致死亡的武器或毒素。

deadly
⇒ 表示「能夠造成死亡的」；也可以用來形容非常危急的情況。

fatal
⇒ 強調某事物發展到最後，必然會造成死亡的結果。常用來形容發生某個事件或出現某種健康狀況的後果。

dangerous
⇨ 在日常生活中最常出現，用來形容任何可能導致傷害或損失的情況，但不一定會造成性命危險。

hazardous
⇨ 形容對健康或安全具有潛在威脅，常在與環境或健康相關的情境中使用。

medication
[ˌmɛdɪˋkeʃən]
n. 藥物治療；藥物

衍 medicate v. 用藥物治療
medical adj. 醫學的；醫療的；醫用的
medicine n. 藥物；醫學

The doctor prescribed a new **medication** to help manage my symptoms.
醫生開了新的用藥來幫助我控制症狀。

❶ Point 重點
medication vs. **medicine**
medication 是經由醫囑，為治療或改善某特定病症而採用的「用藥方案」，可能是具體的單一藥物，但也可能是各有作用的一種藥物搭配組合，常指**醫師開立的處方用藥或長期用藥**。

medicine 指的是**所有能治療或預防病症的藥物**，可以是具體的「特定藥物」，但也可泛指「藥物」的這個概念；除此之外，也可以指「**醫學**」或「**醫療行為**」，指稱範圍較廣。

另一方面，因為英文裡 eat 吃的是食物，因此吃不是食物的藥物必須使用 take，才能更清楚地表達「攝入」或「服用」的行為，應以 take medication/medicine 來表達。
⇨ I need to **take** my medication before breakfast.
　我必須在早餐前吃藥。

聯想單字		
prescription	n. 處方箋，處方
fill a prescription	phr. 拿藥
refill a prescription	phr. 再拿一次相同處方箋的藥

paralyze
[ˈpærəlaɪz]
v. 使麻痺，使癱瘓

衍 paralysis n. 麻痺，癱瘓

A stroke can **paralyze** one side of the body, making it difficult for the patient to move.
中風可能會造成偏癱，使患者移動困難。

❶ Point 重點
paralyze 通常用來描述身體的一部分失去運動能力，陷入麻痺或癱瘓狀態，但也可以用來形容情緒或精神上的無法行動。
⇨ Fear can **paralyze** a person, preventing them from making decisions.
恐懼可以讓人失去行動能力，讓他們無法做出決定。

與「麻痺」或「動彈不得」相關的常見字彙

stun
⇨ 因為過於驚訝而暫時失去感知或行動能力。

freeze
⇨ 因為驚訝或恐懼等原因，使某物或某人突然完全停止動作，且暫時無法移動或活動。

astonish
⇨ 因為過於震驚，造成某人無法立即做出反應。

immobilize
⇨ 使用如綁縛固定等物理手段，使某物或某人失去行動能力，常用於醫療情境之中。

plague
[pleg]
n. 瘟疫
v. 不斷困擾；折磨

Scientists are researching ways to prevent the spread of **plague** in rural areas.
科學家正在研究防止瘟疫在農村地區擴散的方法。

The town was **plagued** by a series of natural disasters last year.
去年這座城鎮遭受了一連串的自然災害侵襲。

> ❶ Point 重點
> **be plagued by** 受到～的困擾，遭受～的侵襲
> ⇨ Many people in the area **are plagued by** allergies during the spring months.
> 這一區裡有很多人會在春天的時候受到過敏的困擾。

scar
[skɑr]
n. 疤，傷疤，傷痕
v. 留下傷疤

After the accident, Ricky was left with a noticeable **scar** on his arm.
在這場事故之後，Ricky 的手臂上留下了一道明顯的傷疤。

The accident **scarred** Wendy both physically and emotionally.
這次事故在 Wendy 的身上和心中都留下了傷疤。

> 聯想單字
> injury　　n. 傷害；受傷
> heal　　　v. 癒合；治癒
> cure　　　v. 治癒，治好 n. 治癒療法；對策

side effect
[ˋsaɪd ɪˋfɛkt]
n. 副作用；未曾預料到的結果

The new medication has some mild **side effects**, such as dizziness and nausea.
這種新藥有一些輕微的副作用，如頭暈和噁心。

> ❶ Point 重點
> 各種常見的「副作用」
> ⇨ dizziness 暈眩
> 　nausea 噁心，嘔吐感
> 　drowsiness 倦怠；昏昏欲睡
> 　muscle soreness 肌肉痠痛
> 　headache 頭痛
> 　diarrhea 腹瀉
> 　constipation 便祕

sprain
[spren]
v. 扭傷（關節）
n. 扭傷

Be careful not to **sprain** your ankle while playing basketball.
打籃球時要小心不要扭到腳踝。

Wrist **sprains** are common in sports like basketball and volleyball.
手腕扭傷在籃球和排球等運動裡很常見。

❶ Point 重點 ⋯⋯⋯⋯⋯⋯⋯⋯⋯⋯⋯⋯⋯⋯⋯⋯⋯⋯⋯⋯⋯⋯⋯⋯⋯⋯⋯⋯⋯⋯
sprain vs. **twist**
sprain 指的是會讓韌帶受損或拉傷，造成腫脹、瘀青和劇烈疼痛等**症狀較嚴重的傷害**。sprain 做為動詞時，常用「**sprain＋body part**（扭傷的部位）」的方式來表達，如 sprain an ankle（扭傷腳踝）、sprain a wrist（扭傷手腕）、sprain a knee（扭傷膝蓋）等。

twist（扭轉，扭到）指的是**沒有造成嚴重傷害、稍微有點不舒服**的「扭到」或「拐到」，例如 twist an ankle（小翻船）、twist a knee（膝蓋拐了一下）、twist your neck（脖子扭了一下）等等。

torment
[tɔr`mɛnt]
n. 折磨；痛苦
v. 折磨；痛苦

衍 tormentor n. 使人痛苦（或煩惱）的人事物

The memories of the accident were a constant **torment** for him.
那場事故的記憶不斷折磨著他。

The loud noises from the market campaign **tormented** the residents nearby for months.
市場造勢的巨大噪音折磨了附近居民好幾個月。

❶ Point 重點 ⋯⋯⋯⋯⋯⋯⋯⋯⋯⋯⋯⋯⋯⋯⋯⋯⋯⋯⋯⋯⋯⋯⋯⋯⋯⋯⋯⋯⋯⋯
與「折磨」相關的其他常見字彙
torture
⇨ 動名詞同形，指對於肉體或精神上的極度折磨，通常**帶有強烈的暴力或迫害意味**。

affliction
⇨ 名詞，表示令人感到痛苦的事物，動詞是 **afflict**，表示**對於他人施加痛苦折磨**，也可表示**受疾病折磨**，通常用於較正式的語境之中。

agony
⇨ 名詞，指**身體或情感上的極度痛苦**。動詞是 **agonize**，除了表示感到極度痛苦或折磨外，也可用來表達「**對於要做出某決定，感到十分苦惱**」。

suffering
⇨ 名詞，指身體或心理上的疼痛、折磨或痛苦，動詞是 **suffer**，特別強調**持續性**，而非短暫受苦。

---

tranquilize
[ˋtræŋkwɪˌlaɪz]
v.（尤指用藥物）使鎮靜（或昏迷）

衍 tranquillizer n.
鎮靜劑
tranquility n.
平靜，寧靜
tranquil adj.
安靜的，平靜的

The zookeepers **tranquilized** the tiger to transport it safely.
動物園的飼育員為了安全運送老虎，對牠施打了鎮靜劑。

---

trauma
[ˋtrɔmə]
n. 精神創傷，心理創傷；嚴重外傷

衍 traumatic adj.
痛苦難忘的，造成精神創傷的；令人恐懼的
traumatically adv.
令人恐懼地；造成嚴重外傷地
traumatize v.
受到精神創傷

The therapist helped her work through the emotional **trauma** caused by her childhood experiences.
這名治療師幫助她處理因童年經歷所造成的情感創傷。

聯想單字		
therapy	n.	治療；療法
therapist	n.	治療師
psychologist	n.	心理學家
session	n.	（從事某項活動的）一段時間（或集會）；一場；一節（上課時間等）

tumor
[ˋtjumɚ]
n. 腫瘤

The doctor found a **tumor** in the patient's lung during the X-ray examination.
醫生在為病人做 X 光檢查時，發現他的肺部有一個腫瘤。

> 聯想單字
> benign　　　adj. 良性的
> malignant　　adj. 惡性的
> cancer　　　n. 癌症

vaccine
[ˋvæksɪn]
n. 疫苗

衍 vaccinate v.
　　給～接種疫苗
　　vaccinated adj.
　　接種過疫苗的
　　vaccination n.
　　接種疫苗

Many countries were working hard to distribute the **vaccine** to their populations.
許多國家當時都很努力要將疫苗分發給民眾。

❶ Point 重點
「接種疫苗」的常用表達方式

get a vaccine
口語化表達「某人去接種疫苗」。
⇨ I need to **get a vaccine** before traveling abroad.
　 我在出國旅行前必須先去接種疫苗。

receive a vaccine
更正式的表達方式，強調接種疫苗的「過程」。
⇨ Patients are encouraged to **receive a vaccine** as soon as it becomes available.
　 我們鼓勵患者在疫苗上市後立即接種。

be vaccinated
被動語態的表達方式，強調已完成接種疫苗的動作。
⇨ All healthcare workers must **be vaccinated** against COVID-19.
　 所有醫護人員都必須接種 COVID-19 疫苗。

get vaccinated
主動語態的表達方式，語意與「**be vaccinated**」相似，但更強調主動性。
⇨ It's important for everyone to **get vaccinated** to help stop the spread of the virus.
為了幫助阻止病毒傳播，大家都去接種疫苗是很重要的。

antibody	n. 抗體
antibiotics	n. 抗生素

vomit
[ˋvɑmɪt]
v. 嘔吐 n. 嘔吐物

衍 vomiting n. 嘔吐

After eating the spoiled food, he began to **vomit** uncontrollably
在吃了壞掉的食物後，他開始無法控制地嘔吐。

Don't step on the **vomit**, I'll clean it right away.
別踩到嘔吐物了，我會馬上去清乾淨。

❗ Point 重點
vomit vs. **throw up**
vomit 可以**當動詞或名詞，用字較正式**，可以用在任何需要描述嘔吐的情況；另一方面，**throw up 是動詞片語，無法做為名詞使用**，且使用上比 vomit 更為口語，通常會在比較隨意的非正式情境中使用。

vomit bag	n. 嘔吐袋
spew	v. 嘔吐；噴出
puke	v. 嘔吐 n. 嘔吐物

vulnerable
[ˋvʌlnərəbl]
adj. 易受傷的；易受影響（或攻擊）的；脆弱的

衍 vulnerability n.
脆弱性；脆弱之物

反 invulnerable adj.
無法傷害的；無法損壞的

The elderly are particularly **vulnerable** to the flu virus during winter.
老年人在冬天特別容易染上流感病毒。

❶ Point 重點

be vulnerable to 易受到～的影響
⇨ Young children **are vulnerable to** emotional distress.
小孩子很容易受到情緒困擾的影響。

vulnerable vs. fragile
雖然 vulnerable 和 fragile 都有「易受傷害的」語意，但兩者無論是在意義或用法上都不盡相同，因此須透過上下文來判斷要使用哪一個字。

vulnerable 的脆弱來自「**外界因素**」的影響，表示某個人事物原本不是特別脆弱，但因為在面對來自外在的攻擊、威脅或變化時的防禦力不足，導致脆弱或易受影響的情形，**常用於形容身體、經濟或心理層面**。

fragile 強調「**內在的脆弱性**」，也就是本質上的容易破碎或損壞，這種脆弱可以是**物理性質**的，例如玻璃製品，但也可以用來表達**心理或情感上**的纖細敏感和易受影響。除此之外，fragile 也可用來形容體質本就不佳的**企業**、**經濟體或關係**等等。

主題分類單字

疾病、醫院、傷病處理、感受

Ch11.mp3

Chapter 11 健康

aging	[ˈedʒɪŋ]	adj. 老化的
antibody	[ˈæntɪˌbɑdɪ]	n. 抗體
asthma	[ˈæzmə]	n. 氣喘；哮喘
cholesterol	[kəˈlɛstəˌrol]	n. 膽固醇
clinical	[ˈklɪnɪkl̩]	adj. 臨床的；診所的
dental	[ˈdɛntl̩]	adj. 牙齒的；牙科的
diabetes	[ˌdaɪəˈbitiz]	n. 糖尿病
disability	[dɪsəˈbɪlətɪ]	n. 失能，缺陷，殘障
dosage	[ˈdosɪdʒ]	n.（藥物的）劑量
dying	[ˈdaɪɪŋ]	adj. 垂死的；即將消失的
hormone	[ˈhɔrmon]	n. 荷爾蒙
limp	[lɪmp]	v. 跛行；緩慢費力地前進 n. 跛行
malaria	[məˈlɛrɪə]	n. 瘧疾
paralysis	[pəˈræləsɪs]	n. 麻痺，癱瘓
pimple	[ˈpɪmpl̩]	n. 粉刺；青春痘
pneumonia	[njuˈmonjə]	n. 肺炎
tranquil	[ˈtræŋkwɪl]	adj. 平靜的；安靜的；安寧的
tranquilizer	[ˈtræŋkwɪˌlaɪzə]	n. 鎮靜劑
tuberculosis	[tjuˌbɝkjəˈlosɪs]	n. 結核病
ulcer	[ˈʌlsɚ]	n. 潰瘍

Chapter 11・疾病、醫院、傷病處理、感受　P.229

Chapter 11 Quiz Time

一、　請選出正確的答案。

1. She was _____ with asthma at a young age and has managed it ever since.

    A. diagnosed
    B. tranquilized
    C. hospitalized
    D. disabled

2. The coastal city is particularly _____ to flooding due to its low elevation.

    A. lethal
    B. infectious
    C. vulnerable
    D. deadly

3. The marathon left her in a state of complete _____.

    A. acne
    B. deficiency
    C. fatigue
    D. tumor

二、請根據下列中文句子，填入適當的英文單字。

1. 慢性壓力可能會對心理和生理健康都造成嚴重的影響。

    C_____ stress can have serious effects on both mental and physical health.

2. 她對花粉過敏,所以春天對她來說常常都很辛苦。

   She's a_____ to pollen, so spring is often difficult for her.

3. 她活在折磨之中,無法逃脫那些揮之不去的痛苦念頭。

   She lived in t_____, unable to escape the painful thoughts that haunted her.

4. 許多士兵在從戰場上歸來後都面臨心理創傷。

   Many soldiers face psychological t_____ after returning from combat.

5. 這名足球員在這場激烈的比賽後全身都是瘀青。

   The soccer player was covered in b_____ after the intense game.

Chapter 12

量測
單位、方位、距離、尺寸、計量、金錢、時間

Ch12.mp3

★核心單字情境對話

Paul　　：Have you seen the **quarterly** report? **Expenditures** have increased massively.
Jordan：Yeah, the **statistics** don't look good. We'll need to **minimize** costs in **subsequent** quarters.
Paul　　：Management might cut **subsidy** programs to **offset** the losses.
Jordan：But won't that **devalue** our brand? We need a more **lucrative** solution.
Paul　　：Agreed. We should schedule a full **appraisal** and evaluation.
Jordan：I think maybe the **massive** marketing cost was the reason for our **deteriorating** finances.
Paul　　：Yeah, the **accumulating** campaign spending could have an **adverse** impact.

翻譯

Paul　　：你看過**季度**報告了嗎？**開支**大幅增加了。
Jordan：是啊，那些**統計數字**看起來不太妙。我們在**接下來的**幾季都得盡量**縮減**成本了。
Paul　　：管理階層可能會把**補貼**計畫砍掉來**填補**那些虧損。
Jordan：但這樣不是會讓我們品牌的**價值下跌**嗎？我們需要更**有利可圖的**解決方案。
Paul　　：我也覺得。我們應該要安排時間做一次完整的**鑑價**和評估。
Jordan：我覺得也許**龐大的**行銷成本是造成我們財務狀況**惡化**的原因。
Paul　　：是啊，宣傳活動的**累積**花費可能會造成**不良**影響。

P.232　國際學村・全民英檢

accumulate
[əˋkjumjəˌlet]
v. 累積，積聚；
逐漸增加

衍 accumulation n.
累積，積聚
accumulative adj.
累積而成的；堆積的

He has **accumulated** a vast amount of wealth through his business ventures.
他透過商業投機累積了大量的財富。

❶ Point 重點

accumulate vs. **collect** vs. **gather**
accumulate 強調「隨著時間推移，自然而然或連續地增加」，也就是「**逐漸累積**」而非驟然增加。
⇨ Dust **accumulated** on the windowsill.
窗台上積了灰塵。

collect 一般都是帶有「**明確目的性**」去收集或聚集某些「**具體的事物**」，例如收集郵票、模型等等。
⇨ He **collects** rare coins.
他會收集稀有的硬幣。

gather 強調將「**散落的東西或人**」集中在一起，這種聚集有時帶有「**迅速**」或「**臨時**」的語意。
⇨ The farmer **gathered** apples from the orchard.
農夫從果園裡採集了蘋果。

adverse
[ædˋvɝs]
adj. 不利的；負面的；有害的

衍 adversely adv.
不利地
adversity n. 逆境；不幸；厄運

同 unfavorable adj.
不利的；負面的；不喜歡的

The project faced **adverse** weather conditions, which significantly delayed its completion.
這項專案遇上了惡劣的天氣狀況，導致完成進度大幅落後。

❶ Point 重點

adverse vs. **averse**
adverse 和 averse 的拼字非常相似，因此有可能會同時出現在選項之中來混淆考生，請特別注意。

adverse 形容**事物或條件**是不利或有害的，可以用與條件相關的 advantage（優點，優勢）來聯想，例如想成「ad 開頭是條件，所以 adverse 是條件不利或有害的」，這樣一來便可加深印象，也就比較不會混淆了。
⇨ **Adverse** circumstances forced him to rethink his plans.
不利的情況迫使他重新思考他的計畫。

Chapter 12・單位、方位、距離、尺寸、計量、金錢、時間　P.233

averse 形容人的態度「**厭惡的**」，後面會出現厭惡的對象，以「**averse to＋N./V-ing**」來表達。
➪ She is **averse to** taking unnecessary risks.
她厭惡冒不必要的險。

聯想單字

adverse reaction	n.（藥物的）不良反應
adverse publicity	n. 負面宣傳
adverse conditions	n. 惡劣條件

appraisal
[ə`prezl]
n. 評定；估價；評價

衍 appraise v. 評定；估價；評價
appraisee n. 被評估者
appraiser n. 估價者，價格評估員

The manager conducted a thorough **appraisal** of the employee's performance over the past year.
那名經理針對該員工過去一年間的表現進行了全面性的評估。

❶ Point 重點

和「評價」相關的其他常用字彙

evaluation
➪ 強調多方考量下的總體評估或分析，而非單一標準下進行的評估。

assessment
➪ 強調標準化且具體的測量與評估，如財產價值、商品鑑價等評估。

review
➪ 強調基於調整、修改或決策的目的，再次回顧或審視已存在事物，並依據重新審視後的結果提出意見。

judgment
➪ 在仔細思考後，基於個人主觀意見所下的判斷與決策，也可指正式的法律裁判或判決。

bankruptcy
[ˈbæŋkrəptsɪ]
n. 破產

衍 bankrupt adj.
破產的;沒錢的;
缺乏～的

After a series of poor financial decisions, the company was forced into **bankruptcy**.
在一連串糟糕的財務決策後,這間公司被迫宣告破產了。

❶ Point 重點
file for / declare bankruptcy 聲請／宣告破產
⇨ The company had no choice but to **declare bankruptcy** after accumulating massive debts.
在累積了巨額債務後,那間公司別無選擇,只能宣告破產。

「破產」的常見表達方式

go bankrupt
⇨ He lost all his savings when his startup **went bankrupt**.
他的新創公司破產時,他失去了所有積蓄。

go into bankruptcy
⇨ Several small businesses in the area have **gone into bankruptcy** due to the economic downturn.
那一區裡的幾間小企業都因為經濟放緩而破產了。

broke [口]
⇨ The business went **broke** after several years of poor sales.
在銷售不佳幾年後,這間公司破產了。

聯想單字
default	v./n. 拖欠債務;違約
sequester	v. 扣押
foreclose	v. 取消贖回(抵押品)權,法拍

Chapter 12 · 單位、方位、距離、尺寸、計量、金錢、時間　P.235

broaden
[ˋbrɔdn̩]
v. (使)變寬；拓寬

衍 broad adj. 寬闊的；廣泛的；概括的
broadly adv. 概括地，大體上地
abroad adv. 在國外；到國外

Traveling to different countries can **broaden** your understanding of different cultures and lifestyles.
去不同國家旅行能拓展你對不同文化和生活方式的理解。

❶ Point 重點
broaden vs. **widen**
雖然 broaden 和 widen 都有「擴大」和「拓寬」的語意，但兩者並非同義字，使用時須透過上下文來判斷該用哪個字。

broaden 尤其強調**抽象事物**的擴展，一般常被用於形容「範圍」、「視野」、「經驗」或「知識」的擴展。常見的表達方式有 **broaden one's horizons**（擴展某人的視野）、**broaden knowledge**（增加知識）、**broaden experience**（拓展經驗）等等。
⇨ Living abroad for a year really helped **broaden my horizons**.
在國外生活了一年確實對於我擴展視野有幫助。

widen 強調的是「**物理**」或「**實際範圍**」的擴大，例如 **widen the road**（拓寬馬路），但也可用於描述「**具體行動範圍**」的擴大，如 **widen the search**（擴大搜索範圍）。
⇨ We need to **widen** the road in front of the school so that cars can pass by easily.
我們必須拓寬學校前面的馬路，讓車輛可以輕鬆通過。

聯想單字		
expand	v.	擴大
diversify	v.	多樣化；(使)多角化經營
extend	v.	延伸；擴大

deteriorate
[dɪˋtɪrɪəˌret]
v. 惡化，變壞

衍 deterioration n. 惡化，變壞

The patient's health began to **deteriorate** after the surgery.
這名病人的健康狀況在手術後開始惡化了。

聯想單字		
degenerate	v.	(品質)下降；退化；行為頹廢的
decline	v.	(逐漸)減少，衰弱，降低
debilitate	v.	使身體虛弱；削弱，使衰弱

devalue
[dɪˋvælju]
v. (使) 貶值；貶低；輕視

衍 devaluation n. 貶值

The government decided to **devalue** the currency to address the economic crisis.
政府決定將貨幣貶值以應對經濟危機。

❶ Point 重點
devalue vs. depreciate
雖然 devalue 和 depreciate 翻成中文都是「貶值」，但兩者在語境、使用範圍以及具體含義上都不盡相同，必須透過上下文來判斷使用。

devalue 是因中央銀行所施行的貨幣政策影響而造成的貶值，換句話說，就是**人為操作導致的貨幣貶值**。
⇨ The central bank may stop **devaluing** the currency if the inflation rate continues to rise.
如果通膨率持續上升，那麼中央銀行可能會停止讓貨幣貶值。

depreciate 是指資產（如貨幣、機器設備、車輛等等）隨著時間流逝或使用次數增加而減損的價值，也就是**自然形成的貶值**。
⇨ Over time, the value of your car will **depreciate** as it gets older and more worn out.
隨著時間過去，你的車會隨著車齡和使用痕跡的增加而貶值。

聯想單字
undervalue	v. 低估；輕視
overvalue	v. 對～估價過高；過分重視
revalue	v. 對～再估價；重新評價

dimension
[dɪˋmɛnʃən]
n. 空間，尺寸；層面，維度

The new policy brings a new **dimension** to the way we work.
這項新政策為我們的工作方式帶來了新的層面。

> **Point 重點**
>
> **dimension** 常用來指**抽象的領域或層面**，不過，在數學和物理學中，dimension 指的是一個**空間的維度**，通常用來描述**空間的結構或物體的特性**，常見的縮寫 3D 之中的 D 就是指 dimension。
>
> ⇨ The **dimensions** of the table are 4 feet by 6 feet.
> 這張桌子的尺寸是 4 英尺乘 6 英尺。

> 聯想單字
> volume　n. 容積；體積；容量
> area　　n. 面積

evaluation
[ɪˌvæljʊˋeʃən]
n. 評估

衍 evaluate v. 評估；評價；估值

The university conducts an annual **evaluation** of all its professors' teaching methods.
這所大學每年都會針對所有教授的教學方法進行評估。

expenditure
[ɪkˋspɛndɪtʃɚ]
n. 全部開支；花費

衍 expend v. 花費；耗費

The company aims to reduce unnecessary **expenditure** in order to increase its profits.
這間公司的目標是要減少不必要的花費以提高利潤。

> **Point 重點**
>
> **expenditure** 通常指的是在一段時間內的整體花費，強調這筆開支是「**全部加總後的結果**」，適用於較正式的場合。
>
> 表達「花費」的其他常見字彙
>
> **cost**
> 指的是為了取得某項商品或服務，必須付出的成本（金錢或時間），強調的是該事物的價值或價格。
> ⇨ The **cost** of this car is NT$ 1.2 million.
> 這輛車的價格是台幣 120 萬元。

P.238　國際學村・全民英檢

expense
指日常生活的花費，花費的東西可以是錢、時間或付出的努力，常用來表達日常開支或公司的開銷。
⇨ Living **expenses** in New York are very high.
紐約的生活開支非常高昂。

spending
為達成特定目的所花費的金錢，特別常用來表示政府單位或特定組織的開銷。
⇨ The government decided to increase **spending** to support low-income families.
政府決定要增加支持低收入家庭的支出。

charge
為獲得某種商品或服務所收取的費用，或是因某些額外服務而產生的附加費用，經常於購物、住宿、餐廳等消費情境中使用。
⇨ The hotel requires its customers to pay an additional **charge** for laundry.
這間飯店要求客人支付額外的洗衣費用。

payment
指的是支付金錢的行為或支付的款項。
⇨ The final **payment** for the car is due next month.
下個月要付這輛車的尾款。

expire
[ɪk`spaɪr]
v. 到期，期滿

衍 expiry n.
 [英] 到期，期滿
 expiration n.
 [美] 到期，期滿

My passport will **expire** in two months, so I need to renew it soon.
我的護照將在兩個月後到期，所以我必須趕快去換新。

聯想單字		
terminate		v. 停止，終止
expiry/expiration date		n. 有效期限
valid		adj. 有效的；有根據的；合法的

gauge
[gedʒ]
v. 測量，量測；判斷，判定
n. 測量儀器；評判方法

The scientists **gauged** the temperature of the water before starting the experiment.
這名科學家在實驗開始前先量了水溫。

The teacher used the students' grades as a **gauge** of their progress.
這位老師把學生的成績當成評判他們進步幅度的方法。

❶ Point 重點
gauge 中的字母組合 **au**，不發成 [aʊ]，而是長音的 **[e]**，這種特殊的發音方式一不小心就會忽略，造成聽錯或說錯，一定要特別小心。

gauge vs. **measure**
gauge 常指**使用特定工具或儀器**來測量出一個數值，尤其常在缺乏精確數據時使用。此外，也常用來表示對某事物（尤其是感受）的判斷。

measure（測量；計量）則**不一定會使用特定工具或儀器**，而是使用各種媒介或方法（例如手掌寬、步伐、碗盤等等）來測量具體（如長度、重量）或抽象（如情感、效果）事物的確切數值或大小。

聯想單字
meter　n. 計，儀，表；公尺　v. 計量
scale　n. 尺度，刻度；比例尺；規模　v. 攀登

installment
[ɪnˋstɔlmənt]
[英] instalment
n. 分期付款；安裝；就任

衍 install v. 安裝；正式任命，使就職
installation n. 安裝；設備；正式就職

He bought the car in monthly **installments** of NT$15,000.
他以每個月分期付款台幣 15,000 元的方式來買了這輛車。

❶ Point 重點
in installments 以分期付款的方式
⇨ Tuition fees can be paid **in installments**, which is convenient for families on a tight budget.
學費可以分期付款，這對預算吃緊的家庭來說很方便。

與「分期付款」相關的其他常見詞彙
down payment 頭期款，首付
deposit 押金，訂金，保證金
rate 利率；費率
monthly payment 每月支付款項
balloon payment（大額）尾款；一次性大額還款

聯想單字
amortization	n. 分期攤還，攤銷（的計畫或程序）
overdue	adj. 逾期的
pay off	phr. 還清債務；得到好結果

lucrative
[ˋlukrətɪv]
adj. 賺錢的，有利可圖的

衍 lucratively adv.
賺錢地，有利可圖地
lucrativeness n.
豐厚利潤

The startup was initially risky but turned out to be extremely **lucrative**.
雖然這間新創公司一開始的風險很高，但最後的獲利卻非常可觀。

❶ Point 重點
lucrative vs. profitable
lucrative 和 profitable 都代表「能創造財務上的利益」，白話來說就是「能賺到錢的」，雖然兩者在許多情況下可以互換使用，但 **lucrative** 更常用來形容「**能拿到高報酬的機會**」，表現出**更積極、想要爭取機會拿到高報酬**的語氣；另一方面，**profitable** 把重點放在「能賺錢」上，**報酬不一定很高，但能穩定獲利，語氣中性**，適合各種規模或性質的收益情境。

聯想單字
earnings	n. 利潤；工資
loss	n. 損失
profit	n. 利潤，盈利
revenue	n. 營收

massive
[ˋmæsɪv]
adj. 巨大的；大量的

衍 massively adv.
極其；非常
massiveness n.
巨大；大量

She received **massive** support from her fans during the concert tour.
她在演唱會巡迴期間獲得了粉絲的大力支持。

● Point 重點

表達「巨大」的常見字彙

huge
⇨ 強調**尺寸或數量**極大。

enormous
⇨ 大到**超過一般預期**的程度，甚至是大到不正常。

gigantic
⇨ 強調尺寸、規模或數量的極端巨大，程度**比「huge」更加誇張地大**。

immense
⇨ 強調範圍極廣、大到無邊無際，帶有「**大到無法判斷到底有多大**」的意味。

vast
⇨ 強調**範圍或空間**的巨大，通常用來描述面積、範圍或領域向外擴張到極為巨大的程度。

tremendous
⇨ 用來形容**數量或程度**極為龐大，或也可用來表達「**極為優秀**」的意思，語氣通常帶有強烈的情緒。

---

minimize

[ˋmɪnəˌmaɪz]
v. 使降到最低限度；使減到最少

衍 minimization n.
極小化；最小化
minimum n.
最小值；最低限度
minimal adj.
極小的；極少的

反 maximize v.
使最大化；使最重要

The company is trying to **minimize** the environmental impact of its manufacturing process.
這間公司正在努力將其製程的環境影響降到最低。

聯想單字		
shorten	v. 縮短
diminish	v. 減少，減小，降低
remove	v. 去掉；排除

monetary
[ˈmʌnəˌtɛrɪ]
adj. 貨幣的

衍 monetarily adv.
金錢上地
monetize v. 轉化為
金錢；變現
monetization n.
轉化為金錢的過程

The government has introduced new **monetary** policies to control inflation.
政府已推行新的貨幣政策來控制通貨膨脹。

economics	n. 經濟學；經濟狀況
fiscal	adj. 財政的
currency	n. 貨幣

monopoly
[məˈnɑplɪ]
n. 壟斷

衍 monopolize v. 壟斷
monopolistic adj.
壟斷的
monopolization n.
壟斷化
monopolist n.
壟斷者

The local grocery store has a **monopoly** on all food supplies, making it difficult for other businesses to compete.
當地的雜貨店壟斷了所有食品的供應，讓其他公司難以競爭。

❶ Point 重點

monopoly on sth 壟斷某一領域
⇨ The company holds a **monopoly on** computer operating systems.
這間公司壟斷了電腦作業系統。

oligopoly	n. 寡頭壟斷
perfect competition	n. 完全競爭
monopolistic competition	n. 壟斷性競爭

offset
[ˈɔfˌsɛt]
v. 補償；抵銷；彌補
n. 抵銷

To **offset** the environmental impact of the new factory, the company promised to plant trees in the surrounding areas.
為了補償新工廠對環境造成的影響，這間公司承諾在周邊區域種植樹木。

The unexpected costs were covered by an **offset** from other departments' savings.
那筆意料之外的費用被用其他部門所省下來的錢抵銷了。

Chapter 12・單位、方位、距離、尺寸、計量、金錢、時間

❗ **Point 重點**

offset vs. **compensate** vs. **counter**

offset 強調用**具體的正面事物**來抵銷或平衡負面的影響，用來補償或抵銷的量**通常經過量化或計算**，常用於財務、會計、工程等領域。
⇨ **Offset** an increase in costs with higher profits.
用更高的利潤抵銷增加的成本。

compensate 將重點放在**補償因發生某事而造成的損失**，這種類型的補償**通常是金錢**，但也可能以其他形式提供，常見於法律、保險、勞資等情境。
⇨ The company **compensated** the employees for their injuries.
這間公司賠償了受傷的員工。

counter 強調用某種**對立的方式來主動應對或回應某事物，表示反擊、反對或對抗**，常用於辯論、政策、策略等情境之中。
⇨ The opposition party **countered** the proposal with an alternative plan.
反對黨以替代方案來對抗這項提案。

聯想單字
balance	n. 平衡；抵銷因素 v. 使平衡；抵銷；補償
counterbalance	v. 使平衡；抵銷；彌補

patronage
[ˋpætrənɪdʒ]
v. 贊助，資助；惠顧

衍 patron n. 贊助者，資助人；老顧客
patronize v. 經常惠顧；以高人一等的態度對待他人

The small local bookstore thrives thanks to the loyal **patronage** of its community.
多虧有來自當地社群的忠實顧客，這間小型的本土書店得以蓬勃發展。

聯想單字
sponsorship	n. 贊助
support	v. 支持；資助 n. 支持；幫助；供養

periodic
[ˌpɪrɪˋɑdɪk]
adj. 週期的；定期的

衍 period n.
　一段時間，時期
　periodical n. 期刊
　periodically adv.
　週期性地，定期地

The company holds **periodic** meetings to discuss progress on ongoing projects.
這間公司會舉行定期會議來討論正在進行中的專案進展。

聯想單字
regular	adj. 定期的；規律的
cyclical	adj. 週期性的
routine	adj. 例行公事的；慣常的

premium
[ˋprimɪəm]
n. 獎金，津貼；附加費用；保險費
adj. 高級的；優質的

Many consumers are willing to pay a **premium** for organic food because of its perceived health benefits.
許多消費者願意多付一點錢吃有機食品，因為他們認為有機食品有益健康。

The **premium** quality of the hotel's services made it a popular choice among luxury travelers.
這家飯店的優質服務使它成為奢華旅客的熱門選擇。

❶ Point 重點
premium 表達的概念是「**比一般情況還要更多的量**」，所以可以用「比一般更多的錢 ⇨ 獎金，津貼；附加費用」或「比一般情況還要更好 ⇨ 高級的」這種概念來記，就可以更快記住字義。在**保險領域中**，premium 是指**投保人按期支付的費用**。另外，premium 做為**形容詞**時，較常用來**描述高品質、奢華或高價的東西**。

be at a premium 非常稀缺
⇨ Parking spaces in the city center **are** always **at a premium**, so it's best to arrive early.
　市中心裡能停車的地方一直都非常稀缺，所以最好早點到。

聯想單字
exclusive	adj. 專屬的；獨有的；昂貴高檔的
high-end	adj. 高價位的，高檔的
elite	n. 精英 adj. 精英的
premium member	n. 高級會員

prior
[ˋpraɪɚ]
adj. 先前的，在前的；更重要的

衍 priority n. 優先考慮的事；優先權

Sabrina had **prior** experience in marketing, which made her the ideal candidate for the job.
Sabrina 有過行銷經驗，這讓她成為那份工作的理想人選。

❶ Point 重點
prior to 在～之前
⇨ The meeting will be held at 10 AM, but **prior to** that, we need to review the documents.
這次會議將於上午 10 點舉行，但在此之前，我們必須把那些文件再看一次。

prior vs. **preceding** vs. **before**
prior、preceding 和 before 都與時間順序有關，但在字義和使用方式上都各有不同，因此必須透過上下文來判斷該使用哪一個字。

prior 強調在某事件或時間點之前，語氣較**正式**且較常於**書面**使用，並**經常與名詞搭配**，如 prior to the event（在活動之前）。

preceding 指具體事物或事件的「**前面**」部分，特別強調事物或事件的**先後順序**，如 the preceding paragraph（前面一個段落）。

before（在～之前）可以做為**介系詞、副詞或連接詞**使用，因此能夠廣泛應用於各種情境之中，此外，除連接**時間點**，如 before 5 PM（在下午 5 點之前），before 也能用來表示在某個「**事件**」或「**動作**」之前，如 before he shows up（在他現身之前）。

prolong
[prə`lɔŋ]
v. 延長，拖延

衍 prolongation n. 延長，拖延
prolonged adj. 延續很久的，長期的

同 extend v. 延長；延伸

They decided to **prolong** the meeting for another hour in order to discuss urgent matters.
他們決定將這次會議再延長一個小時，以便討論緊急事項。

❶ Point 重點
跟「拖延」相關的其他常用字彙

delay
➡ 常用於時間點上發生的延遲，肇因可能是**人為故意**，但也可能是**不可控的因素**，如天氣、天災等原因所造成。

procrastinate
➡ 指**故意拖延或延後**做某事，尤其是指本應立即處理的事情，卻故意拖延不去做，帶有**消極和懶散**的意味。

postpone
➡ 指決定將做某件事的時間向後延，與 delay 的區別在於 postpone 通常是**更正式和有計畫**的推遲。

quarterly
[`kwɔrtəlɪ]
adj. 季度的，按季度的
adv. 按季度，一季一次地
n. 季刊

衍 quarter n. 四分之一；季度；（城鎮的）區 v. 把～切成四部分

The company holds **quarterly** meetings to review its financial performance and discuss future goals.
這間公司會召開季會來檢視公司的財務表現及討論未來目標。

The magazine is published **quarterly**, with the next edition coming out in January.
這本雜誌是季刊，下一期會在一月出刊。

The **quarterly** was delayed due to unforeseen technical issues, but it is expected to be released next week.
這本季刊因為不可預見的技術問題而延誤了，但預期會在下週發刊。

❶ Point 重點
quarter vs. **season**
quarter 指將一年劃分成四個等長的期間，從一月開始每三個月為一季，**這種「季」的劃分具體且固定，不受所在地點或語境類型影響**。

season（季，季節）指的則是自然界的四個季節，即春（spring）、夏（summer）、秋（autumn/fall）、冬（winter），也可用於描述進行特定活動或事件的期間，例如運動賽季或電視劇的季數，season **會受到各種因素影響，造成指稱的月份或時間各不相同**，例如加拿大的春季和澳洲的春季的所指月份就並不相同。

ratio
[ˋreʃo]
n. 比；比例；比率

The **ratio** of students to teachers in the school is 20:1, which ensures individual attention for each student.
學校裡學生與老師的比例是 20:1，這可以確保每個學生都能獲得個別關注。

❶ Point 重點
ratio vs. **rate** vs. **proportion** vs. **percentage**
ratio 是指**兩個數字之間的關係**，通常以分數或冒號表示。
⇨ The **ratio** of boys to girls in the class is 3:2.
這一班中男生與女生的比例是 3:2。

rate 表示某種變化或事件的發生**速度**或在特定時間中發生的**次數或總量**，常翻譯成「**比率；速率**」。
⇨ The birth **rate** in the country has declined over the last decade.
該國的出生率在過去十年間下降了。

proportion（比率，比例）用於描述某一部分與整體之間的關係，與 ratio 類似，但 proportion 更強調「**部分與整體之間的關聯性**」。
⇨ The **proportion** of students who passed the exam was 2/3.
通過考試的學生比例是三分之二。

> **percentage**（百分比，百分率）是一種以百分數（％）來表示的 proportion 形式。
> ⇨ The **percentage** of students receiving a scholarship is 25%.
> 獲得獎學金的學生百分比是 25%。

reverse

[rɪˋvɝs]
adj. 顛倒的；相反的；反向的
v. (使) 反向；徹底改變；推翻；倒車
n. 相反的情況；對立面

衍 reversal n. 反向；逆轉；推翻；挫折

He had to take a **reverse** action and correct his earlier mistake.
他必須採取相反的行動來修正他之前的錯誤。

After the scandal, the company had to **reverse** its decision to launch the new product.
在醜聞發生後，這間公司不得不撤回推出新產品的決定。

The **reverse** of the situation was that they not only avoided bankruptcy but also increased their market share.
情況反轉，他們不僅避免了破產，還提升了市場占有率。

❶ Point 重點
當 **-verse** 加上不同的字首時，會形成許多與**反向**、**對立**或**偏離正道**相關的字彙。
⇨ averse 不喜歡的；反對的
perverse 有悖常理的；故意作對的
inverse 相反的，反面的
adverse 不利的；負面的；有害的

聯想單字
opposite	adj. 全然不同的，截然相反的
turnaround	n. 突然好轉，改善；翻轉，徹底的改變

statistics
[stə`tɪstɪks]
n. 統計數據；統計資料；統計學

衍 statistic adj. 統計上的；統計學的 n. 統計數值
statistical adj. 統計的；統計學的

According to the latest **statistics**, the unemployment rate has dropped to its lowest point in the past decade.
根據最新的統計數據，失業率降到了過去十年間的最低點。

❶ Point 重點

statistics vs. **data** vs. **figure**
data 是最基本的原始資料，沒有經過處理，可以是任何形式。**statistics** 則是整理分析 data 後得到的結果。
figure 指的是具體數字，通常用來描述金額、數量或數據結果，也可以指帶有編號的圖表。

subsequent
[`sʌbsɪˌkwɛnt]
adj. 隨後的，後續的

衍 subsequently adv. 隨後地，接著地

The **subsequent** chapters of the book dive deeper into the historical context of the events.
這本書的後續章節更加深入探討這些事件的歷史背景脈絡。

❶ Point 重點

subsequent to 在～之後
⇨ The product was released **subsequent to** the announcement.
這項產品在公告後隨即上市。

subsequent vs. **consequent**
subsequent 強調事件之間的發生順序，重點放在**時間點的先後順序**。
⇨ The **subsequent** meeting was scheduled for the next week.
後續會議排定在下週進行。

consequent 強調的是事件之間的**因果關係**，表達「因為～而導致隨後發生～的結果」語意，一般常翻成「隨之而來的～」。
⇨ The **consequent** rise in prices has led to widespread public dissatisfaction.
隨之而來的漲價導致群眾的普遍不滿。

聯想單字
sequence　n. 順序；接續；一連串
sequent　adj. 隨之而來的；繼起的

subsidy

[ˈsʌbsədɪ]
n. 補助金；津貼，補貼

衍 subsidize v. 給予～津貼
subsidizer n. 提供資助或補貼者

The government provided a **subsidy** to farmers to encourage the production of renewable energy crops.
政府提供農民補助金，鼓勵生產可再生能源作物。

❶ Point 重點
subsidy vs. **allowance**
subsidy 通常是由**組織龐大的外部機構**（如政府等）提供，針對**某個特定目標（產業、計畫或公共利益）**進行**系統性的資金支援**，例如農業補助、能源補貼等。subsidy 常與動詞 **provide**、**receive**、**give**、**offer**、**grant** 等搭配使用。另一方面，**allowance** 一般是針對**個人或家庭定期給予**，以**滿足日常需求及供應日常支出的生活費用**，如孩子的零用錢或學生津貼等。

聯想單字
aid	n. 幫助；支持；援助
benefit	n. 福利；津貼，救濟金
grant	n. 補助金；給予（物）

taxation

[tækˈseʃən]
n. 課稅，徵稅

The government is considering increasing **taxation** on luxury goods to help fund public services.
政府正在考慮對奢侈品加稅來為公共服務籌措資金。

❶ Point 重點
taxation vs. **tax**
taxation 指的是**政府徵收稅款的這件事**，包括整體系統、流程和政策規範都屬於 taxation 的範圍，而 **tax** 則是具體的**課稅動作**，或指必須繳納的**稅金**。

聯想單字
tax allowance	n. 所得稅免稅額
tax break	n.（因法律變更而）減稅
tax credit	n. 減抵稅額
tax evasion	n. 逃稅
duty	n.（針對特定貨物的）關稅
tariff	n.（針對進出口貿易的）關稅
exemption	n. 豁免

vertical
[ˋvɝ·tɪk!]
adj. 豎直的；垂直的；立式的
n. 垂直線；垂直面

衍 vertically adv. 豎直地；垂直地；立式地

反 horizontal adj. 水平的；與地面平行的

The skyscraper's **vertical** design allowed for the maximum use of limited space in the city.
這棟摩天大樓的垂直設計最大化地利用了這座城市裡的有限空間。

The architect used the **vertical** as the primary axis in the building's design.
這位建築師在設計這棟大樓時採用了垂直線做為主要軸線。

聯想單字
upright　adj. 直立的；挺直的；正直的 adv. 挺直地；豎著
erect　　adj. 直的；豎起的 v. 豎立；使直立

withdrawal
[wɪðˋdrɔəl]
n. 提款；收回；退出；撤軍

衍 withdraw v. 抽回；取回；提取；撤回
withdrawn adj. 孤僻的；畏縮沉默的

He made a **withdrawal** of US$800 from his savings account to cover his rent payment.
他從自己的儲蓄帳戶中領了 800 美金來付房租。

🔹 Point 重點
動詞 withdraw 的三態變化屬於不規則變化（**withdraw-withdrew-withdrawn**），其中過去分詞 withdrawn 也可以做為形容詞，表示「**孤僻的**」或「**畏縮沉默的**」的性格特質。
⇒ She became more **withdrawn** after the incident.
　她在那次事件發生後變得更加孤僻。

另外，withdraw 也可以用來指「**撤回**」或「**退出**」，如從政治、軍事或體育等方面的行動或活動中退出。
⇒ The government decided to **withdraw** its troops from the region.
　該國政府決定從該地區撤軍。

主題分類單字

單位、方位、距離、尺寸、計量、金錢、時間

Ch12.mp3

Chapter 12　量測

adjacent	[əˋdʒesənt]	adj. 毗連的；鄰近的
breadth	[brɛdθ]	n. 寬度；幅度；廣度
broadly	[ˋbrɔdlɪ]	adv. 寬廣地；概括地
clockwise	[ˋklɑk͵waɪz]	adj. 順時針方向的 adv. 順時針方向地
countable	[ˋkaʊntəbḷ]	adj. 可計算的；可數的
counterclockwise	[͵kaʊntɚˋklɑk͵waɪz]	adj. 逆時針方向的 adv. 逆時針方向地
currency	[ˋkɝənsɪ]	n. 貨幣
decimal	[ˋdɛsəml]	adj. 十進位的 n. 小數
density	[ˋdɛnsətɪ]	n. 密度
diagram	[ˋdaɪə͵græm]	n. 圖解；示意圖
diameter	[daɪˋæmətɚ]	n. 直徑
donation	[doˋneʃən]	n. 捐獻；捐款
dual	[ˋdjuəl]	adj. 雙的；雙倍的；雙重的
elevation	[͵ɛləˋveʃən]	n. 海拔高度；提高；（建築）立視圖
graph	[græf]	n. 圖表，圖解
horizontal	[͵hɔrəˋzantḷ]	adj. 水平的；橫的 n. 水平線；水平面
infinite	[ˋɪnfənɪt]	adj. 無限的

Chapter 12・單位、方位、距離、尺寸、計量、金錢、時間　P.253

單字	音標	詞性與中文
lightweight	[ˈlaɪtˈwet]	adj. 較輕的；輕量的 n. 輕量級運動員；一知半解的人
longevity	[lɑnˈdʒɛvətɪ]	n. 長壽；壽命
longitude	[ˈlɑndʒəˌtjud]	n. 經度
magnitude	[ˈmægnəˌtjud]	n. 巨大；重大
measurement	[ˈmɛʒɚmənt]	n. 測量；（測得的）尺寸，大小
metric	[ˈmɛtrɪk]	adj. 公尺的；公制的
millimeter	[ˈmɪləˌmitɚ]	n. 公釐；毫米
millionaire	[ˌmɪljəˈnɛr]	n. 百萬富翁
minimal	[ˈmɪnəməl]	adj. 最小的；極少的
numerical	[njuˈmɛrɪkl̩]	adj. 數字的
previously	[ˈprivɪəslɪ]	adv. 事先；以前
proportional	[prəˈpɔrʃənl̩]	adj. 成比例的；相稱的
proximity	[prɑkˈsɪmətɪ]	n. 接近；鄰近；親近
quota	[ˈkwotə]	n. 配額；限額；定額
radius	[ˈredɪəs]	n. 半徑
ransom	[ˈrænsəm]	v. 贖回 n. 贖金
repayment	[rɪˈpemənt]	n. 付還；報恩
sequence	[ˈsikwəns]	n. 順序；接續；一連串
statistic	[stəˈtɪstɪk]	adj. 統計上的；統計學的 n. 統計數值

subsidiary	[səb`sɪdɪˌɛrɪ]	adj. 次要的；輔助的 n. 子公司；附屬公司
tariff	[`tærɪf]	n.（針對進出口貿易的）關稅
taxpayer	[`tæksˌpeɚ]	n. 納稅人
thickness	[`θɪknɪs]	n. 厚度
ton	[tʌn]	n. 公噸
trillion	[`trɪljən]	n. 兆
trio	[`trio]	n. 三個（或三人）一組
triple	[`trɪpl]	adj. 三倍的；三重的 v. 使成三倍
utmost	[`ʌtˌmost]	adj. 最大的；極度的 n. 極限；最大可能
volt	[volt]	n. 伏特
voltage	[`voltɪdʒ]	n. 電壓；伏特數
watt	[wɑt]	n. 瓦（特）

Chapter 12　Quiz Time

一、　請選出正確的答案。

1. He had to overcome _____ public opinion to implement the new policy.
   A. massive
   B. adverse
   C. periodic
   D. vertical

2. The building's condition _____ due to years of neglect.
   A. deteriorated
   B. prolonged
   C. minimized
   D. broadened

3. Working in the tech industry has proven to be quite _____ for him.
   A. reverse
   B. subsequent
   C. lucrative
   D. prior

二、請根據下列中文句子，填入適當的英文單字。

1. 在手術前必須先全面評估病人的健康狀況。

   A thorough e_____ of the patient's health condition is necessary before surgery.

2. 醫生建議病人要定期檢查來監控她的健康狀況。

   The doctor advised the patient to have p_____ check-ups to monitor her health.

3. 這枚硬幣的反面有著不同的圖案。

   The r_____ side of the coin shows a different design.

4. 在會議結束後，我們會寄出會議記錄給所有的與會者。

   S_____ to the meeting, we will send out the minutes to all participants.

5. 她希望在開設自己的公司前先累積足夠的經驗。

   She hopes to a_____ enough experience before starting her own company.

Answer
(一)：1. B 2. A 3. C
(二)：1. evaluation 2. periodic 3. reverse 4. subsequent 5. accumulate

翻譯：
(一)
1. 他必須嚴謹再三思考，才能進行新的改革。
2. 這種植物的新葉因為多肉而讓人們爭先恐後。
3. 重複證明他對技術工作業的工作熱情永遠非常好轉。

下方以特殊色標記的單字為各章核心單字，主題分類單字則為黑字。

A

abdomen	088
abide	130
abortion	212
absent-minded	124
abstraction	170
absurd	124
abundance	170
acclaim	124
accumulate	233
accustom	124, 151
acne	212
acquisition	130
addicted	152
adjacent	253
administrative	130
adore	124
adverse	233
advertisement	152
advisory	145
aesthetics	186
affectionate	124
agenda	131
aging	229
agricultural	192
aide	145
aisle	047
allergic	212
allocate	131
amiable	106
analogy	186
anchor	071
annoyance	106
antibody	229
anticipate	152
appendix	186
appraisal	234
apprehension	186
architectural	047
archive	186
arena	153
armor	032
arrogant	107
artery	088
artifact	032
assignment	186
assimilate	170
assumption	186
asthma	229
astray	084
astronomer	145
astronomy	186
athletics	154
attendance	186
attendant	186
attic	065
attorney	145
attribute	132
auditorium	048
authorize	132

P.258 國際學村 · 全民英檢

autograph	145
automation	145
aviation	071

B

backpack	032
bankruptcy	235
barbershop	145
barefoot	088
barge	084
barren	192
barricade	072
belongings	033
beverage	009
bibliography	186
biochemistry	186
biological	186
birdie	165
blacksmith	145
bleak	206
blonde	089
blues	165
bodily	101
boiling	009
bonus	133
booking	165
boredom	124
bosom	089
boulevard	072
boundary	192
bout	213
bowel	101
boxer	165
boxing	165
brassiere	043
breadth	253
briefing	145
broadcasting	154
broaden	236
broadly	253
brooch	043
broth	027
brow	101
bruise	213

C

cactus	206
caffeine	010
calf	101
capability	133
capsule	214
carbohydrate	010
cardinal	043
carefree	107
carnation	206
carnival	155
carol	165
carrier	073
carton	065
cashier	145
casino	155
catastrophe	193
catering	011
celebrity	155

Index・索引　P.259

celery	027	comma	186
cellar	065	commend	108
cello	165	commentary	186
Celsius	206	commodity	048
chairperson	145	commute	073
challenged	214	compact	074
chapel	065	compass	065
charcoal	043	compassionate	109
check-in	156	competent	135
chili	027	compile	171
chimpanzee	206	complexion	101
choir	165	complexity	186
cholesterol	229	component	171
chord	165	comprehend	172
chronic	215	computerize	145
chuckle	124	conceive	172
chunk	011	concentrated	173
clam	027	concise	186
clarity	186	condom	065
clinch	048	confusing	124
clinical	229	conscientious	109
clockwise	253	consent	110
closure	165	console	124
clover	027	consumption	012
clutch	193	contaminant	194
coastal	206	contention	173
coastline	206	contractor	145
cockpit	084	contradiction	174
cocoa	027	controversial	174
collaboration	134	convoy	074
collide	073	copyright	186
comet	206	coral	043

core	012	daring	124
cork	027	dart	165
correction	187	daybreak	206
corresponding	175	deadly	215
corrode	206	dealer	145
cosmetic	049	debris	065
counsel	135	decent	090
counselor	145	decimal	253
countable	253	decorative	034
counterclockwise	253	dedicated	175
counterpart	136	deduct	176
courier	145	deficiency	216
courtyard	065	demise	216
covering	065	density	253
cowardly	124	dental	229
cozy	050	despise	124
creativity	187	deteriorate	236
creator	187	devalue	237
crib	065	devastating	194
criterion	187	developed	195
crocodile	206	devour	013
crouch	090	diabetes	229
cruise	075	diagnose	217
crunchy	012	diagram	253
cuisine	013	diameter	253
currency	253	diaper	065
curriculum	187	dilute	027
curry	027	dimension	237
cynical	110	directory	065
		disability	229

D

dandruff	101	disable	217
		disastrous	195

disciplinary	145	embark	076
discreet	111	emigrate	051
disintegrate	065	enclosure	051
dismantle	065	encouraging	124
dismissal	145	encyclopedia	187
displace	145	endeavor	136
disposable	014	enlighten	177
disregard	111	entrepreneur	137
distract	176	equation	187
distress	111	equator	206
distributor	146	erode	206
disturbing	124	erupt	196
donation	253	escort	076
doorstep	065	ethical	177
doorway	065	ethics	187
dosage	229	evacuate	051
dough	027	evaluation	238
drawback	112	evaporate	197
dressed	034	evaporation	206
driveway	065	evergreen	206
drizzle	196	examinee	187
dual	253	excerpt	187
dwarf	090	exemplify	187
dwell	050	exile	065
dying	229	expenditure	238
		expertise	137

E

		expire	239
ecology	206	exposition	156
ecstatic	156	expulsion	146
elevation	253	exquisite	035
eloquent	112	external	091
embargo	075	eyelash	101

eyelid	101

F

fabric	035
faculty	178
fad	165
Fahrenheit	206
famine	197
fatigue	218
fatty	101
feeble	091
feminist	187
fertility	198
fiber	036
fiddle	165
firecracker	065
fireproof	052
fishery	206
fleet	077
footstep	101
frail	219
framework	146
friction	124
frontier	206
frustration	113
furnace	066
fury	124

G

garment	036
gauge	240
gender	092
genetics	179
genre	179
ghetto	066
glacier	207
glitter	036
gloom	124
gnaw	101
goalkeeper	165
good-looking	101
gorge	207
gorgeous	092
gorilla	207
grammatical	187
graph	253
grassy	207
grease	014
greed	125
grill	015
grocer	027
gymnasium	165

H

hacker	146
hairstyle	101
handicraft	037
harassment	138
harmonica	165
hateful	125
haul	077
haunt	157
haven	052
healthful	101

Index · 索引   P.263

hearing	101
heating	066
hedge	198
heir	066
hemisphere	207
herb	207
hillside	207
hockey	166
hometown	066
honk	084
hood	037
horizontal	253
hormone	229
hospitable	053
hospitalize	219
hostile	113
hover	207
humiliate	114
hypocrisy	114
hysterical	114

I

ideological	187
ideology	179
impulsive	115
inaugurate	138
incense	066
index	187
indifferent	115
indignant	125
indulge	125
infectious	220

infinite	253
infrastructure	077
inhabit	053
inhibited	125
inning	166
innovative	139
insecticide	066
insight	180
installment	240
intersection	078
irritate	116
ivy	207

J

jade	043
jasmine	043
journalism	187
jug	066

K

kin	066

L

lame	093
lava	207
lavish	157
lease	054
legacy	054
lethal	220
lifelong	055
lifestyle	066
lighting	066

lightweight	254
lime	027
limousine	084
limp	229
literacy	180
live-in	066
livestock	199
lizard	207
locomotive	084
lodge	056
logo	146
lollipop	027
lonesome	125
longevity	254
longitude	254
lottery	166
lotus	207
lounge	056
lucrative	241
lunchtime	027
lure	125

M

magnitude	254
maiden	066
mainstream	199
malaria	229
mammal	207
manifest	078
masculine	093
massive	241
mastery	146

mattress	066
mayonnaise	027
measurement	254
medication	221
melancholy	125
mellow	207
merchandise	146
mermaid	207
metallic	038
metric	254
migrate	057
mileage	084
millimeter	254
millionaire	254
minimal	254
minimize	242
mining	200
mint	027
monetary	243
monopoly	243
moody	125
motherhood	066
motorist	084
motorway	084
mower	066
muscular	094
mustard	027
mutton	016

N

naive	116
nanny	146

Index・索引　P.265

navel ··········· 101
navigation ··········· 079
nearsighted ··········· 094
necktie ··········· 043
newlywed ··········· 066
nightclub ··········· 166
nightingale ··········· 207
nostril ··········· 101
notion ··········· 187
novice ··········· 181
numerical ··········· 254
nurture ··········· 200

O

oatmeal ··········· 027
obsession ··········· 125
octopus ··········· 207
odor ··········· 095
offset ··········· 243
offshore ··········· 201
offspring ··········· 066
olive ··········· 028
optical ··········· 101
optimistic ··········· 117
orchard ··········· 028
ornament ··········· 066
ostrich ··········· 207
outfit ··········· 038
outgoing ··········· 125
outing ··········· 158
outrageous ··········· 117
outsider ··········· 146
outskirts ··········· 058
oversee ··········· 146
overwork ··········· 146
oyster ··········· 028

P

paddle ··········· 079
pane ··········· 066
paralysis ··········· 229
paralyze ··········· 222
parsley ··········· 028
part-time ··········· 146
password ··········· 066
pastime ··········· 158
pastry ··········· 016
pathetic ··········· 125
patronage ··········· 244
pavement ··········· 080
peacock ··········· 207
peck ··········· 207
peddle ··········· 166
peddler ··········· 159
pedestrian ··········· 080
peek ··········· 096
peg ··········· 067
pendulum ··········· 067
peninsula ··········· 207
penis ··········· 101
pension ··········· 139
perch ··········· 208
perennial ··········· 201
periodic ··········· 245

perseverance	118
persistent	119
personnel	139
pesticide	067
petroleum	208
pickle	028
picturesque	201
pier	080
pimple	229
plague	222
plantation	028
playwright	146
pneumonia	229
poach	028
poetic	187
populate	058
porcelain	067
posture	096
potter	146
premium	245
presidency	146
previously	254
prey	202
prior	246
produce	017
prolong	247
propeller	081
proportional	254
prosecutor	140
provoke	120
proximity	254
psychiatrist	146
putt	166

Q

qualifier	146
quarrelsome	125
quarterly	247
questionnaire	181
quota	254
quotation	182

R

rack	058
radiator	067
radish	028
radius	254
ragged	039
ransom	254
ratio	248
realm	208
rebellious	120
reckless	120
recording	067
reef	208
refreshment	017
refuge	059
rein	081
rejoice	125
reliability	121
reliance	125
relieved	125
relish	017
removal	140

Index・索引　P.267

repayment	254		scent	097
reproduce	203		scorn	125
reptile	208		sculptor	146
resent	125		seasoned	018
residential	060		seduce	126
retailer	159		self-esteem	126
retired	146		seminar	182
retirement	140		senate	146
reverse	249		senator	147
rhetoric	182		sensation	126
rhetorical	187		sensitivity	126
rhythmic	187		sentimental	122
ridicule	125		sequence	254
roam	159		shareholder	147
rocky	208		shear	102
rouge	101		shipment	082
row	082		shudder	126
ruby	039		side effect	223
rugby	166		silkworm	208
runner-up	166		simmer	019
rustle	208		skeptical	122
ruthless	121		skull	102
			slate	067

S

saddle	084		sled	084
salmon	018		sleigh	084
sandal	043		slum	060
sandy	043		sniff	102
satisfied	160		soak	019
scar	223		sober	020
scarecrow	208		socialize	188
scenic	203		sophomore	188
			sorrowful	126

spacious	061	stumble	098
specialize	140	sturdy	099
specify	183	submit	147
specimen	208	subsequent	250
spectacular	204	subsidiary	255
spine	097	subsidy	251
sporting	166	suite	160
spouse	067	sulfur	043
sprain	224	superiority	141
sprawl	098	superstitious	123
squad	183	supervise	141
stale	021	surveillance	147
stall	082	swallow	022
stammer	126	swamp	208
standpoint	184	syllabus	188
stanza	188	symbolic	185
staple	147	symbolism	188
starch	028	syndicate	147
starter	028	synonymous	188
startle	126	systematical	188
statistic	254		
statistics	250	**T**	
stature	102	tablespoon	028
steamer	028	taco	028
stepchild	067	tailor-made	040
stern	084	takeaway	023
stew	021	tan	041
storage	061	tango	166
strait	208	tariff	255
strap	039	tasteless	023
striker	147	tavern	024
stripe	040	taxation	251

Index・索引　P.269

taxpayer	255	torrent	208
teamwork	185	tournament	161
teaspoon	028	tract	067
teller	147	tractor	083
tempest	208	trample	099
temptation	161	tranquil	229
terminate	142	tranquilize	225
termination	147	tranquilizer	229
terminology	188	transcript	185
terrace	067	trauma	225
terrestrial	208	treacherous	204
territorial	204	tread	100
textile	042	trillion	255
texture	042	trio	255
therapist	147	triple	255
thermometer	208	triumphant	162
thermos	067	trivial	062
thesis	188	trophy	162
thickness	255	tropic	208
thigh	102	tuberculosis	229
threshold	062	tuition	188
thrill	126	tumor	226

U

		ulcer	229
		ultraviolet	166
		undergraduate	188
thunderous	208	undo	042
tile	067	unemployment	142
tint	043	unpleasant	126
toddle	067	unwilling	126
tollbooth	084	upbringing	067
tollway	084		
ton	255		
tonic	102		
torment	224		

utensil	024
utilize	147
utmost	255

V

vacancy	143
vaccine	226
vacuum	062
valve	102
vanilla	028
vegetation	208
velvet	043
versatile	162
vertical	252
veteran	147
veterinarian	147
vicinity	063
victorious	163
viewer	166
villa	163
villager	063
vine	208
vineyard	028
vintage	024
visa	166
vocation	143
vocational	147
vogue	163
volt	255
voltage	255
vomit	227
vulnerable	228

W

wallpaper	067
walnut	025
wardrobe	042
warranty	064
watt	255
wed	067
whisk	028
whiskey	026
widow	067
wig	043
withdrawal	252
wither	205
woodpecker	208
workforce	143
workman	147
workplace	147
wretched	123

Z

zeal	164

Index · 索引　P.271

台灣廣廈國際出版集團 Taiwan Mansion International Group

國家圖書館出版品預行編目（CIP）資料

全新!NEW GEPT全民英檢單字大全. 中高級/蔡宜庭著. -- 初
版. -- 新北市：國際學村出版社, 2025.08
　　面；　公分
ISBN 978-986-454-435-6(平裝)

1.CST: 英語 2.CST: 詞彙

805.1892　　　　　　　　　　　　　　　　114007691

國際學村

全新！NEW GEPT 全民英檢單字大全【中高級】

作　　　者/蔡宜庭	編輯中心編輯長/伍峻宏・編輯/徐淳輔
	封面設計/陳沛涓・內頁排版/菩薩蠻數位文化有限公司
	製版・印刷・裝訂/東豪・紘億・秉成

行企研發中心總監/陳冠蒨
媒體公關組/陳柔彣
綜合業務組/何欣穎

發　行　人/江媛珍
法　律　顧　問/第一國際法律事務所 余淑杏律師・北辰著作權事務所 蕭雄淋律師
出　　　版/國際學村
發　　　行/台灣廣廈有聲圖書有限公司
　　　　　　地址：新北市235中和區中山路二段359巷7號2樓
　　　　　　電話：（886）2-2225-5777・傳真：（886）2-2225-8052
讀者服務信箱/cs@booknews.com.tw

代理印務・全球總經銷/知遠文化事業有限公司
　　　　　　地址：新北市222深坑區北深路三段155巷25號5樓
　　　　　　電話：（886）2-2664-8800・傳真：（886）2-2664-8801
郵　政　劃　撥/劃撥帳號：18836722
　　　　　　劃撥戶名：知遠文化事業有限公司（※單次購書金額未達1000元，請另付70元郵資。）

■出版日期：2025年08月　　ISBN：978-986-454-435-6
　　　　　　　　　　　　　版權所有，未經同意不得重製、轉載、翻印。

Complete Copyright 2025 © by Taiwan Mansion Books Group.
All rights reserved.